PRAISE FOR STINA LINDENBLATT

Decidedly by Chance

"...a truly unique and utterly swoon-worthy romance." —Mary Dubé at Frolic/USA Today's HEA

"Decidedly By Chance is a well written emotional story that will tug on your heart strings."—MI Bookshelf

"This is a great read, fresh, funny, sweet and romantic, with amazing characters and lots of surprises." – Blog on the Run

"Stina Lindenblatt writes an emotional, heartfelt story about single parenthood, friendship, and love. Add to that great chemistry and tons of feels and this is a great book for anyone who enjoys this trope." – Ari at Red Hatter Book Blog

"Their slow build from friends to more was filled with so much heart melting goodness and swoon it honestly didn't even feel like a slow burn to me. And that's when you know a slow burn has been done right!" – Britt at Red Hatter Book Blog

Other Books By Stina Lindenblatt

"A feel good, sensual, intoxicating and sexy love story; if you love contemporary romance you do not want to miss *Decidedly Off Limits.*" —Slick, Guilty Pleasures

"Sweet, sexy and invigorating, *Decidedly off Limits* is a friends to lovers story that is truly a breath of fresh air!"—Read & Share Book Reviews

"Oh my goodness this book was so much fun!!!"—For the Love of Books (*Decidedly With Baby*)

"There are steamy moments but you are just left with feel good melty moments more."—Books Are Love (*Decidedly With Baby*)

"Be warned dear reader, this book will have you giggling and blushing as you devour it."—The Subclub Books (*Decidedly With Love*)

"I can't wait for more Daniels brothers."—Mary at USA Today HEA (*Cowboy Most Wanted*)

"Are you in the mood for a fun, hot, sweet, romantic read that will have you blushing, laughing and glued to the pages then look no further than *Cowboy Most Wanted.*"—The Subclub Books

"HOLY HOTNESS!! Not only this book was a fun read, but it was so sexy as well!"—Blog on the Run (*Cowboy Most Wanted*)

"I'm loving this series!"—Red Hot Blue Reads (*Once Upon a Cowboy*)

ALSO BY STINA LINDENBLATT

Contemporary Romances

Carson Brothers Series

One More Chance

One More Secret

One More Betrayal

One More Truth

Spicy Romantic Comedy Novels

By The Bay Series

Decidedly Off Limits

Decidedly with Baby

Decidedly with Love

Decidedly with Mistletoe

Decidedly by Chance

Decidedly with Luck

Decidedly with Wishes

Copper Creek Series

Cowboy Most Wanted

Once Upon a Cowboy

Fix Me Up Cowboy

Visit stinalindenblattauthor.com for more books

DECIDEDLY BY CHANCE

SPECIAL EDITION

STINA LINDENBLATT

*For the readers who asked if
Wes was getting his own happily ever after...*

DECIDEDLY BY CHANCE

1

HANNAH

November

Dr. St. Clair moved the Doppler across the warm gel on my lower belly. In the background, a tiny galloping sound could be heard in the otherwise quiet room.

Even Emma, sitting on a chair near the exam table, was holding her breath, her own little bundle of joy safe in *her* belly.

My eyes misted like the early morning San Francisco fog, obscuring my vision...the same reaction they always had each time I heard the beautiful sound.

What was it?

My baby's heartbeat—the reason I had endured hormone shots so an anonymous donor could knock me up.

Yep, I know—that doesn't sound very romantic.

But neither was the way Little Bean had become one with my uterus.

There was no candlelight dinner. No quickie against a brick wall.

No husband. No boyfriend. No one-night stand.

Little Bean's start in the world was thanks to modern medicine.

I turned my head to see my best friend's reaction. Emma was grinning at me, tears threatening to knock down the dam, her hand resting on her protruding stomach.

I was fifteen weeks pregnant; Emma was five months. Everything about her was glowing, including her curly red hair.

I grinned back at her, then returned my attention to Dr. St. Clair. "And everything is okay?"

"We'll arrange the ultrasound once you're finished here, but things are progressing nicely." She wiped the gel off my still-flat belly with a towel.

The belly that was the result of years of karate as I trained to earn my black belt. A goal I had temporarily put aside to start my own family.

Why not go the more traditional route of meeting a man, falling in love, getting married, and then beginning a family a year or two later? The same path Emma had gone down when she and her now-husband, Travis, hooked up? Although in their case, their relationship had begun as nothing more than a ruse. A way to throw a wrench into his grandmother's matchmaking schemes. She'd wanted to be a great-grandmother. And now, she was finally getting her wish.

Yes, the traditional route was the dream, but it wasn't always the reality.

And my reality wasn't so pretty. Or at least it hadn't been while I was growing up.

Ready for a bedtime story?

Don't worry, it's short.

Once upon a time, a girl met a boy. He got her with child, then disappeared into the yonder, never to be heard from again.

The girl had the baby (me). And met another boy. Who didn't last long.

She then met another boy.

And another.

And another.

None of these men stuck around for long. None were interested in being saddled with someone else's child.

Fair enough.

One day, when the child was six years old, her mother ran off to Vegas with the latest boyfriend, leaving the child on her own.

Neither the mother nor the boyfriend returned. Something to do with a drug deal gone wrong. They went RIP, and the authorities moved the little girl to foster care, where she bounced around from foster home to foster home. Eventually, she ended up with a loving family who wanted to adopt her.

But something changed before she was adopted, and she was tossed back into the system.

There, she met a girl who would one day become her best friend. A girl who'd had similar struggles but had the physical scars to show for it.

I smiled at Emma once more. The scar on her chin had faded over the years—but our friendship hadn't.

Both of us had dreamed of one day finding someone who loved us as we deserved. Emma got lucky with Travis. Me?

Not so much. But I guess that was partly my fault. It's hard to trust your heart to another when it's been beaten down so many times. Before any guy had a chance to walk away, I was already sprinting out the door.

Most guys didn't make it past the first date.

But I was hardly one-of-a-kind in that department. Some women with a background similar to mine married young, yearning for the loving family they hadn't been part of growing up. Others, like myself, ran from those who professed their love to them.

Why?

Because we feared we'd be abandoned down the line—something with which we'd had lots of experience.

The only difference between me and the majority of those women? I never gave guys a chance to get close to the part where they believed they were in love with me.

But not a problem. Thanks to modern technology, single women didn't need a man if they wanted to procreate.

Okay, you're right. Modern technology hasn't gotten to the point where it can create sperm without a man. But I'm sure that possibility is right around the corner.

In the meantime, thanks to a sperm donor's generosity, Little Bean was cozy inside me. No complications. No messy relationship. And no having to worry about the father one day walking away from us—as my own parents did.

Once Dr. St. Clair had left the exam room, I climbed off the table and straightened my clothes.

"Does Travis know you're here?" I asked Emma.

She shook her head. "I haven't told him you're pregnant, if that's what you're asking. But you do realize I hate lying to him?"

"Technically, you're not lying. It's not like he's asked you if I'm pregnant." I felt my eyebrows rise. "He hasn't asked, right?"

Little Bean wasn't noticeable yet. Definitely not to the extent where someone would be posting my photo on social media, a circle drawn around the small stomach bulge with the question "Baby bump?" in block print.

"No, not yet. But he will eventually start to wonder. *People* will eventually start to wonder." Her gaze pointedly dropped to my breasts, which were fuller than they had been fifteen or so weeks ago. Her gaze then continued down to my stomach.

She was right—I wouldn't be able to hide my condition for much longer.

"I just want to wait another week, and after that you can tell him."

"But if he asks me before that if you're pregnant...?"

I opened the exam-room door. "If that happens, you can tell him the truth. I don't expect you to lie to your husband on my behalf." I grinned at her, knowing she'd been practically busting at the pregnant seams to share my news with Travis and our other friends.

All of whom already had babies or little kids of their own.

Except for Wes Chiasson.

Confirmed bachelor and workaholic.

Whom I hadn't seen in several months.

I booked my next doctor appointment; then Emma and I left the medical office and started walking the short distance to the elevators.

"I need to go to the ladies' room first," she said. "This baby is playing hockey with my bladder again."

Did I mention her husband was a hockey player with the San Francisco Rock?

Yes, I had met a few guys on the team because of that.

No, I wasn't interested in any of them. Hockey players weren't my thing.

"Go ahead," I told her since Little Bean was currently leaving my bladder alone. "I'll wait for you here."

She disappeared down the hallway leading to the ladies' room. I retrieved my phone from my purse and checked if there were any messages.

The door behind me clicked open. Without looking to see who it was, I continued reading an email.

"What do you say we go get some ice cream, Everly?"

At the deep sound of Wes's voice, my heart stumbled, and this time I did check over my shoulder. The stumbling heart was a new side effect I'd been experiencing whenever I'd seen him, but I didn't know why.

While my heart's reaction wasn't unexpected, seeing Wes with a little girl hugging a floppy bunny was.

Heck, I hadn't anticipated seeing him at all—especially not in *this* building.

His jeans and Henley top clung enticingly to his tall, athletic body. His short, light-brown hair beckoned for me to run my fingers through it. My lady bits released a dreamy sigh —and not just because I was dealing with pregnancy hormones.

Focus, Hannah.

Without meaning to, I let my gaze dart to the obstetrician's office. It was clearly marked as that. Maybe he would think I was coming from the...

My gaze did another quick dart in the opposite direction to the...orthodontist's office.

Great. Clearly, the building was trying to screw me over. All right, orthodontist's office it was.

Wes looked in my direction, and his eyes widened. "Hannah, what are you doing here?" Non-surprisingly, he quickly surveyed the other two offices on the floor.

And just like that, my explanation vanished from my brain. All I was capable of doing was opening and closing my mouth like a pregnant fish out of water. "I'm...I'm...here to see a therapist." Which was the third office located on this floor—the office that he had been coming from.

Face, meet palm.

But that was okay. I could work with that.

A confused frown crinkled on his brow. "You're here to see a child therapist?"

"Yes...I...I have a date. With one...there." I vaguely gestured in the direction he had come from. It was official. I had pregnancy brain.

That was a thing, right?

"You have a date with a therapist in that clinic?" He enunciated the words slowly as if I was an idiot. Which at that moment didn't feel too far from the truth. "You mean like an appointment or a *date*-date?" His confusion had bailed, replaced by amusement if his voice was an indication.

"Well, not so much a date as an appointment."

Nice save, Hannah.

The corners of his mouth turned up. He really did have a sexy mouth.

I meant a nice mouth.

Not a sexy mouth.

Just a regular old nice mouth.

"That's good to know," he said, "considering all the therapists in the clinic are females."

"Right," I said, "I knew that."

"Is there any particular reason you're seeing a pediatric psychologist?"

"Pediatric?" My gaze flicked to the sign by the office door. The one I hadn't paid much attention to the first time. *Oops.*

Chuckling, he nodded. "Yeah, you know. A psychologist who specializes in kids. But as a *pe-di-a-tric* nurse, you probably already know that."

"Hey, Wes," Emma said from behind me, and coming to my rescue.

Maybe.

Possibly.

Okay, definitely not. Not unless she had suddenly developed the ability to read minds.

He smiled at her. "Travis mentioned your obstetrician's office is in the same building as Everly's play therapist. I didn't realize you had an appointment there today."

Emma no doubt saw what had to be a panicked expression on my face and unfortunately misread it. "Yes, I did. But Travis was unable to join me, and Hannah came to give me moral support instead."

I inwardly cringed, knowing I would have to make it up to her, big-time. Especially if Wes mentioned seeing us here to Travis. There was no way Emma's amazing husband would miss out on a prenatal appointment. Not unless his team was on the road.

And they weren't.

I knew that. Emma knew that. And Wes knew that.

"That's me," I said, smiling on the outside and cringing some more on the inside. "The supportive friend who would do anything for her *best friend*."

Time for a change of topic.

I crouched in front of the cute little blonde girl, who had been paying more attention to her stuffed animal than us. She was wearing cream-colored tights under her velvet navy dress, the cable pattern twisted awkwardly around her legs. Whoever had put them on her hadn't done a good job. She also had on an adorable red duffle coat.

"Hi, what's your bunny's name?" I asked.

She took a small step back, almost colliding with Wes's legs, and hugged her animal tighter. "Snuggle Bunny." She smiled, and an angelic dimple sprung to life.

Wes crouched next to her, and she threw her arms around his neck. He returned her hug and pushed himself to his feet.

"Everly, these are my friends, Emma and Hannah." He pointed to each of us in turn. "And this is my niece."

A small noise, almost a gasp, fell from Emma's mouth and her eyes went wide. I had a feeling I was missing something, something Emma knew.

I looked back and forth between them, puzzling out what was going on.

"I'm so sorry about your brother and sister-in-law," she said, her eyes tearing up like they had in the doctor's office when we heard Little Bean's heartbeat.

Oh.

Wes smiled again, but this time it was twisted with the pain he was struggling to keep off his face. For Everly's sake. I'd heard that his brother and sister-in-law had died five months ago. I sent him a condolence card as soon as Emma told me. But I hadn't known that they had a daughter.

But that would explain why I hadn't seen him in a while.

"I'm sorry, too." The words emerged from my throat, thick and heavy, like peanut butter squeezed through a drinking straw.

How I kept from bursting into tears was a medical miracle in itself.

"Thanks. That's why we're here." He nodded at the office he and Everly had come from. "They're helping her deal with what happened." He directed his smile at his niece; only this time he succeeded in keeping the pain out of it. The smile was lethal—designed to melt all hearts, young and old. "Did you have fun playing the games today, Everly?"

She nodded and grinned, flashing her dimple again. "We get ice cream now?"

"That's right. Now we get to eat ice cream. Would it be okay if Hannah and Emma join us?" Wes looked at Emma. "Or do you have your appointment now?"

"No, we're already done," she said. "But unfortunately, I won't be able to join you. My store called. They need me to return due to some fountain emergency."

Emma's store? No, it didn't sell fountains. But it did have one in the center of it. People threw coins into the water and made wishes, mostly of the love variety, and Emma donated the money to a youth center for underprivileged kids.

So what did her store sell? Anything to do with love.

Don't tell anyone I said this, but she's also Dr. Lovejoy. Yes, *the* Dr. Lovejoy, who writes what is now a popular sex and relationship column for a local San Francisco indie newspaper.

"But why don't you go with them?" Emma said to me. "I know you were getting hungry." There was no missing the conspiring wink in her tone.

Except I had no idea what it meant.

I opened my mouth to tell her my stomach and I were fine, but my stomach betrayed me, making a noise rivaling that of a bear waking from a long winter nap.

Traitor.

Everly giggled.

"Is it okay with Snuggle Bunny if I join you and your uncle Wes?" I asked Everly.

She nodded.

The elevator door pinged open, and the four of us entered.

"The place is just around the corner," Wes explained as the doors closed. "It has the best ice cream around."

On the main floor, Wes, Everly, and I exited the elevator.

"I'll talk to you later." Emma nodded at him, and her eyebrows danced up her forehead.

Fortunately, Wes's back was to her.

I'm not interested, I mouthed.

It wasn't a complete lie. Lightning wasn't going to strike me.

At least not while I was in the building.

2

WES

The last person I expected to see when I took Everly to her play-therapy session was Hannah. She was the woman I'd been attracted to—and was still attracted to—from the first moment I met her almost two years ago, when Emma was pretending to be Travis's fake girlfriend.

But within a few minutes of meeting me, she had erected a wall. Did I feel bad? Not at all. Turned out, I was part of a not-so-elite group of men. Except the difference between those dumbasses she went out with and me was that they never lasted beyond the first date.

They were all ancient history; I was still in her life.

For the most part.

Why? Because we had never been on a date. We were casual friends—nothing more—who saw each other whenever the rest of our friends got together.

This would be the first time she and I were together. Alone.

Along with Everly.

"So, if I'm buying," I said as we walked down the block, "does this count as a date?"

She laughed. "Usually a date involves kissing at the end of the night. So that would be a no."

"Are you saying you'll be able to contain yourself and not kiss me?"

She made a face for a second as if pondering my question. Then she nodded, her one-sided smile matching my own. "That's exactly what I'm saying. In case you didn't realize, I have tremendous willpower."

Everly stopped and pointed at a store window with a Christmas tree in it. "Pretty."

"Do you want to go inside and check it out?" I asked her, willing to do whatever it took to make her happy.

Because a happy Everly was a lot easier to deal with than one who wondered when her parents were coming home.

She was struggling with the concept that they were permanently gone. Struggling to understand that the accident she and her parents had been in had ended their lives. The therapist we were seeing was trying to help Everly distinguish between reality and her version of reality. We weren't there yet.

She skipped to the store door.

"I guess that's a yes," Hannah said with a laugh.

"Is that okay with you?" I asked her. Lots of people got cranky if a store put up decorations and played Christmas music before Thanksgiving. I didn't know if Hannah was one of them.

Her attention was on the tree in the window, but her smile was breathtaking. And she was glowing like a little kid on Christmas morning after discovering Santa had visited during the night.

"Absolutely. I love Christmas." Her tone matched her thrilled expression. "I didn't have much of it growing up, so I'm making up for lost time."

She hurried to the store door before I could ask her what

she'd meant. She pulled it open for Everly, and they both disappeared inside. I followed them.

Normally, I loved Christmas, too. I had spent every one of them over the past few years with my brother and sister-in-law. This would be the first Christmas I would be without family. Other than Everly, who was the only close family I had left.

The two girls approached one of the fake Christmas trees that had been set up near the front of the store. The awe on Everly's face was priceless. She and Hannah inspected the decorations at Everly's height, both of them super excited about each one.

"Isn't that pretty?" Hannah pointed to a frosted glass angel with gold wings and a halo, who was holding a baby. Hannah gently stroked her finger down the angel's dress, mesmerized by the decoration.

She turned to see what Everly was looking at after my niece pointed to a decoration slightly higher up. She laughed. "Yes, that angel is pretty, too."

The angel in question was a small teddy bear, also with wings and a halo. Except these wings were a shiny burgundy fabric.

They spent a few more minutes examining the trees near the front of the store before wandering down the different aisles. At the back of the store, several miniature Christmas villages had been arranged, complete with fake snow and tiny people. I picked Everly up so she could see them better.

"Train!" She pointed at the small steam train making its way along the track.

"That's so adorable," Hannah said. "Look at the toy store, and there's a candy shop...." She pointed to each one. Then she and Everly identified all the different buildings in the village.

Or more like Everly excitedly pointed to each one, and Hannah told her what they were.

If this was what they were both like now, when it was only the first week of November, what would they be like on Christmas Eve?

I suspected their excitement wouldn't diminish; it would only be more heightened.

Or at least, I hoped it would still be that way for Everly now that her parents were gone.

Without meaning to, I hugged her a little tighter, afraid to put her down and lose her like I'd lost her father and mother.

She squirmed in my arms and gestured at something else she wanted to check out. I lowered her to the floor and she took off, darting around the legs of various strangers.

"Everly, don't run," I told her, not that she listened. When she set her mind to something, there was no stopping her.

I'd learned that the hard way.

Hannah and I trailed after her. Even with the scent of artificial pine clinging to the air, I could smell Hannah's familiar light, floral aroma. It was soft and sweet—a contrast to the woman wearing it, who was compassionate, strong, and stubborn.

"Thank you for the card," I said, keeping an eye on my niece. "It meant a lot to me." I had received it a few days after I'd told Travis about the accident. I still had the card. In my bedside table drawer. Next to a box of condoms.

"You're welcome. And I really am sorry for your loss." And then Hannah did something else entirely unexpected. She hugged me.

And naturally, I made the most of it and returned her hug.

Christ, she felt good in my arms.

She pulled away, face flushed, and returned her attention to my niece. "Is Everly living with your parents or with one of your siblings?"

"My brother was my only sibling, and my parents are both dead." Mom died of cancer while I was in college, and my father died of a heart attack a few years ago. "She's living with me. I'm her legal guardian and I'm currently in the process of adopting her."

Which was crazy when you thought about it. I was still figuring out how to parent a three-year-old. Before the accident, being a father hadn't exactly been on my to-do list. I had been a bachelor—a bachelor who spent long hours at work.

Before the accident, you could have easily fit what I knew about having kids on a pinhead.

My knowledge base had only marginally grown since then. But after talking to an attorney specializing in family law, I'd decided that the right thing to do—for Everly and for me—was to legally adopt my niece.

The entire process could take six months, including adoption classes and interviews. I had only recently started the paperwork.

Hannah's jaw dropped open, wide enough that I could've fit a Christmas bauble in her mouth, and the flush of her face was now gone. "You're her guardian?"

I couldn't tell from her tone if she thought that was a bad idea or if she was still in shock over the news. "It would seem so."

Everly was unaware of our conversation. She had discovered a wooden rocking horse—well, more like a rocking Rudolph the Red-Nosed Reindeer—and had climbed on it. She was riding it like she was one of Santa's elves in charge of exercising his transportation.

"She's so sweet," an older woman with short white hair said, moving between Hannah and me. "Looks like someone can't wait for Christmas. You two are lucky parents."

Hannah's face turned the shade of Rudolph's nose again, and she riffled through her purse.

"Thank you," I told the woman because I didn't feel like

explaining the situation to a stranger. Besides, for all intents and purposes, I was Everly's parent.

Even though I wasn't ready to be one.

"So what do you say, you two?" I said to Everly and Hannah after the woman had left us. "You ready for ice cream yet?"

Everly scrambled off the rocking reindeer, and Hannah quit searching through her purse for whatever she was pretending to look for. She glanced around her; then her shoulders sagged in relief. "Yes, let's get out of here before that lady gets any more crazy ideas."

Before I could respond, she and Everly headed toward the store exit.

The ice cream café wasn't busy when we entered it a few minutes later. Had it been summer, there would've been a line out the door and partway down the block. The place was popular due to both the delicious ice cream flavors and the old-style ice-cream-parlor atmosphere, with a black-and-white checkered floor and comfortable teal seats.

I lifted Everly so she could see the flavors. Well, more like so she could pick her favorite color. Pink, in case you were wondering.

That accounted for several choices. I convinced her to narrow it down to one.

"Strawberry," I said. "Good choice."

"What are you going to have?" I asked Hannah.

"Hmm. I have an immense craving for mango," she said, gazing longingly at the jumbo tub of ice cream. It was a familiar expression I'd seen on my sister-in-law several years ago.

I laughed. "Are you pregnant or something?"

She continued staring at the ice cream, to the point where I thought she was about to start drooling. "Sorry, I didn't realize loving mango was a crime."

"No crime. At least none I know of. You just had the same

expression as my sister-in-law whenever she craved something while pregnant with Everly."

Hannah gave me a "whatever" shrug.

I ordered our ice cream while Hannah took Everly to a table near the window and helped her onto the booster seat. "Better make hers a double mango," I told the woman behind the counter.

Maybe I'd have a better chance of scoring a kiss after our non-date date with the double scoop of mango ice cream.

Not that I was expecting Hannah to kiss me.

Did I want her to?

I certainly wouldn't complain...not unless it put me in the same standing as the idiots she had gone out with in the past. The ones riding the train of "Don't call me because I won't be calling you."

Or maybe the problem had nothing to do with the guys and everything to do with the way they kissed.

Maybe their kisses were sadly lacking in a way that mine weren't. No, that wasn't my ego talking. It was the truth.

My gaze shifted to Hannah.

Was I a man who loved a good challenge? Damn straight I was.

Was I a man who enjoyed being kicked in the nuts? What do you think?

But I had a feeling that was exactly what would happen if I tried to kiss her. However, that didn't mean I couldn't try to get *her* to kiss *me*. For fun.

Hey, don't look at me that way. It wasn't like Hannah was looking for a happily ever after. If she were, she wouldn't be treating men like they were a one-night stand...minus the sex.

And I wasn't looking for a relationship either. Now that I was Everly's guardian, my dating days were behind me. My life only had room for one girl, and she was the three-year-old sitting at the table with Hannah.

While the woman scooped my ice cream flavors out of the large tubs, I delivered Everly's and Hannah's ice cream to them.

"Here you go, ladies." I handed them their cones.

"A double?" Hannah traced the tip of her tongue up her ice cream and moaned—and the crotch of my pants suddenly felt a little snugger.

Great.

Not helping me here, Hannah.

3

HANNAH

I gave the ice cream another lick, slowly dragging the tip of my tongue up the yummy goodness. *Oh, God.* It tasted amazing.

Did I usually love mango? Not at all. It wasn't something I typically ate. But one look at the tub of ice cream, and it was like nothing else mattered.

I needed that flavor *yesterday*.

A weird expression crossed Wes's face for a fleeting second before his standard cocky smile returned. "Good, huh?"

I smiled back at him. "The best."

He went to pay for the ice cream. While he was gone, I checked to see how Everly was doing. She was enjoying her ice cream as much as I was enjoying mine.

He returned a minute later with his cone in one hand and a thick stack of napkins in the other, which he placed in the center of the table. "We'll be needing these soon enough." He nodded at Everly, who was offering ice cream to her stuffed bunny.

"Do you think she might like carrot ice cream more?" I asked her.

Everly made a face of disgust; Wes and I laughed.

This wasn't the first time Wes and I had hung out together, but it was the first time our friends weren't also there. Usually, Emma and Travis joined us. But not in the way you're thinking. We were never together as a couple.

But this time things felt different. Only I couldn't figure out why.

It felt...nice.

That was not to say that hanging out with him in the past hadn't been pleasant. I always had a good time when we got together with our friends.

But maybe being with Everly made all the difference. Maybe deep down, I'd felt a little out of place because everyone else in the group was part of a couple.

I just hadn't realized how out of place I had felt until now.

"What kind of ice cream do rabbits like to eat?" Wes asked his niece.

Everly thought about it for a moment. "Chocolate!" She giggled and licked her ice cream, accidentally smearing it on her chin and around her mouth. Wes grabbed a napkin and wiped her face clean.

Which she thought was especially funny.

We continued eating our ice cream and asking Everly all kinds of questions about Snuggle Bunny. Like what was her favorite bedtime story?

Don't Let the Pigeon Drive the Bus!

What was her favorite drink?

Strawberry lemonade.

What was her favorite food?

Apparently, it wasn't carrots like real rabbits ate. It was chocolate cake.

Everly nodded at her toy as if it had asked a question. "Snuggle Bunny wants chocolate cake for dinner tonight." She flashed Wes a hopeful expression, cranking up her persuasive superpowers with a single look.

"Sorry, Snuggle Bunny," he said to the stuffed toy, "but you've already had ice cream. So it looks like it's going to be chicken and pasta with spinach, tomatoes, and mushrooms for you."

"Wow, that does sound yummy," I said to Snuggle Bunny. "You're one very lucky bunny indeed."

"Then you can eat with us," Everly said in earnest. Melting ice cream dribbled down her cone and hand, but she didn't seem too concerned.

I was about to politely decline, but Wes had other ideas. "I think that's a great suggestion," he said. "I could use some adult company for dinner." While he might have said it with a smile, there was a slight desperation to his tone.

This wasn't a man who was used to having a young child in his life twenty-four seven. This was a man who until recently had been a workaholic bachelor. A man who had suddenly been thrown into the unexpected role of father to a preschooler. A man who had made a choice even though he hadn't been interested in becoming a parent at any point.

A man who refused to turn his back on his niece and let the higher powers put her into foster care.

Because he most likely knew that unless she got lucky and quickly found a loving home, she would end up going the route that Emma and I had traveled. Yes, Emma and I had turned out fine despite our struggles for most of our childhood and the feeling of being unlovable because no one had wanted us. But not every kid left the system the same as when they had entered.

They came out broken, their futures uncertain.

Fortunately for Everly, that wasn't her fate—thanks to Wes. Even though he no doubt felt like he'd plunged into the deep end and was drowning at times, he was there for her.

Something inside me stirred, and an unexpected warmth toward the man flickered like a firefly in my belly.

I had always liked Wes, as a casual friend, as part of the gang, but for the first time, I was seeing a different side to him, a side I admired.

Did that mean I wanted to ride off into the sunset with him?

Heck, no.

Little Bean was my first priority, and I had no room in my life for men.

However, I did have room for friends.

And since Wes had never been interested in settling down with a woman and raising a family, our friendship would remain uncomplicated.

And uncomplicated was good.

Especially given my new situation.

Both Wes and Everly looked at me expectantly.

"I'd love to join you for dinner," I said.

Everly let out a squeal of delight. Her ice cream was now melting onto the table, and she resumed her attack on it.

After we finished and Wes gave me directions to his condo, we headed our separate ways.

I was parked on a side street a couple of blocks away. A chill wrapped around my body as the damp wind picked up. The weather wasn't cold enough for the threatening rain to turn into snow, a feat that rarely happened in San Francisco. But it was chilly enough to make me shiver.

I pulled my coat closed and began the long walk to my car, cursing the fact that I'd had to park so far away from the OB's office. Cursing the fact that I had just eaten ice cream instead of something warmer.

And while I was listing the things I was cursing, how about we add the part where I was suddenly tired?

I'd been lucky during my first trimester. I hadn't suffered through morning sickness like some of my colleagues. I'd been able to ward away any threatening nausea with crackers and hard ginger candies.

But the one thing that almost knocked me off my feet was how tired I was most of the time.

Not a problem, I told myself. I just needed a short nap before I joined Wes and Everly for dinner, and everything would be fine.

The need to yawn overpowered me. I barely covered my mouth in time.

A few other individuals were also striding along the sidewalk, too preoccupied with escaping the cold to pay attention to me and my humongous yawn.

I walked down the street I'd parallel parked on and kept on walking. Right past the spot where I was positive I'd left my car.

But instead of *my* car, another vehicle was parked there.

Oh, God. Someone had stolen my car? No sooner had the thought crossed my mind, than I could feel the blood in my head rapidly pool in my feet.

This couldn't be happening.

Breathe in. Breathe out. Stressing out wasn't good for Little Bean.

But apparently, the heavens thought dumping water on my head was a better idea. The sky opened up and pelted me with rain. And of course, my umbrella was. In. My. Car.

I fought the urge to stick my tongue out at the clouds...or at least flip them the bird.

First things first. I needed to find my vehicle.

Then I could give the heavens a piece of my mind.

Maybe I had parked it somewhere else and thanks to my pregnancy brain, I'd confused the real location with this one.

I scanned the street. Nothing. Was I even on the right road? Maybe I had parked down a different one.

I surveyed the businesses lining the street. No, I was positive it was this one. I remembered the florist. A good-looking man had stepped from the store with a large bouquet when I'd been walking away from my car. He'd been hard to miss.

What were the chances of an identical florist being in the area?

Yeah, I didn't think it was very high either. We weren't talking about Starbucks here.

"Do you need help, miss? You look lost."

The woman from the Christmas store, who had thought Wes and I were Everly's parents, was standing in front of me. Her bright-red umbrella protected her head from the slaughter of rain.

"I was looking for my car. I parked it here, but it's not here anymore." I had no idea why I was telling her this. It wasn't like she could make it magically reappear.

"What did it look like?"

"Blue. Small. A hatchback."

She flashed me a pitying look, and my stomach dropped like a rubber ball released from the top of the Empire State building. "The city towed it not long ago."

I blinked. "Towed it?"

She nodded. "I don't know what it is about this neighborhood. It's like the tow trucks are hungry vultures, waiting for someone's time to run out before they swoop in and tow the vehicle."

I inwardly groaned. The area had free parking for up to two hours, but between my OB appointment, bumping into Wes, visiting the Christmas store and the ice cream café, I had been parked here for over two hours.

More like two and a half hours.

"Where's your husband?" she asked.

"My husband?"

"Yes, that nice, tall man you were with in the store. He was quite the hottie."

"He's not my husband. He's just a friend." Who had driven

Everly home for a nap. So I couldn't call him, even if I wanted to.

"If you would like, I can get my grandson to drive you to where they towed your car. He'll be picking me up in a few minutes."

Ever watched a criminal show? This is the part were the sweet little old lady lures the poor unsuspecting, drowned rat of a girl into her car...only for her psychopathic grandson to bludgeon the girl to death.

Note to self: No more watching those shows. They probably weren't healthy to watch when you were pregnant.

And when you had young children.

"Oh, that's okay." I took a step back. "I don't want to be any trouble." And another step. "I can call a cab."

"It won't be trouble at all. You'll like my grandson. He's a very nice man. And he's single." She winked at me and those stranger-danger alarms blared in my head again.

Along with the image of my obituary in the newspaper after my body was recovered months later.

I retreated another step, prepared to go into full fight-or-flight mode. Fortunately, I'd spent the past eight years working toward my black belt, and I'd taken some self-defense classes.

A girl could never be too careful.

"And there he is now."

A black SUV pulled up into the empty space in front of where my car used to be.

Of course. What better way to transport a body than in a black SUV? Then they could bury my body far from San Francisco, in some off-road location.

A man climbed out of the driver's side. I couldn't see his face, but I memorized the top of his head—the only part I could see—in case I needed to describe it later.

He was obviously tall. His black hair was shaved short, hugging a nicely shaped head.

Right, not the best choice of adverb for a potential killer.

He came around the front of the vehicle, giving me a glimpse of his light-brown skin. The familiar light-brown skin of a certain hot someone who worked in Emma's building.

"Hey, Hannah," Jayden said, flashing me his perfect white teeth.

"You two know each other?" his grandmother asked, clearly surprised and delighted by the turn of events.

No more than I was. Why? No, I wasn't interested in hooking up with him.

I knew him enough to trust him for a ride to wherever the city had impounded my poor baby, though. Jayden wasn't about to murder me and bury my body so that no one found me until the spring.

It didn't mean Mr. Former Navy SEAL wasn't capable of doing that. From all accounts that I'd heard, he and the rest of crew at Quade Security and Investigations were highly skilled and able to do that.

All except maybe their receptionist, Isabelle, although I wouldn't put anything past her.

"My best friend has a store in the same building where his work is located," I explain to Jayden's grandmother.

I turned to him in time to see him visibly wince.

Uh, oh. Did I say something I shouldn't have?

"You mean where his *store* is located," his grandmother said.

"Right. His store." I raised my eyebrow at him in silent question.

He gave me a negligible shake of his head that I didn't think his grandmother noticed.

"Jayden, we need to drop Hannah off at the city impound so she can retrieve her car. They towed it while she was shopping with her non-husband and his daughter."

"She means Wes," I clarified. "But you really don't need to

do that. I can grab a cab." Which would cost money...on top of the parking and towing fines.

Money that was supposed to be for Little Bean and not for stupid expenses like these.

I added a few more mental curses directed at the car-towing fiend.

"I can definitely take you," Jayden informed me. "But you'll need to go to the nearest police station first to obtain a vehicle release form. Then I can drive you to the impound to retrieve your car."

"That's a lot of bother to get your car back," his grandmother said with a groan. She pointed to Jayden's SUV. "Now get in before you catch your death from this cold."

I opened my mouth to protest but didn't get too far. A shiver rippled through me, proving her point.

"*Tut-tut*, just get in." She strode determinedly to the front passenger door, opened it, and waved me in.

Woof. The deep, welcoming bark could come from no other than...

"Mojo!" I said as the adorable Bernese mountain dog stuck his large, grinning head between the front seats.

He barked again.

"You better do as she says." The corners of Jayden's eyes crinkled with suppressed laughter, and he nodded toward his grandmother. "She's stubborner than a mule."

"But I'm soaking wet. I'll ruin your seats."

"Have you been rolling around in mud?"

"Not lately, no." That was Mojo's specialty.

"Then it shouldn't be an issue. You're at greater risk of being covered in dog hair from Mojo." The big bear of a dog happily barked at the sound of his name.

I climbed onto the seat, and my cheek was immediately the recipient of wet doggy kisses.

Which I'm sad to report was the first time I'd been kissed in many months.

By either man or dog.

"Mojo—in the back." The words flew from Jayden's mouth like M&M's from a BB gun. Mojo gave him a disappointed whimper before doing what he was told.

Liam Quade—Jayden's boss and the owner of the company he worked for—most likely paid his employees really well. The inside of the SUV was a helluva lot fancier than my car. The leather seats? A very nice touch.

His grandmother pulled herself onto the seat behind Jayden's. "By the way, I'm Ruth."

I turned to her. "Thank you for rescuing me. I was beginning to think my car had been stolen."

Well, technically it had been. The mean person who towed my vehicle couldn't have just given me a parking ticket. That would have been bad enough.

But to tow me? It seemed a little excessive. Like something Ebenezer Scrooge would do to Santa's sleigh on Christmas Eve.

Bah, humbug.

4

WES

All the ingredients I needed for dinner were arranged on the kitchen counter. "So what's it going to be?" I asked Everly, who was standing on the kiddy step next to me so she could watch me work. "Spaghetti or rotini?"

"Saghetti."

"All right, *spaghetti* it is."

I filled the pot with water and turned on the heat. The chicken breasts had been marinating for the past hour in a lemon-and-herb sauce. It was my mom's special recipe. A recipe she had passed down to both of her sons when we were teens. She had felt it was important that her boys know how to cook so that one day we could impress our future wives.

While I might not have used my skills to land me a wife, they had certainly come in handy for helping me get laid.

Too bad those days were long gone.

Now the only female I cooked for was the pint-sized variety in the form of my niece.

And now Hannah.

"So what did you think of Hannah?" I asked while cutting the vegetables. It seemed like a safe enough question.

"She's pretty," Everly said matter-of-factly and continued cutting invisible carrots with her toy knife.

"She is very pretty."

"And she's nice," Everly added.

"She is very nice. And she's smart too. She's a nurse."

"What's a nurse?"

"That's someone who takes care of people who are sick."

"Like Mommy does?"

I mentally cringed at her use of present tense. "No, your mommy was a doctor. Nurses help the doctors make their patients feel better again."

"So that makes Hannah super nice."

"You're right. She is super nice and super special."

Eventually, Everly got bored with helping me, climbed down from her booster step, and went off to watch *Dora the Explorer*.

A short while later, the intercom buzzed, and I let Hannah into the building.

As I made my way to the apartment door, I rounded up a few of the toys that had claimed the living room floor as their home. "Everly, Hannah is here. Turn off the TV."

She cheered and happily obliged—which wasn't usually the case when it came to her favorite shows. She had a brilliant future as a lawyer.

That, or I sucked when it came to negotiating with a three-year-old.

I tossed the armful of toys into her toy chest in her bedroom as the apartment doorbell announced Hannah's arrival. I strode to the door and opened it.

She was standing in the hallway in light-brown suede boots and a burgundy dress that reached an inch above her knees. A narrow width of skin peeked from between the boots and the hem of the skirt. With her long brown hair cascading in loose waves down her shoulders, she looked like my new favorite kind of sexy. Understated but definitely there.

"Sorry I'm late." She smiled, but it was as if the corners of her mouth didn't have the energy to tilt up all the way. "Turns out an overly zealous parking patrol officer monitored the spot where I was parked this afternoon. And he has a thing for towing cars instead of ticketing the owners."

I moved aside to let her in. "They towed your vehicle?"

"Yep."

"How did you get it back?"

"Jayden Price was picking up his grandmother—who, by the way, was the same elderly woman from the Christmas store who thought we were married. He took me to the police station to get the vehicle release form, and only then could we retrieve my car. Which I finally got about an hour ago."

I took her coat from her and hung it in the foyer closet. "You look like you could use a glass of wine."

She didn't respond—too busy taking in my fancy-ass condo to say anything, her mouth half-open in shock. "I knew you lived in a nicer place than me. I just didn't realize how nice. Is this a penthouse?"

I nodded—not that she noticed. The place had that effect on people, especially with the large open-concept design, the white walls, and the hardwood floor. They were great, but the real selling feature was the view: the huge, picturesque windows that overlooked the bay and part of downtown. Because the sun had already set, the buildings were lit up like Christmas trees.

I'll admit the three-bedroom condo was a little excessive for one person—now two with Everly—but I loved it here. It proved my father wrong when he had said I'd never amount to anything. In his mind, I'd been nothing more than a gamer, wasting my life away.

Too bad he wasn't alive to see how wrong he had been.

"It's gorgeous. Did you decorate it yourself?"

I laughed. "Definitely not. I hired an interior designer." One of my friends had recommended her.

"It's really impressive."

"You want to see my room?" Everly scrambled off the oversized, super comfy couch.

Hannah beamed at her. "I would love to see your room." She bent down and removed her boots.

Once she was finished, Everly grabbed hold of her hand and led her to the guest rooms. We entered Everly's room, and she flicked on her light. The curtains had been drawn for the night.

Hannah gaped at what was obviously a little girl's room—one that belonged to a princess. The walls were light pink, as were the curtains, the canopy on the four-poster bed, the bedding, and the armchair in the corner. The only things that weren't pink were the mural, the off-white furniture, and the rug. But even though the rug had lots of green on it, it also had a pink border and pink roses.

"Wow, this is amazing. Did Travis paint the mural?" Hannah asked.

The mural in question was a picture of a deciduous forest with cute woodland critters keeping an eye on Everly.

My friend—a defenseman for the San Francisco Rock—was a talented artist who had also painted murals for the kids of some of our friends. At least when he retired from the NHL, Travis had a potential career to fall back on.

"That's right," I said. "You love it don't you, Everly?"

She nodded enthusiastically and showed Hannah her room like a princess showing off her castle. Not a single item was skipped.

At one point, Hannah yawned, unable to cover her mouth fast enough. "Sorry, I'm just a little tired."

"Why don't I finish showing you around, and then dinner

should be ready." From the looks of her, I wasn't sure if she would even last through the meal.

Clearly running around the city to retrieve her car after it had been towed had taken a toll on her.

Next on the tour was the guest room. The only guests who had ever stayed in it were my brother and sister-in-law. Usually, if I had a sleepover guest, they were in my room. But that didn't happen too often. There was no point in bringing a one-night stand to your place unless you were really hoping for more than one night—as I had learned the hard way.

One look at my condo and the woman would imagine herself as the future Mrs. Chiasson, complete with full access to my bank account.

And those women were harder to shake than a fistful of burrs on your sock.

Another lesson I'd learned the hard way.

I only invited Hannah for dinner because I knew she wouldn't suddenly declare her love for me after seeing my condo. Yes, that had happened with another woman.

Hannah's gaze swept over the room. "The view's incredible. You can't see much of anything from my apartment, other than the building across from me. But it really is a nice brick building." She laughed softly, the exhaustion momentarily chased from her face.

The tour ended with the master bedroom.

"Oh, God. I finally know what Heaven looks like," Hannah declared after we stepped into my room. "I can tell you now if this was my room, I'd never leave it."

If you were in this room, I'd never let you leave it. I'd spend all my days happily fucking you in the bed and in the shower and in the Jacuzzi.

The thought stopped me short. I mean it was true. I would be more than willing to screw her in all those places. But I had no intention of getting married or ending up in a permanent relationship with a woman.

That just wasn't for me.

My company was the only thing I wanted to be married to... till death do us part.

Hannah yawned again, and for a fleeting second, I saw desire on her face. Only it wasn't the desire to fuck me in my bed or the shower or even the Jacuzzi. She looked like she wanted to crawl onto my bed for a long nap.

She shook her head slightly as if waking herself up. "Can I help you with dinner?"

"Nope. Everly and I have it all under control."

Hannah looked down at Everly, who had scaled my bed and seemed ready to use it as a trampoline, a mischievous gleam in her large blue eyes.

"You helped Uncle Wes make dinner?" she asked Everly, who nodded. "Then I bet it will be delicious."

"Uncle Wes says you're very pretty." Everly flopped back onto the bed and giggled.

Hannah's face flushed, and her gaze went to anywhere but me. "That was sweet of him to say."

I knew it couldn't have been the first time Hannah had heard that she was pretty, gorgeous, or breathtaking, but maybe when the other men said it, it was clear the compliment came with strings attached.

"Well, sweet is my middle name. But don't let that get out. It might ruin my reputation." I winked at her, and she laughed.

"Oh, goodie. Blackmail." She rubbed her hands together in gleeful malice...except there wasn't a single malicious bone in her hot body.

A sudden urge to kiss that expression from her face surged through me.

I pushed the urge aside. Even if Hannah had no issues with

me kissing her, I wasn't about to make out with her in front of my niece.

Besides kissing her now would suck all the fun out of my game. The game where I got *her* to kiss *me.*

I gestured for us to head to the dinner table. Everly climbed into her booster chair while I served everyone the food.

I went to pour white wine for Hannah, but she shook her head.

"I'll have what she's having." She pointed to Everly's glass.

"You want milk?" I'd eaten out with Hannah several times, and she always ordered wine with her food.

Maybe that's just a restaurant thing with her.

Except, when we had dinner at Emma and Travis's condo, she always had wine then, too. At least she did until Emma became pregnant. Out of sympathy for her friend, Hannah switched to milk.

Maybe she really likes milk now.

Hannah took a bite of the food. "Mmm." The fork slowly slid from between her lips, the sound probably more erotic in my head than it had been in reality. "You two are amazing chefs."

Look away from her lips. With some effort, I got my eyes to obey.

Dinner was fun. It was easy to see that Everly enjoyed having Hannah there. She wasn't the only one. Hannah seemed more relaxed than usual. *Everly Magic.* It was incredible what a three-year-old could do—especially *this* three-year-old.

But Everly wasn't the only one with the magic touch. The three of us ate and talked and laughed, and for the first time since the accident, Everly was her old animated self. It was no wonder Hannah was a pediatric nurse. She had a way with kids.

Once dinner was finished, Hannah and I cleared the dishes while Everly went off to play.

"You're doing an amazing job with her," Hannah said quietly, lowering the plates onto the kitchen counter. "And I can't believe how adorable her room looks. If I were a three-year-old girl, I'd be very jealous."

"So your parents never painted woodland critters on your wall?" I asked, laughing.

A smile appeared at the corner of Hannah's mouth. It wasn't a happy smile. It was the same sad smile I'd seen a few times when the topic of parents was brought up among our friends. She and Emma were always quiet on the subject.

So was Josh, who I knew hadn't had a good childhood. His grandparents raised him because his own parents couldn't be bothered.

"Definitely not," she said. "I never knew my father. And my mom was always too preoccupied with her latest boyfriend to worry about giving me a princess room. And when it comes to foster parents, many care more about the money they earn than making the kid feel like a princess. Or at least that was my experience."

She lifted her shoulders in a *What-can-you-do?* shrug. "That's why I think it's so great you're doing all of this for Everly"—she gestured toward my niece's bedroom—"to help her cope with what happened."

She leaned in and kissed my cheek. The kiss wasn't the kind I was aiming for, but the impact was the same. An electrical hum crackled beneath my skin.

Without thinking about what I was doing, I moved my upper body closer to her.

"She's lucky to have you as an uncle." Her voice was low and smoky, and her gaze flickered briefly to my mouth.

The patter of bare feet against the kitchen tiles behind me was the only warning I got that we were no longer alone.

I stepped away from Hannah and turned to my niece. "Are you ready for your bath and then bed?"

That was the advantage of having a kid who was three years old. They went to bed early.

The disadvantage? They woke up early, too. Forget sleeping in on the weekends. With Everly, those days were gone.

Not that I had slept in late very often even before she moved in with me, the workaholic that I was. But it would have been nice to have the option.

She nodded. "And a story. Snuggle Bunny wants a story."

"Of course. I wouldn't have it any other way." I lifted her into my arms. "This won't take too long," I told Hannah. "Why don't you make yourself comfortable on the couch? Maybe turn on a show or something?"

I wasn't ready for her to leave yet. And it had nothing to do with my goal of getting her to kiss me again...only this time not on my cheek.

I wanted to find out more about what we had been discussing in the kitchen before Everly interrupted. Emma had once mentioned that she and Hannah had grown up in foster care. I'd never brought it up with Hannah after Emma's little insight into their past, figuring she would tell me when she was ready.

But now I was curious. Now I wanted to know more about that period in her life, which was partly responsible for the woman she had become.

By the time I returned to the living room, after tucking Everly into bed, Hannah's eyes were closed, her head was on the armrest of the couch, and her breathing was slow and even.

I crouched in front of her and brushed strands of hair out of her face. She didn't so much as stir.

After contemplating what to do, I turned down the bed covers in the guest room and returned to the couch to get sleeping beauty. I gathered her in my arms. The skin on the back of her thigh, where her skirt had raised, was warm and soft against my arm. Fortunately, the skirt stayed mostly in place.

Hannah stirred but remained asleep. All the excitement from retrieving her towed vehicle really had worn her out.

I carried her to the guest room and laid her on the bed. She immediately turned to her side, facing me. In the dim light of the bedside table lamp, she looked like a sleeping dark-haired angel, her full lips slightly parted.

Didn't the prince in *Sleeping Beauty* kiss the princess and wake her from a deep sleep? I wasn't exactly sure. I remembered something about Snow White waking up from the dead after a prince kissed *her*.

There's a word for that: necrophilia.

And if you asked me, that prince was one sick dude.

That was one fairy tale I wouldn't be reading to Everly.

I covered Hannah with the bedding, turned off the lamp, and left the room, shutting the door behind me.

In the kitchen, I removed my phone from my back pocket and sent Jayden a text.

Me: Thanks for helping Hannah earlier.

He responded a minute later as I turned on the Rock's hockey game. Tonight they were playing the Vancouver Canucks.

Jayden: I take it she told you.

Me: Yes, she came over for dinner and mentioned it.

Jayden: My grandmother will be disappointed.

Me: ??? That Hannah had dinner with me?

> Jayden: I think she was hoping to set me up with Hannah.

I'd be lying if I said it didn't feel like sour chocolate milk had turned in my stomach at his text.

> Me: I didn't realize you're interested in Hannah that way.

It was official. Next time it was my turn to bring coffee to Quade Security and Investigations for a meeting, I was dumping a bottle of hot sauce into Jayden's cup.

> Jayden: Ha! And risk you removing my balls? Not a chance man.

> Me: And what's that supposed to mean?

> Jayden: I swear you and Hannah are the only two people who haven't figured out you have it bad for her.

> Me: I'm not sure I should dignify that with an answer.

> Me: And you're wrong by the way.

Cheers broke out on the TV. I didn't have to look to know the Rock had scored.

> Jayden: Then I guess you won't mind if my grandmother sets me up with Hannah. Hmm. I wonder where I should take her on our first date.

> Jayden: Any suggestions?

> Me: Fuck. Off.

Jayden: Googling "Fuck. Off." now…

5

HANNAH

The familiar woodsy scent of a man's aftershave mixed with his yummy smell filled my dreams. Yes, I was dreaming. That was the only explanation for why I could smell Wes so clearly.

In my dream, my head was resting on his chest.

Except I had no idea why I was dreaming about Wes. Maybe I could blame it on the pregnancy hormones. I was positive the dream-thing was listed somewhere in the pregnancy book I'd bought but hadn't quite gotten around to reading yet.

I'd been afraid of jinxing things.

If I were lucky, the book would explain why I was dreaming about Wes, specifically. Not that it was a hard puzzle to solve. I'd had dinner with Wes and Everly last night.

I attempted to yank myself out of my dream. While doing that, I played the movie montage in my head of yesterday. The OB appointment. Bumping into Wes. The Christmas store and the ice cream café. My car being towed. I paused the montage for some serious cursing at the asshole who'd towed my vehicle.

Okay, back to the montage...

Jayden and his grandmother rescuing me.

Eating dinner with Wes and Everly.

Him leaving to give her a bath.

Me sitting on the couch.

Us talking?

I strained to remember that part of the evening, along with me leaving his condo and the drive home.

All of it came up blank.

My eyes fluttered open, but instead of my bedroom greeting me, a less familiar one popped into view.

Holy. Shit.

And that was when the remainder of the movie montage in my head came into focus. I'd been so tired from being pregnant and from running around to get my car back from the impound. When Wes had given Everly her bath, I'd closed my eyes.

For a second.

Or at least that was what I had promised myself.

But I must have fallen asleep instead.

Throwing the covers off my body, I pushed myself to sit. The room was dark, which meant it had to be before seven in the morning. I didn't feel as exhausted as I had last night, so I must have slept for at least a few hours.

The rest of the condo was dark and quiet when I stepped from the guest room. I slowly navigated my way to the living room, allowing my eyes to adjust to the darkness. Fortunately, the typical morning bay fog hadn't rolled in far enough to block the glow of the moon. And thanks to the large windows, there was enough light for me to find my way to the couch, where I'd left my purse and phone.

I checked the time on it. 5:16 a.m. Quietly, I retraced my steps to the foyer, slipped on my boots and coat, and vacated the condo. The door clicked behind me, but I didn't think it was loud enough to wake anyone. Neither Wes's nor Everly's rooms were close to the entrance.

As I walked to the elevator, I brushed my hand over my hair, attempting to make it look more presentable. I hadn't had a chance to look in a mirror, but something warned me I looked like I was doing the walk of shame when that couldn't be the furthest thing from the truth.

My bladder cursed me for that little oversight. The oversight that involved me going to the bathroom before leaving the apartment. I had been so desperate to avoid any awkwardness from bumping into Wes, I had ignored the part where I had to pee. Badly.

I pressed the down button of the elevator and willed it to be fast. The door eventually—after several impossibly long minutes—pinged open and I stepped inside.

To be met by a woman in her seventies, impeccably dressed in black slacks and a hunter-green silk blouse. She wore makeup that was perfectly applied, and her long gray hair was pulled back in a neat bun. She looked ready to step into the boardroom of a Fortune 100 company.

Her gaze gave me a cursory once-over, and it was clear she wasn't impressed with what she saw. I had no idea why. She didn't know me. And I doubted she knew every resident in this building to guess that I was sneaking out like a one-night stand who had overstayed her welcome.

I smiled and nodded at her, but that was the extent of my interaction. I just wanted to get home, pee, and shower—in that order.

"What apartment are you coming from?" Her tone was blunt but still sharp enough to cut steak with a fair bit of effort.

I widened my smile. Unlike before, the movement felt forced. But thanks to my years as a pediatric nurse, I had developed the skill so that even my painted-on smiles appeared genuine. "I'm sorry, but I'm not sure how it's any of your business."

"If it has to do with this building, then I make it my business."

Well, okey dokey. Good for her. "That's nice, but I don't see what that has to do with me. I'm not here to renovate it or inspect the elevator or putter around in the garden. I was visiting a friend."

"During the night?"

"You make it sound like a boarding house for young women from the turn of the twentieth century."

Clearly, the woman didn't find that as amusing as I did. She snorted with disgust.

Did she seriously believe I was here to soil some guy's reputation?

I almost burst out laughing. In the time that I'd known Wes (about two years for those keeping track), I'd seen him with a number of dates. He wasn't a player. He was too busy with work to be one. But he was as much a monk as I was a nun.

"Not that it's any of your business, but I was visiting a friend and fell asleep on the couch." No need to point out that said friend had put me to bed. In the guest bed, not *his* bed.

She gave me a brisk nod that I had no idea how to translate. Not that I needed to. The elevator door pinged open, and I made my escape like a woman on a mission.

Or a woman who desperately needed to get home so she could pee.

A point I didn't feel like mentioning to the elderly lady. If she thought she was the reason I couldn't get away fast enough, so be it. She probably enjoyed the power trip.

The early Wednesday morning traffic added a few minutes to my drive time. Under normal circumstances, the time difference wouldn't be a big deal.

But that was when my bladder wasn't a ticking time bomb, ready to explode at any moment.

By the time I arrived at my building, I was ready to do the pee-pee dance—the dance little kids do when they need to go badly. Okay, I might have done precisely that while waiting for the elevator to get to my floor.

C'mon. What's taking so long?

Was it trying to get into the Guinness Book of World Records for being the slowest elevator? Because if that were the case, then I'd say it had succeeded.

The door finally opened on my floor, and I hurried down the hallway in a near sprint. The only reason I didn't actually sprint was because I didn't think my bladder would appreciate it.

I slipped my key into the lock. "C'mon," I muttered to it. Now wasn't the time for it to get stuck.

The key finally turned. I opened the door, quickly kicked off my shoes, and rushed toward the bathroom...only to be brought up short at the squishing of wet carpet underfoot.

Oh. Shit.

The *plop, plop, plop* of water drops against a hard surface caused my stomach to sag against my bladder. Water was dripping in rapid-fire from the ceiling. And I'm not talking about from only one spot. It had sprung multiple leaks, including over my couch.

But my bladder didn't care about that, and I returned to my original goal of heading to the bathroom. The leaking ceiling would have to wait a few more minutes.

Once I finished relieving myself, I grabbed my phone from my purse and called the building manager.

He answered as I stepped into my bedroom.

Oh. Double shit.

My bedroom was in the same condition as the living room; just switch the wet couch for the wet bed.

I explained the situation to the manager. Thirty minutes later, he and the maintenance guy were standing in my apartment, assessing the damage. The water had already been turned off, and the shower in my apartment the weatherman had not predicted last night had ended.

"You'll need to find somewhere to stay while your apartment is being repaired," the manager said.

"Don't you have a vacant apartment you can move me to?"

He shook his head. "Had this happened last month, I could have moved you to apartment 509. But I just leased it out last week. There's nothing else available."

I inwardly groaned. That was not what I was hoping to hear.

On the other hand, I had planned to find a new place to live because my one-bedroom apartment wouldn't be big enough once Little Bean was born and mobile.

But I'd thought I had five months until my lease was close to expiring before I had to worry about it.

After the manager and building maintenance departed my apartment, I called my insurance company. Fortunately, they would cover the majority of my damaged possessions.

Now I needed to find a place to stay while I searched for a new apartment. And I needed to do this and pack my stuff *before* the beginning of my shift at the hospital that afternoon.

With a *Why-is-this-happening-to-me?* sigh, I began packing up my apartment. I'd been working for almost two hours when my phone pinged from my bedroom dresser—the only furniture without puddles on it.

Emma had texted me.

Emma: I'm standing outside your building on
the off chance you're home. Are you home?

Me: I am, I replied. I'll buzz you up. I'll be in my bedroom. Don't bother removing your shoes... unless you want to go swimming in what used to be my living room.

Emma's text didn't exactly surprise me. She and I used to show up all the time at each other's apartments without calling first, back when she was single and we used to live near each other.

But then she and Travis got married and moved into a condo of their own. Now, she no longer lived near me, but her store was still not far from my soon-to-be ex-apartment.

A few minutes later, I heard the apartment door click open.

Silence poured in for several moments, followed by, "Oh, that's not good."

I turned to the bedroom doorway as Emma entered my room.

"I know you've always wanted a house with a swimming pool, but common wisdom says you don't place it in your living room."

"I don't know. I think it's the most overlooked location. I won't have to worry about the weather outside. My swimming pool will always be a pleasant temperature."

Emma's gaze shifted to the bedroom ceiling and the very noticeable wet stain that wasn't there the last time she was in my apartment. "What the hell happened?"

"A water pipe burst in the apartment above mine. Because the couple upstairs is away on vacation, and I didn't come home until this morning, no one realized there was an issue with the plumbing until a few hours ago."

I retrieved my wet nurse's uniform from my closet and tossed it into a large garbage bag. "So now I need somewhere to stay while I look for a new apartment." I also needed to do laundry before my clothes turned mildew-y.

"You're staying with Travis and me." Emma said as if it were a given. A smile grew on her face. "But first let's get back to the part where you didn't come home until this morning. When I left you after the OB appointment, you were going to have ice cream with Wes and Everly. How did that go from ice cream to a sleepover?"

"You're assuming I was with Wes last night."

Her eyes widened. "You were with someone else? Wow, just how many dates did you have yesterday?"

I didn't think she could get any more excited at my little revelation than if I had announced I was getting married to royalty.

"Having ice cream with Wes and Everly doesn't count as a date. She invited me for dinner, and I fell asleep on the couch while he was putting her to bed." I explained about my misadventures with the tow truck.

"You should have called me," she said once I was finished.

"You were working. But everything turned out okay, in the end, thanks to Jayden and his grandmother."

"And if they hadn't shown up? Then what were you planning to do?"

I smirked. "Wish on a shooting star...anyway, back to the part about me staying with you and Travis. Shouldn't you at least ask your husband first?" I added a pair of jeans to the plastic bag.

"I can do that, but you know he won't have an issue with it. And we have the extra room." She nodded at the bag in my hand. "And we have a washer and dryer." Which was more than I could say for my small apartment. I had to wash and dry my clothes in the equally small laundry room downstairs.

"Are you sure it will be okay?" The location wasn't the best when it came to the hospital, but it was better than staying at a hotel.

"I'm positive. But if it will make you feel better, I can talk to

Travis now." Her gaze scanned the room again. "I'll definitely call him right away."

She stepped from the room to phone him while I continued packing my clothes.

She returned a few minutes later, grinning. "The best husband in the world is heading over in a few minutes and will help us pack up your stuff. Especially since you shouldn't be lifting anything given your condition."

"You told him I'm pregnant?"

She shook her head. "Nope. It's your job to tell him."

"So how do I do that? I don't think there's any conversation that would lead to the one where I announce I'm pregnant by an anonymous donor."

What was I supposed to say? *Guess what, Travis? Your wife isn't the only one here who's pregnant. I'm pregnant, too. But I have no idea who the father is. Little Bean was conceived in a petri dish.*

Talk about a conversation stopper—which was why I had put off announcing I was pregnant for as long as I had after my first trimester.

"When the time is right, you'll know what to say. Besides, it's not like you're telling some guy you went out with one time that he's going to be a father."

"True." *Thank God I got to skip that awkward conversation.*

6

HANNAH

Emma and I were stuffing my clothes into plastic bags when Travis buzzed my apartment to be let in. I continued packing while Emma went to the living room—probably so she and Travis could make out for a few minutes first.

I was used to that. I knew being married to an NHL player was tough, even more so now that Emma was pregnant. Travis was on the road more times than she would like. So whenever they were together, they were like horny teens, always making out.

It was sweet and cute and often made me wish a man like Travis existed somewhere out there for me.

But I knew better than to get sucked into that fairy-tale fantasy.

Because even if I did find this wonderful man, there was no guarantee he would stick around. If history had taught me one thing, it was that I wasn't worth sticking around for.

No need to bring out the pity-party decorations. I was only stating the facts. But thanks to modern technology, it wasn't something I had to worry about anymore. I was creating my own family. Yes, my family unit wouldn't have a father, but I did have male friends who were now fathers and would be great role models for Little Bean later on.

Besides, this was the twenty-first century. The old family model of father plus mother plus kids (and a dog) was ancient history.

I didn't need a man to make me complete.

I did, though, miss making out with the human male species.

Emma and Travis eventually stepped into the bedroom. Emma's lips appeared happily satisfied, and her curly red hair was messier than it had been before she left the room.

"I'm pregnant." The words just tumbled from between my lips. Had I meant to say that? Not at all. I was going to give them a hard time for being gone for so long.

Well, I guess that cat was out of the proverbial garbage bag now.

Travis looked at Emma as if expecting her to start laughing because I was punking him. The faint *plop...plop...plop* could be heard coming from the living room, from one of the few places in the ceiling still leaking. The water drops were landing in a bucket maintenance had set up in that room.

Emma nodded. "It's true."

"So does this have anything to do with you being at the OB's office yesterday when you didn't tell me you had an appointment there?" he asked her.

Oops. Busted.

"Wes told you he saw me there yesterday, huh?" she asked.

Travis nodded.

"That was my fault," I said. "I didn't want anyone to know until I was out of the first trimester"—which ended two weeks ago—"and Emma, being such an amazing friend, let me have my way, even if it meant keeping a secret from you." I grinned at him. "But let me assure you that she didn't *want* to break the oath you guys made on your wedding day. The one about keeping secrets from your spouse when they have nothing to do with him."

"Does Wes know?"

"Nope. Only Emma and now you know."

"Are you planning to tell him?"

"What difference does it make if I tell him or not? Either way, in a few months it will be hard to miss." I gestured to Emma's belly.

Travis leaned his hand high against the doorframe. "What about the father? Does he know?"

"You mean the baby's daddy?"

He nodded again.

I felt the corners of my mouth move ever-so-slightly, eager to stretch into a bigger smile. I fought back the urge. "I don't think he'll care either way."

"How do you know that? Just look at Josh and Holly." Holly and Josh were mutual friends of ours. Their daughter was the same age as Everly.

The pair got drunk one night, and their daughter, Lily, happened. But they were already friends beforehand.

They simply got the nursery rhyme all mixed up: First comes the baby carriage. Then comes love; then comes marriage.

"I'm pretty sure when my baby daddy left his donation, he didn't care if he knocked me up or not."

A confused frown scrunched between Travis's eyes. "Am I missing something here?"

Emma chuckled. "She went to a sperm bank and was artificially inseminated."

I snorted a laugh. "Ooh, you make it sound so romantic when you put it that way."

"So there was no guy?" Travis asked, still looking a little confused.

"Nope, no guy. I mean other than the one who made the donation in the plastic cup. And as long as he got paid, he didn't care if I got knocked up or not."

"That doesn't sound like much fun."

He did have a point there. At least getting knocked up the old-fashioned way was more fun—most of the time. Getting knocked up the scientific way? Not so much.

But it was worth it in the end. And I didn't have to worry about things getting complex because the father wanted to be in the picture, and I didn't want him there.

Sure, things had worked out great for Holly and Josh, but that didn't mean it would've been so simple if I had asked a random guy to knock me up...or had asked someone I knew to get me pregnant.

The other option would have been to have lots of one-night stands until one of them got me pregnant, but don't get me started with the list of reasons why that was a bad idea.

And yes, I did have a list.

"It wasn't about having fun," I told him. "It was about getting pregnant."

Although in retrospect, I would have preferred to do it the old-fashioned way. Travis was right. Sex was more fun than a date with a turkey baster.

He looked down at his wife, the adoration on his face hard to miss. His hand moved to her belly, and he smiled softly at her.

Something deep inside me ached for a man to look at me that way.

I ignored it. I had Little Bean. What more could I want?

Travis's gaze returned to me, but his hand remained on his growing baby. "Well, then, congratulations." His smile told me he meant it.

He wasn't judging my choice on how I became a mother.

Even though my pregnancy wasn't news for Emma, that

didn't stop her from coming over to me and throwing her arms around me. "You're going be an amazing mom."

I returned her hug. "You, too."

"So now that Travis knows, are you going to tell anyone else?"

I assumed she meant our mutual friends. "Yes, but I'd prefer to be the one who did that, so I can explain my decision."

"Are you telling everyone you didn't do things the fun way?" Travis asked. "Or are you going to invent a fake story for the father to explain why he's not in the picture?"

"You mean how I fell in love with a CIA agent, but he was sent overseas before we could get married and died on a secret mission?" I grinned, and Emma laughed.

"Well, that would certainly be a more interesting version of the truth," she said, still laughing.

Travis leaned back against the doorjamb, a cocky grin on his face. "While you're at it, how about you say the father was a god from Mount Olympus and your baby is a demigod?"

"Yes, because that's so much more realistic than Hannah's version." Emma kissed him on the cheek, and his eyes went soft for her.

It was another of those cute moments between them that always melted my heart: that moment when you're slightly jealous of what they have, but at the same time also happy for them.

The building manager had told me I could leave my stuff in storage until I moved back into my apartment. So we first transferred as much of the salvageable items that we could fit into the small space.

By we, I meant mostly Travis, since he was the only one who wasn't pregnant. He loaded my luggage and plastic bags into the bed of his truck, and we drove to their condo.

By the time I'd finished moving into their place, and my

clothes were washed and in the drier, I felt like I'd just run a marathon.

And I still had an eight-hour shift to go at the hospital.

I flopped down on the couch and finally looked at my phone for the first time in several hours. Travis was due at the rink because his team had back-to-back games tonight. Emma was having a nap.

The lucky girl. But I knew if I lay down, I might not wake up in time for my shift.

Wes had texted.

> Wes: How's Sleeping Beauty doing? I heard you had a run in with the dragon this morning in the elevator.

> Me: Fortunately, she was more frosty than fire breathing. But she's one nosy tenant. Does she grill all your visitors?

> Wes: Only the pretty ones. And only the ones she feels are a threat to my reputation. ;)

> Me: LOL Yes, because your reputation is ever so sparkly, Mr. Virgin.

> Me: So is that how you keep your one-night stands from reappearing at your condo after you're finished with them? You set the dragon lady on them? Very clever.

> Wes: First, I hope you're not telling me she scared you away. Everly and I would like you to visit the princess castle again soon.

I laughed.

> Me: I guess as long as I don't do any more sleepovers, I should be fine.

Wes: How about tonight? Are you busy? Or is that against the rules?

Me: Rules?

Wes: Yes, the dating rules. Like you have to wait three days after a woman gives you her phone number, so you don't come off as desperate.

Me: I thought that was five days.

Wes: You see, I keep getting it all wrong.

Me: Well, you don't have to worry about the 3-5 day wait period. We're not dating. So unless you have some strange friendship rules I don't know about...

Wes: Does that mean you're coming over for dinner tonight?

Me: Sorry, I can't. I have to leave soon for a shift at the hospital. Rain check?

I meant it when I told Wes that I was sorry I couldn't join him and Everly for dinner. Hanging out with them last night had been fun.

Would I have joined them if I didn't have a shift tonight?

Yes—because like I told him, it wasn't a date.

For starters, most dates I went on didn't have a chaperone in the form of a three-year-old.

And most dates weren't that much fun.

I caught my lower lip between my teeth, waiting for his reply.

Hoping his answer would be yes.

7

WES

I texted Hannah back, letting her know that I would be happy to accept her rain check.

I knew it shouldn't be a big deal that Hannah couldn't make it for dinner tonight, but I'd be lying if I said disappointment didn't slither through me like a snake flushed down the toilet.

It was the same disappointment I'd felt this morning when I discovered she had slipped out of the condo like a one-night stand.

A one-night stand who had a run-in with the Dragon.

Or as the other members of the resident board called her, Mrs. Marylou Hitchcock.

She was *that* person you hear about all the time. The one who sat on the board and flailed her power around like a sword from *The Lord of the Rings*. If she didn't like someone who was applying to be a resident, she would do everything she could to convince the other board members to vote her way.

Even if there was nothing wrong with the applicant.

Even if they were an outstanding member of society.

If she didn't like them, too bad for them.

How did I know?

Let's just say I hadn't been her number one choice when it came to buying my condo. Nor had I been even at the bottom of the list or anywhere in between.

She saw what I did for a living and translated that to mean I was a stoner.

I had no idea how she came to that conclusion.

The building was now my home, thanks to one equally persuasive board member. The same person who took care of Everly while I worked: Mrs. Beth Jenkins, grandmother extraordinaire.

I swear, the woman was actually a superhero disguised as a sixty-year-old. She'd have to be to keep up with Everly's endless energy.

Isabelle strode into my temporary office at Quade Security and Investigations. Her black, chin-length hair with blue chunks had its usual I-don't-give-a-fuck waves that made the unsuspecting believe she was unorganized and a flirt.

All right, the flirt part was true, but the unorganized part definitely wasn't.

"Liam, Jayden, and Connor are in the conference room."

Why wasn't I in my own office down the hall, where my assistant was busy fielding all kinds of questions about the building I owned? The building where Liam's Quade Security and Investigations and Emma's Aphrodite's Boutique (aka the love shop) resided?

Because I was dealing with some of Liam's highly classified files, and he didn't want to risk anything happening to them. Plus the change of scenery was nice.

"Donuts?" I asked.

All right, while I'll admit the change of scenery was nice, the donuts Connor supplied from his secret source were even better.

"Absolutely," Isabelle said. "I even secured you a raspberry jam one."

My favorite.

"You're the best."

"Don't I know it."

I gathered up my laptop and walked into the conference room. Liam, Jayden, and Connor were there waiting for me, already eating the donuts and drinking coffee.

"Ah, the breakfast of champions." I sat in an empty chair and petted Mojo's large black head. He was sitting next to Jayden as he usually did during their group meetings—unless he was snoozing in the front office, keeping Isabelle company.

"I don't see you turning down the chance to have one of these," Jayden quipped back and sunk his teeth into his chocolate-glazed donut. Mojo's hopeful brown eyes followed the movement of the sweet treat. The poor dog was practically drooling.

"Never. Not until Connor tells my assistant where he gets these from."

The three men burst out laughing. Not because Connor would never tell any of us where he got them from—which was true. But because my assistant was not only brilliant, she was a major health food nut. Anything less than health food in the confines of my company office would affect the *feng shui* thing she was always talking about.

And in her opinion, that would disrupt my genius status.

I personally believed my so-called genius would be enhanced by a daily dose of these donuts.

"How's Hannah doing?" Jayden asked.

The other two men looked at me expectantly. Liam's fiancée, Ava, was friends with Hannah. The two of them hit it off immediately when Liam's mysterious fiancée, whom he'd broken up with over ten years ago, reappeared in his life.

"Did something happen to her?" Liam asked, frowning.

"She's doing fine," I told them. "So far she's managed not to get her car towed by some overly eager asshole today."

Liam's frown turned to one of confusion, and Jayden explained what happened yesterday.

"I've heard through the grapevine there's been issues with people parking in the area and getting towed prematurely." Liam turned to Connor, their regular computer techie. "See what you can find out about the city employee who's doing that." If dirt on the guy existed, Connor would be the one to find it.

Jayden leaned forward in his chair and folded his arms on the table. "What's the plan, boss?"

"No plan yet. We'll do some standard recon first to see what we're working with." Liam's mouth curved to one side in a way that made me glad he was on my side.

You never wanted to mess with anyone who mattered to him.

And that included Hannah.

"And then we'll decide what to do," he said. "In the meantime, how's the program going, Wes?"

"Fine. I've had some setbacks, but I should be on schedule again in the next day or two."

Liam nodded, knowing full well what the setback had been. Becoming Everly's guardian hadn't exactly been conducive to the long work hours I was used to keeping.

Ever since becoming her guardian, I'd cut down on my work hours while I struggled to figure out how to parent a three-year-old. I still had no idea what I was doing. My brother had made it look so easy, had been better equipped to handle her many stubborn moments and temper tantrums.

I was as equipped to handle those—and everything else— as I was to walk down the feminine protection aisle and buy a package of whatever for Hannah.

"Remember, you're a single father now," Liam said. "You're not a robot."

"So I've heard," I said dryly.

"Okay, we've established that Connor is going to do some digging on the towing asshole," Jayden said, "and Wes has been reminded that he's not a robot. Is there anything else we're going to discuss, or can I get back to pulling intel on the security breach at the mayor's home?"

Liam shook his head. "He canceled our services, so you're helping Wes today with whatever he needs."

I smirked at Jayden. "I could use more coffee from downstairs in about an hour." All these late nights after Everly went to bed, so I could catch up on my work, were starting to get to me.

Jayden flipped me the bird.

I laughed but then got serious. "Right now I'm the only one who can do the rest of the programming. So unless you're expecting Jayden to take over my role as Everly's guardian—make her dinner, play little-girl games, bathe her, and read her a bedtime story—so I can work during the evenings, he won't be much help."

Liam's gaze shifted to Jayden.

Jayden raised his hands. "Hey, don't look at me. I know nothing about taking care of little girls."

I snorted a laugh. "And you think I do? I'm still as clueless about these things as you are. It's not like she came with an instruction manual." A how-to manual would have made life so much easier.

"Yes, but you're her uncle."

Connor laughed. "I don't think that makes much of a difference."

"He's right," I said. "And it's not like I was around in Everly's life much prior to the accident. Not like I had been for the first two years of her life. I was always too busy with work to visit my brother and his family."

Guilt pummeled me in the gut like a kung fu fighter, as it tended to do at random moments since the accident.

"So how exactly are you expecting me to help Wes with his project?" Jayden asked Liam. "I mean, unless you want me to sit in his office and ask him every three minutes, 'Are you done yet? Are you done yet? Are you done yet?' "

"Because *that* won't get boring after the first time," I said with an eye-roll of a tone.

"All right, you can work on one of your other cases that also needs your attention."

Isabelle entered the room. "Sorry to interrupt, guys. Wes, you have a call on line two about Everly. She said it's important."

8

HANNAH

It was almost 11:30 p.m. by the time I finished my shift at the hospital and arrived at Emma and Travis's condo.

The place was quiet when I entered. Travis's team was playing tonight, although from what I'd gathered on the radio as I drove home, they had won. Emma texted me that she was going to bed early because she was tired.

I could relate.

I was ready to curl up on the floor and go to sleep.

The only thing keeping me from doing that was the thought of Travis coming home and tripping over my sleeping body.

Although judging from how tired I was, I probably wouldn't notice if he did. Heck, I'd probably even sleep through a hurricane...if one should happen to hit the west coast.

My stomach pointed out that it was hungry. The rest of my body said *screw that*. My body won, and I trudged to the room where I would be staying until I found a new apartment.

I grabbed my sleep T-shirt and shorts, as well as my toiletries, and headed to the bathroom to quickly get ready for bed.

I could practically hear it beckoning me.

A few minutes later, I crawled under the covers and closed my eyes.

Dreamland, here I come.

Normally, I would read a chapter before turning off the light, but given my current condition, I doubted that I would last a paragraph before dozing off.

Knowing my luck, I'd accidentally drop the e-reader on my face.

The faint clicking of the front door registered in the back of my mind. Heavy footsteps walked past my room.

Travis must be home.

That, or someone just broke in.

I snuggled farther under the covers, too tired to investigate. For some strange reason, the image of Wes popped into my head, and I smiled unexpectedly at the thought of him.

Which made my body suddenly venture from the land of dead-tired to the continent of horny.

Well, that's new.

Murmured voices drifted through the wall behind my head. Emma must be awake now.

A giggle.

A moan. Definitely Emma.

Another giggle.

Travis must have said something funny.

Instead of letting me drift off to sleep, my brain had other ideas. It returned to thinking about Wes.

Of him kissing me. *Oh.*

He groaned softly.

A giggle.

Wait. I didn't giggle.

A slightly longer pause followed it, and then, "Oh, yes." The voice was soft but definitely female and definitely not mine.

That horny sensation sneaking through my body? It increased tenfold.

Brilliant.

It wouldn't be so bad if I at least had someone to help me deal with it. But I didn't. I was on my own.

No wonder older women frowned at those of us who were single and pregnant, knocked up by a guy who wasn't in the picture. It wasn't that they thought we had loose moral values.

It was because they knew the torture we would go through with no one to help us deal with the increased horniness after the first trimester.

Apparently, my body had cranked up the horniness to a level that put a teenage boy to shame.

And to add to my torture, Emma and Travis seemed to have forgotten I was in the room next to theirs.

Or maybe they were being quiet, and pregnancy had improved my hearing to that of a bat.

The only thing I knew for sure was that I had entered the land of porn radio, my best friend and her husband the starring act.

And with each moan, each groan, each "oh, God," it was like the tap had been turned on and my previous exhaustion drained away...for now.

"Yes, yes, yes!"

Clearly, sex with Travis was good. Not that I had doubted it before now.

Because my brain and body had decided to play traitor and co-conspirator, a single thought trickled through my head: Was Wes as talented in bed as Travis?

No, no, no, I told myself. *We're not going there.*

Emma was. Or at least she was going someplace. The same place I hadn't been to in a long while, if you didn't count my ability to service myself.

Emma wasn't the only one of the duo who was having fun. By the time Travis came, I was wide awake and doing my best *not* to imagine Wes was responsible for that very satisfied grunt that came from Emma's husband.

My body hummed, hoping there was a second act, but this time with me as the heroine.

I was of a different opinion. And if I was lucky, Emma and Travis were now ready to fall asleep.

Except that was not what happened. A short time later they were ready for round two.

Oh, God, she's so lucky.

And then round three.

Fortunately, they ran out of steam after that.

My horniness and wide-awake status? Not so lucky.

All I could do was turn on my light and read the new romance I had started last night.

But an hour later, my brain and body were still riled up with the need to have sex, helped along by the heroine and hero of the book who were also getting more action than I was.

I turned off the light and shimmied out of my shorts and panties. The room next door was quiet.

Even though I tried to conjure up some fictitious man to play my lover in my little fantasy, Wes's image returned to my head.

Oh, well. I was up for whatever it took so I could finally fall asleep. It wasn't as if I would be finding out if sex with Wes in real life was the same as with my fantasy version of him.

I removed my T-shirt and closed my eyes. Then pretending that Wes's big strong hands were the ones touching my breasts, I played with them, teased them, tormented them.

A throbbing between my legs demanded attention, too. So while one hand continued to give my breasts the attention they craved, the other hand drifted south, much to the delight of my clit.

The whole time I was doing this, I thought about the sound

of Wes's smooth rumbling voice, his cocky smile, his deep laugh that made my lady bits tingle.

And thanks to my crazy hormones, I came in record time.

I also had an aching suspicion that, with the way my hormones were acting, the next time I saw Wes, I would come in record time at the mere sight of him.

Maybe even try humping him.

Crap. I was in serious trouble.

9

—————

HANNAH

Four days later, I received a text from Emma to let me know she couldn't get away from the store to help me with my apartment hunting. But not to worry, she was sending someone to join me, so I didn't have to deal with the realtor on my own.

Travis and his team were away on a road trip, which meant he wasn't the mysterious person.

The building intercom near the front door squawked like a vulture being sat on.

I pressed the intercom button. "Hi, can I help you?"

"I'm here to pick you up," the voice on the other end said.

"Wes?"

"Who else were you expecting?"

"Let me get this straight. You're the one Emma just texted me about? The one who's helping me with apartment hunting?"

"That's right. She didn't tell you it was going to be me?"

"Apparently not."

"Are you coming downstairs, or are we continuing this conversation on the intercom?"

My body had been craving him for the past four days, so having this conversion via the intercom versus seeing him in person sounded like a brilliant idea. But since that wouldn't help me find a new place to live... "I'll be right down."

Remember, fantasy Wes is not the same thing as the real deal. You have no reason to want to hump him. Just think of him as Emma's couch. It's not like you're planning on humping that. Right?

Right.

I pulled on my knee-high boots, gathered my purse and coat, and headed downstairs.

Wes was waiting for me in the lobby.

And my body instantly called me a liar. Fantasy Wes was a poor distant cousin to the real deal. I mean the jury was still out about his lovemaking abilities, but it wasn't like fantasy Wes had been all that amazing when you thought about it. My hands had been the ones that made me come, and kissing hadn't been involved.

The real deal is probably so much better, my body not-so-helpfully pointed out.

"So I take it you heard what happened to my apartment?" I said as we walked to his car.

"I did. Will they be able to fix it?"

"I guess so."

"You guess? But you want to move out anyway?"

"Eventually, yes. My lease is expiring in seven months, and I need to move to a larger apartment by then. I thought I'd have a little more time to find a new home, but since I've been displaced for at least a month, I might as well start my search now." Because of the situation with the apartment, as soon as I found another place to live, the old lease would be terminated if I wanted.

Wes laughed. "So you're not interested in staying with Travis and Emma that long?"

"Oh, God, no. I love them dearly, but their sex life is driving me insane."

Oops. Hadn't meant to say that.

I cringed.

That made him laugh harder. "Are they really that loud?"

Shit. What was I supposed to say?

This is your chance to tell him the truth, the logical voice in my head said. *You're in the second trimester now. You can tell everyone that you're pregnant, and this is the perfect opening.*

Good point—if the circumstances were different and I was married.

What difference does it make? This isn't the 1950s. You're a modern woman. Nor, may I point out, are you the first and only woman to go your route. There are plenty of single women opting not to settle for a man just so they can have kids. They're taking matters into their own hands and doing what you did.

Again, all good points. But I already knew that because I'd had this conversation with myself numerous times before finally going through with the medical procedure.

My choice had been the right one for me, and it was time I let the world—or at least Wes—know it.

"Probably not under normal circumstances," I said. "But I'm pregnant, and I swear it's given me super hearing."

That sound? My pulse pounding in my ears to the tune of *here we go.*

Wes stopped abruptly. "You are?" His face lacked emotion. No surprise. No disgust. No indication he was happy for me.

Because he doesn't know that's what you want.

I smiled and nodded. Before, I had been worried about what people would think when I announced my news. But I really had nothing to worry about. I wasn't ashamed of my status. It was what I wanted.

You own it, girl!

My smile widened. "Yes, I am."

"I didn't realize you were seeing anyone."

"I'm not. I've never even met the guy."

Wes's eyebrow rose, confusion and amusement ongoing in his expression. "So what was it? An immaculate conception?"

I laughed. "No, it definitely wasn't that. I was artificially inseminated with an anonymous donor's sperm."

The confused look on Wes's face switched to a frown. "But why?"

"Why what?"

"Why didn't you do it the old-fashioned way? Boy meets girl. Boy and girl have sex. Boy knocks up girl." His hand waved back and forth through the air as he talked. "It's been working great since the beginning of time."

"True. It has. But I haven't found the right guy, and this seemed the simplest way of doing things." Okay, that wasn't exactly true. Having sex with a guy and getting knocked up was so much simpler than going the donor route.

Wes didn't say anything for a full thirty seconds, clearly warring with himself at how to respond. But then he smiled, the movement big and genuine—and my stupid heart fluttered hopelessly in my chest. "Well, congratulations." He hugged me.

Instantly my body went into overdrive, and it was all I could do not to dry-hump him. It didn't help that he smelled amazing.

Realizing that his hugging me might not be a good idea, I pulled away. "So anyway, back to my super hearing. I don't think Emma and Travis mean to be noisy. And they probably aren't to most people. But they are to me and to make things worse, my pregnancy hormones make me super horny. Every time they go at it in their room, it's like listening to porn."

"And you have something against porn?"

"Can't say that I've ever watched it, and I'm not planning to start. But my point is, I'm horny and hearing them having sex—and it's never just once or twice—is killing me. It's all I can do not to go knocking from door-to-door in their building and find some random guy who wants to pound into me and help me deal with this insatiable ache between my legs."

All right, I'll admit that was probably a little TMI, but Wes was a guy. He could handle it.

His eyes darkened, and his Adam's apple bopped up and slid down.

"I'm supposed to meet the realtor at the first apartment building in twenty minutes." Fortunately, it wasn't far from Emma and Travis's condo. Unfortunately, it was farther from the hospital than I would've liked. "Are you sure you have time to help me with this? Don't you have work to do?" He was a workaholic after all.

"I do. But it's Sunday and Liam's ordered me not to work this weekend because I need to spend more time with Everly."

I glanced around. "Um, I hate to tell you this, if you're supposed to be spending more time with her, it probably would be easier to do that if she's with you." My mouth dropped open. "You didn't leave her in your vehicle, did you?"

"No, she's with my neighbor. The one who usually looks after her while I'm at work. She volunteered to look after Everly for a few hours." He gestured for me to walk to the visitor lot where his car was parked.

"What about Everly's other grandparents? Your sister-in-law's parents? Do they help you out?"

"I've never met Kristin's parents. I only know she was estranged from them and had no siblings. I have no idea if her parents are even still alive."

That would explain why Wes was Everly's guardian.

"So it's just you and Everly?" I asked.

"Yep, that's about right."

"Does she have any other kids her age to play with?"

"She's met Josh and Holly's daughter, Lily, and they have

fun playing together." He unlocked the doors to his SUV with his key fob, and we climbed in.

"New vehicle?"

He used to have a BMW.

"I figured an SUV would be a safer bet now that I have a kid."

More durable too where kids were involved. "Good idea. So, have you and Josh considered taking the girls to Wonder Play?"

"What's that?" He turned over the engine and drove forward. Aerosmith's "Love in an Elevator" poured from his speakers.

"It's this amazing play gym designed for little kids. There are tunnels, fun squishy shapes to climb and slide down on, wooden bridges, parachute playtime, songs. Kids love it. It's a great way to spend time with your child because it's parented. That means the parent has to attend the class with their child."

"That's the first I've heard of it. Where are we going first?"

I told him the address. "Holly would know about Wonder Play. She took Lily there before James was born. You should talk to Josh about taking the girls there. The next session starts in January, so you'll want to register early to get in. From what I've heard, it's extremely popular."

"That's not a bad idea. Mrs. Jenkins said it might help Everly adjust better to her new situation if she had some friends to play with regularly."

"How is Everly doing?"

"It's hit and miss. Some days she's fine and only asks about her mom and dad a few times. Other days she wakes up in the middle of the night because of nightmares."

My heart tightened at what both she and Wes were going through. It was a good thing he was driving or else I might have been tempted to hug him again—while doing my best not to rub up against him. "Does she understand that her parents are dead?"

"I don't know if she really understands what that means. The play therapist has been trying to help her, but Everly still believes they're coming back."

"It will take time. All you can do is what you're already doing. You have a lot of friends who are fathers. Make the most of that. Get their advice when it comes to being a parent."

Emma and I had already been sharing with each other about being pregnant. I was looking forward to announcing my news to Holly and Kelsey, too, so I could benefit from their wisdom. Kelsey had given birth to Ethan four months ago.

"Are you doing the same with your mommy friends?" he asked as if reading my mind.

"Is that your way of asking if Holly and Kelsey know about my bun in the oven?"

"Yep. I guess I'm wondering if I was the last to know that you got intimate with a turkey baster." His gaze briefly flicked to me before returning to the road.

"Will you ever get over that I went the sperm-donor route?"

"Eventually. It's just that fucking is so much more fun."

I laughed. "I'll have to take your word for that. It's been a long time since I last had sex. I've almost forgotten what it's like."

"How long are we talking about? A month? Three months?"

"I'd say two years."

The SUV swerved, not enough to cause an accident, but definitely enough to be noticed. The car behind us honked.

"Christ, Hannah, no wonder you're so horny right now. But what about all those losers you were dating last year?"

"I never ended up having sex with any of them. Like you said, they were losers, and I tend not to put out when it comes to that breed of men." That was when I realized I had to stop looking for love and move on with my goal of starting a family on my own.

"So you really haven't had sex in all that time?"

"Is that so hard to believe? Right, look who I'm talking to. You probably had sex last week."

"Not exactly. It's been a couple of months. I was busy with work, and then Everly moved in with me. She's my priority now when it comes to females, which means my dating days are over for some time to come."

"By dating, do you mean sex?"

"The last time I picked up a woman at the bar and took her home was back in college. I tend to take women out on a date first."

"Followed by banging them," I filled in for him.

"Not always. There have been a few I couldn't get away from fast enough. They might have been hot, but something about them irritated the hell out of me, and the thought of having sex with them wasn't all that appealing."

"Ooh, a man with standards. I like that." The sarcasm in my tone was light and bubbly, like a glass of cherry soda.

He smacked his hand against his chest. "I'm offended. Clearly, you think I'll fuck anyone who bats their eyelashes at me."

I might have believed that he was telling the truth—that I had offended him—if it weren't for the sexy one-sided grin on his face.

My lady bits hummed in excitement.

Get a grip, girls. It's not happening.

They booed me.

Besides, I inwardly added, *I'm pregnant, and I'm positive Wes isn't interested in screwing a pregnant woman. Remember, he does have standards.*

And I wasn't within a hundred miles of them.

10

WES

"This apartment is perfect for a small family," Janice, the realtor said, standing in the middle of the living room.

Small family? Sure, if we were talking about a family of mice.

Everly's bedroom closet was larger than what would be the baby's room.

What did I think about Hannah's pregnancy news?

Once I got over the initial shock, I really was happy for her.

But it did change things when it came to my game—the game that involved me getting her to kiss me without her realizing what I was doing.

Her news complicated things.

Why? Because before her news, it would have been nothing more than fun and games between two friends. But now that she was pregnant, her hormones were all over the place, as her confession about her state of horniness proved.

Which meant her emotions would be all over the place, too.

And what if she really was looking for Mr. Right, someone

who would one day be a father to her baby? That wasn't something I could be.

I was clueless when it came to fathering Everly. I couldn't imagine parenting a baby on top of that.

"It's nice," Hannah said, in a tone that implied the opposite. Except you had to know her as well as I did to recognize it for what it was. "It's just a little cozier than I had in mind. Especially once my baby is more mobile." She rested her hand protectively on her still-flat stomach. "Once I put furniture in here, there won't be much room for the baby to explore."

Janice nodded, but it was obvious she hadn't listened to a word Hannah said.

"The kitchen has been recently renovated." She walked toward it, not that she needed to go far to be in the kitchen.

This was recently renovated? What did it look like beforehand? A wood-burning stove and an icebox? Even the cupboards looked like they were several decades old.

"The apartment doesn't exactly fit what I'm looking for," Hannah explained once more. "It's smaller than I need."

"Fair enough. I've got several more apartments on the list to check out."

Janice told us the address for the next location, and we followed her in my SUV.

"This isn't exactly near your hospital," I said, pulling into the visitor parking lot. The commute was at least an hour, more if she got stuck in rush-hour traffic. "Did you want to be this far from there?"

"Not really, but Janice told me there aren't many rental properties available that fit what I'm looking for, in that general area."

We went inside the building and checked out the apartment, but it wasn't much better than the last place we had looked at. And neither were any of the apartments after that.

"This apartment is better," Hannah said as we walked

through the last location on Janice's list. We'd already been doing this for the past few hours, and she looked ready for a nap.

Now that I knew she was pregnant, her falling asleep at my apartment last week while I was getting Everly to bed made sense. Between dealing with her towed vehicle and her being pregnant, I was surprised she'd lasted as long as she had when she came over for dinner.

"There's a great daycare nearby if you're planning to go that route with childcare," Janice said. "But I recommend putting your name down now for a spot. They have a long waiting list."

Hannah nodded, her expression thoughtful, as she examined the larger bedroom.

"Now, the rent for this apartment is slightly higher than the amount Emma said you were willing to pay." She itemized all the great features to the place—and tornado sirens blared in my head.

Just how *slightly* above the amount were we talking about?

"But as you can see, it's definitely worth the price," Janice concluded.

"How much is the rent?" I asked.

At the amount, Hannah's mouth dropped open, and the excited spark in her eyes fizzled. Her hand went to her stomach as if to protect the baby from the bad news. "That's too expensive. We'll have to keep looking."

Janice nodded, and they made arrangements for the next time they could meet.

"I was really hoping it would be easier than this," Hannah said as we drove toward Travis and Emma's building. "I guess it was too much to hope for that I would find the perfect place today so that I could move in right away." She covered her mouth with her hand, attempting to stifle a yawn. She had already yawned several times in the past hour.

"Unfortunately, these things are rarely ever quick, unless

you get lucky. I was looking for several months before I found my condo." And then it took another month on top of that for the board to approve my application.

I kept that part to myself. Hannah was only looking to rent an apartment. She wasn't looking to buy a condo.

But what was supposed to be a motivating speech fell flat, if her defeated expression was anything to go by.

All right, I could have been a little more optimistic. That might have helped. "But I'm sure it won't take you that long to find your dream apartment."

She shot me a look that said she wasn't buying it and released a long sigh. "Maybe I'm too fussy."

"I hardly think wanting an apartment big enough to move around in can be considered being too fussy."

"That's because you're not three months pregnant, horny, and living with two highly sexually active roommates."

"Not so fast on that. You might have me on points one and three, but I'm a thirty-two-year-old male who is currently looking at a life of celibacy for some time to come. I'm horny, but I can't do anything about it. Once you find a new place to live, you can have all the sex you want."

She laughed. "Yes, because every man's sexual fantasy is to fuck a pregnant woman, especially when she's not *his* woman."

Yeah, she might have had me there. But I could only speak for myself.

"I guess we're both pitiful cases then," she said. "Both of us are horny. Neither of us will be having sex any time soon. But I'd rather not become my mother. I want Little Bean to not feel like an afterthought and that her mom's boyfriends are more important than she is."

"Little Bean?"

"It's what I'm calling my baby until he or she is born."

"Well, I know you well enough to know Little Bean will never feel like an afterthought, boyfriends or not. You know, if you want, you can always stay with Everly and me until you find a new apartment. That's if you don't mind living with a three-year-old, which I'm assuming you don't because you're going to have a baby."

Whoa. What was I saying? Having Hannah live under the same roof as me was not a good idea, even if it ended up being only for a short time. Just because I was now living the life of a monk, it didn't mean my body didn't crave sex, as Hannah and I had already established. And when we were talking about Hannah, my thoughts definitely weren't wholesome.

"That's sweet of you, but I'm sure I'll find a new place soon. And Travis is gone for the next few days, so I'll have a reprieve from the audio porn during that time. I bet I'll be living in a new apartment by the time he returns."

"Are you sure?"

"Positive." She gave a firm nod of her head.

Except...two weeks later she still hadn't found a new home.

11

HANNAH

"It looks like someone was murdered there." Emma pointed to a stain on the beige carpet in what was the sixth rental unit we had looked at that day.

Correction. Most of the carpet was stained, but this particular patch was broader and darker than the rest.

My stomach sagged in defeat. She was right. That was exactly what it looked like had happened.

"According to the information the landlord gave me," Janice said, her tone matter-of-fact, "the carpets have recently been cleaned."

In that case, they'd missed a spot...like the entire floor.

"I think I'll pass. I'm not too eager to have my baby crawling on that one day. Who knows what kind of allergens are lurking in it?"

Besides, every time I looked at that stain, which would be impossible to hide with furniture because of its location, I'd wonder if someone had been murdered there, the missing body yet to be located.

Shit. I was never going to find a new apartment. I had been looking for two weeks now, and I still hadn't found anything close to what I wanted. And the sad part? I really didn't think the must-have items on my list were asking too much.

While the place didn't have to be close to the hospital, I also didn't want to live on the other side of the city from my job. I wanted a home near a playground, so Little Bean and I could play there every day once she was old enough. I wanted an apartment we could call home for many years to come, which meant it needed to be near a good school and in a good neighborhood.

I wanted a home that didn't look like someone had been murdered in it, and I wanted an apartment that had room for a growing baby and me. And most of all, I wanted a home that wouldn't drain all my monthly income just so we could have a roof over our heads. As a nurse, I earned more than some single mothers, but after I factored in childcare and other expenses, it didn't leave me with a lot of money to waste—especially if I was planning to keep saving for the future.

After I left the foster care system, I had worked hard to make something of myself, desperate not to fall down the same hole my mother had gone down after she left home. She hadn't attended college. She had worked as a grocery clerk in a local store, barely making enough to support us. The money probably would have gone further if she hadn't wasted it on booze and deadbeat boyfriends.

I guess deep down she had hoped to one day find Mr. Right. The guy with a nice income who would want to marry her and take us away from the life we were barely living.

Great dream. Too bad she had been a magnet to losers like pollen to bees.

At least none of the guys I had dated over the years had been anywhere near as bad, but neither had they come close to being someone worth spending the rest of my life with. None had been interested in having a family one day.

Not wanting to follow in my mom's disastrous path, I

worked hard in school, never taking anything for granted when it came to my education. It hadn't been easy because I had been bounced from foster home to foster home. That meant I had never stayed in the same school for more than one or two years. And with some foster homes, the kids were just there as paid labor. By that I mean, the kids did the labor and the state paid the foster parents to keep us so that we could do all the work around the house.

And that seriously cut into my study time.

But I had kept my eye on the prize: a scholarship to a state college.

And a future I hadn't dared to imagine before.

The added bonus? I learned to juggle working and my studies.

Not bad, huh?

And the best part was, I'd learned at a young age to rely on myself. I knew I didn't need to find a man to take care of me.

I could take care of myself.

"I'm with Hannah on this," Emma said. "This is not the ideal place to raise a child. What's next on the list?" Her gaze was as hopeful as ice cream was cold.

Ooh. Speaking of ice cream. *I really could go for mango ice cream right now.*

And Little Bean thoroughly agreed.

I was practically drooling at the thought of it.

Emma's phone pinged. She briefly glanced at the screen, grinned, and returned her attention to Janice. But I knew that smile. Travis's plane—the team's plane—had touched down at the airport.

And for tonight's porn pleasure...

"That's all I have available to show you today." Janice's tone was sitting on the fence. On one side was sympathy. On the other side was a *Will-you-just-fucking-pick-one?* attitude. Right now she was leaning more toward the latter than the former.

"There haven't been any new listings since we looked two days ago," she said.

This time it was *my* phone that pinged.

Wes had texted me.

> Wes: Have you been craving mango ice cream lately?

Okay, that was kind of freaky. What, now he could read my mind?

> Me: How did you know?

> Wes: I didn't. But Everly has another play therapy session soon, and we want to know if you would like to join us afterward for ice cream.

"I can let you know once another listing comes up," Janice was saying, although she didn't sound too enthusiastic or optimistic.

"That would be great," Emma replied, the more upbeat of the two of them.

> Me: Right now, I could really go for some mango ice cream.

> Wes: Good, see you there in 1 1/2 hours?

> Me: Sounds good.

> Wes: And Hannah…

Another text pinged on my phone from him.

> Wes: Try not to get yourself towed.

Me: Thanks for the advice. I'll do better this time. ;)

Emma and I said our good-byes to Janice and returned to my vehicle.

"Wes texted. He and Everly have invited us for ice cream. Did you want to join me, or are you and Travis planning to spend the afternoon catching up?" The innuendo in the last part was thick like chunky peanut butter.

"Are you okay if I skip the invite?" The smile on her face told me all I needed to know. My best friend was horny for her hot husband, and she had every intention of making the most of the time while I was away, showing him how much she missed him.

"That's more than okay. Go see your husband." I dropped her off at her condo. I had some chores I needed to do first before I could meet up with Wes and Everly.

After finishing my tasks, I parked in the same place as the last time and set the timer on my phone, so I didn't get a ticket or towed. Then I walked toward the ice cream café where Wes and Everly would be meeting me soon. But since I was ten minutes early and they were still in therapy, I entered the Christmas store first.

My mouth slid into a big grin the moment I stepped inside. Move over, Disneyland. This location was indeed the happiest place on the planet.

I walked to the decorated pine trees and smiled at the cute woodland critter decorations. The fox. The mouse. The rabbit. All sported either a little elf hat or held a Christmas stocking. The cheery tune of "Jingle Bells" played in the background.

The glass angels I saw the other week were still on the tree, including the one holding the baby. It was so beautiful and delicate and perfect.

"Is there anything I can help you with?" a man's voice said beside me.

I turned to find a tall, good-looking man dressed in a suit. The suit alone looked out of place here. "You don't actually work here, do you?" I said with a smile.

He grinned at me. "What gave it away?"

I waved at the suit. "You look more like a lawyer or someone who works in an office, making cutthroat deals."

He chuckled. "You got the lawyer part right."

"So let me guess, you're the guy who makes sure the bad guys aren't locked away." The type I would never want to date.

"Not at all. I'm a contract lawyer."

"So more of a boring-type lawyer?"

His chuckle upgraded to a laugh. "You're probably right about that. Contract law isn't known to be thrilling. But don't let that make you think I'm boring, too." He winked at me, and I smiled some more.

"And you usually come into this store to help their customers find what they're looking for?"

"Nope. You would be the first. Am I doing a good job of it? Do you think they would hire me to help with the Christmas rush?" He grinned again, and my lady bits took that to mean I'd be getting down and dirty with him.

Not so fast, girls.

I didn't think this was the time or place to deal with my hormonal overdrive.

And who knew if he was interested in one day becoming the father to someone else's baby?

Whoa. Who's talking about walking down the aisle with him? We're talking about having fantastic sex. Pleeeease.

They did have a point. It wasn't as if I had to marry the guy. And a quickie would make staying at Emma and Travis's a little less torturous. At least until Little Bean began showing and the guy bailed.

And then I could come up with Plan B.

Like humping a tree.

"Maybe they will hire you. You have *me* convinced I should buy something," I said.

"I didn't realize I was that good."

"You are, and maybe they should give you a bonus."

"Or you could give me your phone number."

"Maybe I have a boyfriend?" Well, what do you know? Being horny gave my voice the smoky sound of a seductress. It was a superpower the pregnancy books didn't tell you about.

"Do you?"

I shook my head. "Which means I might be free to go out with you sometime."

He pulled a business card out of his breast pocket and handed it to me. "So are you free for drinks tomorrow night?"

"I might be." The seductress tone was back, amped up to a new level. I told him my number, and we planned for a time and place to meet.

That was right. The following night he and I would be having sex.

Unless he was the kind of guy who didn't like to bring women to his place. Which would be a problem since I couldn't very well bring him to Emma and Travis's condo. It was one thing for them to have sex in *their* home. It was another for me to bring a man there.

Besides, I didn't want Emma to get the wrong idea. I knew that even though she was happy for me when it came to Little Bean, she would be even happier if I had a man in my life to share it with...like she had Travis.

But what did I expect? She did own Aphrodite's—a store that was all about love.

"Was my son able to help you find everything you're looking for?" a woman wearing an ugly Christmas sweater asked.

By ugly, I meant it was adorably ugly, with a large Rudolph standing in the snow, a red pom-pom for his nose.

"Your son?" I looked at Philip, who was standing on the other side of me.

He nodded. "Does dropping in to check on my mom earn me brownie points?"

"No, but it does explain why you're in this store." I just thought that maybe he liked Christmas as much as I did.

To his mom I said, "I'd love to get one of those cute mouse decorations." I pointed to the one in question, and Philip and I made plans to meet for a drink the next night.

A few minutes later, I stepped into the ice cream café, clutching a paper bag with my new mouse friend inside.

Wes and Everly were already at the counter, checking the different flavors. At the sound of the bell above the door, Wes looked in my direction and the corners of his mouth curved into a grin.

And my lady bits threw a huge party, putting their reaction at the thought of having sex with Philip to shame.

Clearly, they had their priorities all screwed up.

"Hannah!" Everly exclaimed.

Wes lowered her to the floor, and she ran over to me and hugged my legs.

"She's been excited to see you ever since I told her you'd be joining us for ice cream," he explained.

She let go of my legs, grabbed my hand, and pulled me over to her uncle.

"Are you ready to order yet?" the woman behind the counter asked.

We told her what we would like, then sat at a table near the window while we waited for our order.

"I love the braids," I told Everly. "Did your uncle do them?"

The braids in question? One was higher than the other, and one part of the braid had been divided thicker than the other two. On top of that, strands of blonde hair had gone rogue from both and were sticking out in all directions.

Wes laughed. "That obvious, huh?"

"You just need a little practice. But for the record, I think it's adorable you at least tried. Most men wouldn't." My heart might have melted a little at that. "I hope you weren't waiting too long for me. I went to the Christmas store and bought a mouse decoration." I removed it from the bag to show Everly as I said, "And I got a date while I was there." Philip's business card fell out of the bag and onto the table.

Everly squealed and reached for the cute decoration. Wes picked up the card and read it.

"You got yourself a date in the Christmas store?" he asked. "With whom? One of Santa's elves?"

"Unless Santa's elves are now tall, dark, and handsome, I'm going to say that would be a no. He's a lawyer, and his mom owns the store." But Wes already knew my date was a lawyer. It said so on the card.

"And you're going out with this stranger?"

Wow. Who knew Wes had it in him? He sounded like a father. His tone didn't hold an edge of curiosity. It was more along the lines of what happens right before you're grounded.

"Apparently so. He and I are having drinks tomorrow night."

"But you're pregnant."

"What's that got to do with anything? I'm not drinking anything alcoholic."

Everly was busy introducing the mouse decoration to Snuggle Bunny, so she failed to notice Wes frowning.

"Does he know you're pregnant?"

I opened my mouth to answer but didn't get that far.

The ice cream woman approached our table and handed Everly her cone. She then passed Wes and me our ice cream. "Is there anything else I can get you?"

Wes and I told her we were all good. The woman walked away.

"Does he know you're pregnant?" Wes asked again.

"It didn't exactly come up." I licked my ice cream. *Mmm. This is so much better than I remembered.*

"So when exactly are you going to tell him?" His tone reminded me of an elastic band being held taut. Not quite at the point of snapping, but definitely not the casual tone I would expect for this conversation.

"I guess when I feel like it's the right time to tell him. Who knows if we'll survive the first date?"

All right, I'll admit it. I hadn't thought things through. When I accepted the date, I wasn't thinking about happily ever afters or anything else.

I was thinking with my horny body.

Or rather, it was doing all the thinking for me.

Oh, well.

"Have you given any thought to moving in with Everly and me while you look for a new apartment?" And just like that, the overwrought elastic band was released. Wes's tone returned to his casual one.

"Not really." Which was a little bit true. I hadn't thought about his offer for the past forty-five minutes. But I had definitely thought about it when Emma and Travis were in their room late at night, getting in some exercise...if you know what I mean. Or when they were being cute and cuddly on the couch while we watched TV.

Or when I caught them kissing in the kitchen.

But I wasn't feeling out of place in their condo because of my amped-up horny hormones. Those pesky hormones only made me want to have sex. It was Emma and Travis's adorableness that reminded me I had no one like that in my life.

And the reminder was getting a little stale.

"The offer still stands," Wes said.

"Okay."

"Okay, as in, you'll consider it? Or as in, when can you move in?"

"Are you sure my being there won't cramp your style?"

"Exactly which style are we talking about?" His gaze flicked to Everly.

"Point taken. But I have no idea how long it will take to find an apartment. So far it hasn't gone too well."

Understatement of the century.

"Doesn't matter. Take a long as you need."

"Are you sure about this?" Because a part of me was screaming, *Bad idea!* The rest of me was thinking the opposite. Maybe once I was no longer exposed to the sex happening in the room next to mine, the horniness factor would dial down a couple of notches.

It certainly couldn't get any worse.

Wes and I had a strictly platonic relationship, so there was no reason to think otherwise.

Or so I thought...

12

WES

The next morning, I walked into Connor's office without knocking first. "What can you tell me about a Philip Stevenson? He's a lawyer at Long and Fairbrother."

"Any reason why you're asking?"

"A friend of mine might be doing some business with him, and I want to make sure there's nothing sketchy about him."

All right, that wasn't exactly the truth, but it was close enough. Business. Date. They were pretty much kissing cousins on the grand scale of things, especially where Hannah was concerned.

I knew Hannah's dating life wasn't any of my business. It was *her* choice if she wanted to date some loser—as long as said loser wasn't also a big creep.

Which was why I was in Connor's office. As Hannah's new roommate, it was my duty to ensure things were on the up-and-up with this Philip guy.

"Give me three hours, and I'll see what I can find," Conner said.

"Great. Thanks. I owe you one."

"You owe him what?" Jayden asked, strolling into the office. He handed Connor a short stack of files. "I need a level-four background check on these five guys."

"I'm right on it."

"Great. So let's return to what Wes owes you..." He looked between us, expectantly.

"Have you considered the possibility that it has nothing to do with you?" I inwardly groaned. That was the worst thing I could have said to Jayden. It only spiked his curiosity.

"I have—for maybe one second. Two, tops. So spill it. What's going on here?"

"Wes needed to run a check on some lawyer," Connor told him.

"Why does Wes need you to do that?" Liam's voice came from the doorway behind me.

I twisted away from the desk. "Why is everyone suddenly curious about what I'm doing?"

Jayden smirked. "Because we know whatever you're up to is bound to be entertaining."

Connor adopted an identical expression. "He's got a point there."

"Looks like we're all in agreement." Liam crossed his arms, demonstrating the bad-guy-beware stance he had perfected while with the SEALs.

"All right, if you really must know. A stranger asked Hannah out on a date, and I want to make sure she's not going out with someone who's bad news."

"Are we talking about Hannah Morrell? The woman who's one step away from getting her black belt, the woman who knows how to look after herself?"

The smirks on Connor's and Jayden's faces grew wider.

"That would be the one. Normally I would agree that she knows how to take care of herself. But she's pregnant now, so I don't think it's a bad idea to ensure that she isn't in over her head."

All three men exchanged looks.

Shit.

"And for the record, you didn't hear about the pregnant part from me. She's going to tell everyone"—I looked pointedly at Liam—"including your fiancée, when she's ready."

Did you hear that? That was the sound of a pin dropping against Connor's desk. That was how quiet the room was after my little announcement.

Liam was the first to get over his shock. "Hannah is pregnant?"

"I don't suppose you're the father?" That would be Jayden.

"Why would you even think that?"

"Because everyone knows you used to have a thing for her." Jayden might have said it, but his tone implied I still had a thing for her.

"I didn't have a thing for her, and I still don't." *Right, just be happy that lightning can't hit you inside a building, dumbass,* an annoying voice in my head said. "And no, I'm not the father."

"Do you know who the father is?" Liam asked. "Connor can do a background check on him. Just to be sure she won't be dealing with some major headaches down the line."

"Is that the guy you want me to do the check on?" Connor asked. "Is he the father?"

I shook my head, even though I had no idea if Philip the lawyer made a recent deposit at the sperm bank. Even if he had, chances were slim that Hannah ended up with his sperm. "No. He's just a stranger she met in a store yesterday, and he asked her out on a date."

"Okay, Connor, do the background check on Hannah's date first. And then report back to us."

"Us?" I asked.

"Yes, us. We want to know what we're dealing with. We all

like Hannah, and she's my fiancée's friend. If Ava even suspects I haven't done my due diligence when it comes to Hannah's dating life, I could end up losing my balls. And I've grown quite attached to them, no pun intended."

I almost felt sorry for Hannah's idiot date if Connor did turn up dirt on him. If the guys' expressions were anything to go by, he'd be canceling soon after.

But none of this surprised me. The team had already dealt with the individual who had been fast on the draw when it came to towing Hannah's vehicle. Connor had found dirt on him, and Jayden and Liam had a little chat with the douchebag to make sure he demonstrated restraint in the future.

"Is he picking her up for the date, or is she meeting him somewhere?" Jayden asked.

"She said she's meeting him at Swizzle Sticks Lounge." It was some fancy-ass place I'd taken a couple of dates to in the past.

"Time?"

"That part didn't come up in our conversation yesterday." I was lucky I even found out his name and where they were meeting up.

And that was only because she wasn't expecting me to crash the date.

"Not a problem," Liam said. "We can set up a detail to follow her from Travis's building."

"What exactly are you guys planning to do?"

"Quite simple. Jayden and Isabelle will show up at the meeting and make sure everything goes smoothly."

My gaze shifted to Jayden. "You mean you two will be pretending to be on a date?"

"More like two colleagues going out after work to discuss work-related matters."

Plausible? Quite possibly. "There's only one problem with

that plan," I said, stalling on revealing the next part. "Hannah isn't staying with Travis and Emma anymore."

Liam's eyebrows raised in either surprise or disbelief. "She's already found a new apartment?"

"Not exactly. She's moving into my condo this afternoon."

Whatever emotion Liam had experienced with my first revelation had just done an unexpected U-turn. It was now fully in the disbelief zone.

"She's moving in with *you*?" Liam asked, enunciating each word slowly.

"Well, not permanently. Just until she finds a new apartment. She wanted to give Travis and Emma some alone time before they become new parents."

I'd already revealed the part about her being pregnant. I had no intention of also mentioning about the audio porn and her heightened level of horniness, thanks to the pregnancy.

A level of horniness her dumbass date might get to appreciate —unless Jayden and Isabelle succeeded in disrupting his plans.

What does it matter if she and the dumbass have sex? the annoying voice in my head asked.

I ignored it.

"But why with you?" Liam asked.

"Because I invited her to stay with me while she's searching for a new apartment. But you have to admit, it's a brilliant move on my part. She's a pediatric nurse, and who knows kids better than a nurse who specializes in them? She's about five steps ahead of where I am as Everly's guardian and uncle."

I had expected them to see the genius behind my inviting Hannah to stay with Everly and me. Instead, skepticism stared back at me.

"Are you sure that's a good idea?" Liam finally voiced.

"Why wouldn't it be? She needs a place to stay. And now she has plenty of time to find the right apartment to move into.

She doesn't have to settle for less. I've seen some of the locations she's been looking at. If you'd seen them, you would agree with me, too. They weren't the right apartments for her to raise her baby." And because I was on a roll, I threw in for added benefit, "Apartment hunting is exhausting and stressful enough when you aren't pregnant. Hannah doesn't need that extra stress now that she *is* pregnant."

Slam. Dunk.

Clearly, the guys didn't agree with me. The skepticism had been turned up several notches.

"Honestly, there's nothing going on between us. So don't make more of this than there is. I'm just being there for her as a friend. Any of you guys would do the same if you were in my situation."

Yep, that didn't do much to erase their disbelieving expressions either. "Do you want me to text you when she leaves for her date?" I asked Jayden.

"That will work. But first things first. I need to check that Isabelle is free tonight."

"Tell her it's for work," Liam called after him. "She's been after me to let her be more hands-on with our cases," he added once Jayden was out the door. "Hopefully this will appease her for a while."

Connor leaned back in his chair. "It's one of our least dangerous cases."

Right—not dangerous at all. *Unless Hannah puts two plus two together when Jayden and Isabelle mysteriously show up at the same location as her and her dumbass date.*

I kept that thought to myself.

Jayden returned a few minutes later to let us know Isabelle had agreed to the scheme. Connor got to work on gathering intel on Hannah's date, and the rest of us returned to our own jobs.

Several hours later, we were in his office again, ready to hear the dirt on Philip Stevenson.

"I swear, he has to be the most boring man on the planet," Connor said. "He's a contract lawyer with no dings on any aspect of his work ethics. He hasn't had a single speeding ticket, parking ticket, or accident. He has lived in San Francisco his entire life. His mother owns a store that specializes in Christmas and his father is an accountant. He volunteers once a month at the food bank and plays racquetball twice a week with a colleague, who was also his best friend in high school."

By boring, I assumed Connor was referring to the man's lack of a criminal record.

Or an indication that Hannah was in for a very dull night.

None of this matters, I reminded myself. *As long as she has fun and he's not a jerk, that's all that matters.*

Nope, I didn't believe that either.

13

HANNAH

"How do I look?" I asked Everly as we both studied our reflections in the bathroom mirror. She was standing on the closed toilet lid while I applied my makeup for my date.

"Pretty." She surveyed the array of makeup containers scattered on the counter, picked up the lipstick, and handed it to me.

"You don't think red will be a little too much?"

That's right. I'm taking advice from a three-year-old.

She shook her head. "Red is pretty."

She was right. With my dark hair and the black dress, the color would be perfect. But not for the reasons Everly was thinking. It said sexy...as in I wanted to get laid, but without screaming my intentions.

"All right, red it is." I lightly applied a coat and checked to make sure it hadn't ended up on my teeth. "Okay, I think I'm ready for this." As ready as I ever would be.

Wes was in the living room, watching a hockey game when Everly and I entered.

"What do you think?" I asked him.

He turned around and looked me over. "You're not planning on wearing that, are you?"

I checked my dress in case there was a big smudge I hadn't noticed. Nope, it still looked good, especially paired with my thigh-high boots. "What's wrong with what I'm wearing?"

Wes looked at Everly, who was watching the exchange. "It might send the wrong message."

"What, that I want to have a good time?" Not waiting for an answer, I crouched to Everly's level. "Keep him out of trouble while I'm gone, will you? Maybe read him some stories."

She giggled and ran off to her room, possibly to fetch some picture books.

"Enjoy your game," I said to Wes. "I won't be late since I have work tomorrow morning." That was part of the reason I had agreed to meet Philip for drinks tonight. Work gave me an excuse for bailing early if my date turned out to be good-looking but dull.

Maybe I should have been annoyed at Wes's comment, but I knew he hadn't said it to be a jerk. Okay, he hadn't said it to be a *complete* jerk. Just a partial one. He was being a good friend and looking out for me. Except for Emma when we were in foster care together, no one had done that for me growing up.

I'd been the one who always looked out for myself and for those kids who were younger than me. It was kind of nice, for once, to have someone else do the same for me.

I walked to where he was sitting on the couch and planted a quick kiss on his cheek. "Thanks for being such a good friend, Wes."

I pulled away, surprised at how my lips tingled from the kiss —the same sensation spreading through my body.

Always a bonus when you're about to go on a date with a man who wasn't the one you just kissed.

"Not a problem." An emotion flickered on his face, too fast

for me to register what it meant. Then his expression quickly morphed into a smirk. "Have fun."

"I will. Have fun reading to Everly."

FORTUNATELY, THE RAIN FROM EARLIER HAD STOPPED, SO I DIDN'T have to worry about getting wet when I walked from my parked car to the restaurant. I entered the building and headed toward the lounge.

Philip was already sitting at a table when I arrived. He stood to greet me. "You look beautiful." His words were a huge step up from what Wes had said before I left to come here.

I smiled. At least someone appreciated how I looked. "Thank you. You look great, too."

And he did. He was wearing a lightweight, dark-green sweater and black slacks. Both accentuated his athletic body nicely. "I hope you haven't been waiting too long."

He returned my smile. "Not at all. I just got here."

I took the seat across from him. Jazz music played softly in the background, loud enough to be heard, but low enough so it didn't drown out the conversation. The lounge wasn't busy, probably because it was only Tuesday. I imagined it was popular on the weekend and Friday nights.

"Do you have any big plans for Thanksgiving?" he asked. The holiday was in two days.

"I have to work in the morning, but I'll be joining some friends for Thanksgiving dinner. What about you?"

"Same deal, minus the working part. But I'll be spending it with my family, which is always interesting. I come from a big family, and it usually gets a little crazy and competitive when it comes to my brothers."

The cocktail waitress approached our table. "Hi, what can I get you to drink?"

"I'll have a virgin bloody mary."

Philip ordered a pilsner.

And that was when I noticed them. Jayden and Isabelle. They were sitting at a table not far from us, deep in conversation. Isabelle laughed at whatever Jayden had told her. Her gaze then landed on me, and she smiled.

She said something to him, and the next thing I knew, they were heading our way.

Without asking first if they could join us, they sat in the two vacant chairs at our table. Isabelle reached across it so my date could shake her hand. "Hi, I'm Isabelle, a friend of Hannah's. And this is Jayden. Also a friend of Hannah's." She smiled sweetly at Philip, but there was no missing the warning undertone in her voice. The undertone that almost made me laugh. "You don't mind if we join you, do you?"

"Not at all," Philip replied, although I had a feeling what he said and what he meant were on opposite ends of the spectrum.

I introduced them to him.

Did I care that they were crashing my date? Kind of—but not enough to shoo them away. Their presence reduced some of the pressure of being on a first date.

Maybe not for Philip, but definitely for me.

The downside? It was a lot harder to flirt with him if my goal was to get laid tonight. I was hardly bringing on my flirting skills in front of Jayden and Isabelle.

I looked between them. Jayden appeared comfortable, leaning casually back in his chair. Maybe a little too comfortable. "I didn't realize you two are dating."

"Oh, we're not dating," Isabelle said a little too quickly. "Jayden isn't the type of man I usually date." Her gaze scanned the area to either find the kind of man she did date...or to avoid eye contact with me.

Interesting.

"So how come you're here, together?"

This time she looked me squarely in the eye. "To discuss work. You know, the usual boring stuff. So Philip, what do you do for a living?"

He explained his job, which was duller than when he had first told me about it. Jayden and Isabelle nodded as if it were the most interesting occupation in the world.

And then came the questions about what we were doing over Thanksgiving.

"How many siblings do you have?" Jayden asked after Philip had explained his plans for the holiday.

"Five. Three brothers and two sisters."

"Are you looking to have a big family, too, one day?" Isabelle inquired.

"Maybe. I haven't given it much thought. My goal is to make partner eventually, and that doesn't leave me time to focus on having a family right now. But later, I would be amicable to the idea of having two or three kids."

"But not yet," Jayden replied, pretty much repeating what Philip had already told us.

What the heck were he and Isabelle doing? And why did it feel like they were interrogating Philip? Was this what they usually did on dates? Eliminate their date early in the game so that they didn't waste too much time on the individual?

Do you want kids? No? Okay, date's over.

Besides, shouldn't *I* be the one asking the questions? It was *my* date after all.

Both Jayden and Isabelle looked at me, waiting for me to respond—or maybe for me to lobby the next round of questions.

"That's too bad," Isabelle said. "Hannah, weren't you hoping to have kids one day soon?"

Huh? If I didn't know better, I'd say that she and her partner in crime knew about my pregnancy. But that was impossible. Only myself, Wes, Emma, and Travis knew about it.

I narrowed my eyes at Jayden.

"So Jayden. Isabelle. When was the last time you spoke with Wes?" My gaze darted between them, the truth serum of gazes.

Neither of their faces betrayed what they were thinking or confirmed my suspicions. This wasn't a surprise when it came to Jayden. The man was trained to be stone when it came revealing his emotions.

"He was at the office today. Why?" Isabelle's tone was sweet as honey, cunning as Yogi Bear.

Even without looking at him, I could tell Philip was watching our exchange with great interest.

"No reason in particular," I replied, tone matching hers. "I was just curious."

I also had a sneaky suspicion their presence at the same time as my date hadn't been a happy coincidence.

"But now that you've done what you came for," I said, "time to run along and report to your boss."

"And what exactly are we supposed to report to Liam on?" Jayden said it a little too smoothly, like he knew exactly what I was talking about. He then looked to Isabelle, as though she had the answer.

"That's not the boss I was referring to, and you know it. You've done your job. Now it's time to let me enjoy my date. Without you two." I motioned for them to amscray. "And while you're talking to your boss, let him know that I'm on to him, and he and I will be talking about it when I get home."

I flashed them both meaningful looks.

Jayden chuckled. "Wish I was going to be around to see that." He pushed himself to his feet and held out his hand to Isabelle. "How about we finish our drinks over there?" He jerked his head to where they were sitting earlier.

She picked up her drink from the table and stood. "Good idea. And then we can brainstorm some ideas for how I'm going to survive Thanksgiving with my relatives. My grandmother is still hoping you're going to show up and remove your shirt. She said that would give her something to be truly thankful for."

The two of them returned to their table. Jayden sat with his back to me, but once again Isabelle had a clear view of us.

My phone pinged.

Even though it wasn't a polite thing to do on a date, I checked the text from Isabelle.

Isabelle: Just so you know. He didn't pay us to do this. We did it because we're your friends and we care about you.

I gave her a small nod and smiled.

I would like to say the date improved after that, but sadly that wasn't the case. I spent more time dwelling on what to say to Wes for sending Jayden and Isabelle to spy on me than I paid attention to Philip.

That was not to say I didn't enjoy getting to know him. He was a nice guy. Second date material?

Maybe.

After a couple of drinks, we headed out to the parking lot. Jayden and Isabelle hadn't left yet, but I knew they were giving us space so as not to scare Philip off.

"Soo...?" He left the rest of the question hanging, but it wasn't hard to guess where he was hoping things were heading. His heated gaze locked on to mine.

Except I was certain the level of heat in *my* gaze didn't come close to matching his. The hum my body had experienced when I kissed Wes's cheek was playing shy. Even when Philip touched my arm earlier, it had stayed away.

Before I was willing to take this any further, I had one more test to do. "I had a good time." I kissed him on the lips.

It was a barely-there kiss. Mostly to see if there were any sparks...or if this date would end in a fizzle.

Philip saw things differently...he pressed me against my car, and then his tongue was in my mouth.

Let's pause for a moment to discuss the different types of kisses:

There's the tentative kiss. It's sweet but also sexy when done in the right way.

There's the inexperienced kiss. Usually not great, but with practice, the kisser becomes better with time.

There's the playful kiss, which involves tongues. It's fun and it's sexy and it's the prelude to so much more.

There's the dirty, demanding kiss that melts you to the core and usually results in clothes flying across the room.

And then there is the kiss that defies all description—and not in a good way. This is the sloppy kiss that is all levels of not sexy, and includes, as an added bonus, the guy's tongue jammed down your throat.

I don't think I need to tell you which category Philip fell under.

And that...was the end of our date.

Somehow I managed to pry his face off mine. It was like a space alien that had suctioned its tentacles to your face.

"Well, I should get going," I said, spotting Jayden and Isabelle hovering a few vehicles down. "I have the early shift at the hospital tomorrow."

He smiled. "I'll call you."

Oh, boy. Now for the part I hated the most. "It's probably not a good idea. You're a great guy. But I don't think it would work out between us." Never mind that I was just over four months pregnant.

He didn't need to know that.

"You're probably right." He waved at Jayden and Isabelle. "Have fun with those two."

"I'm really sorry about them."

"Don't be. They were only looking out for you. Not everyone has great friends like that."

We said our good-byes, and I got into my car.

Jayden and Isabelle were still standing next to his SUV when I drove past. I waved bye to them.

And my body sighed.

Not because I wasn't going home with Philip. It was actually quite relieved, given how terrible his kiss had been.

My body was sighing because I was returning to Wes's condo, and my body remembered how amazing it had felt when I'd kissed his cheek earlier.

Why couldn't it have been that way with Philip?

It was 8:30 p.m. by the time I arrived at the condo. Early to be coming home from a date—late for Everly to still be awake.

I pushed open the door and removed my boots. I was positive that by now Wes would have received Jayden's full report on my date.

The TV was on in the living room, but no one was watching it.

"You're home early." Wes's voice was low and came from the kitchen. "How was the date?"

I laughed. "As if you don't already know." I walked up to him and smacked him on the chest. He barely flinched. "That's for sending your goons to spy on me."

His deep chuckle set off a flicker of heat in my lower belly. *Not good.* "Apparently, my goons need to work on their spy skills."

"Hopefully they do a better job undercover when working for Liam."

That got another round of chuckles, much to the detriment of my body. "So bad date, huh?"

Needing something to distract myself—and possibly to extinguish the heat—I grabbed a glass from the cupboard and filled it with tap water. I chugged some of it back, washing away the remnants of Philip's kiss.

"It wasn't bad," I said once I'd finished drinking enough water to drown a goldfish. "The guy wasn't the most exciting man in the world, but he was nice."

"But you want more than nice? Like maybe someone to be a father to your baby?"

"I didn't go on a date with him because I was hoping he'd be Little Bean's dad one day. Which was just as well because he wasn't looking to have kids for quite a few more years."

He nodded, already knowing this because it was part of the comprehensive report he would have gotten from Jayden.

"I'm not looking for a husband or a father for my child," I told him. "As I said before, Little Bean is my number one priority."

"So why did you go on a date with him?"

"Because I wanted to have sex. And maybe because I know it won't be much longer before men are no longer interested in me. I wanted to make the most of things before it's just my baby and me."

"But you didn't have sex with him?"

I laughed softly, not wanting to wake up Everly. "I take it your spies told you that part, too?"

"They told me you two kissed, and that was the end of the date. He went his way and you went yours."

"They were very thorough with their report."

"So what happened? Why did you change your mind?"

I set my glass on the counter. "Because his kissing was awful. And I was worried that if his kisses were bad, then…"

"Then the sex would be just as bad?"

I nodded, and my gaze dropped to Wes's lips. For a second, I allowed in, once again, the thought of what kissing him would feel like. I had no doubts whatsoever it would be a helluva lot better than kissing my date.

My eyes flicked up to his. "As it is, I'll probably have to bleach my brain to forget his kiss. I think I have kiss PTSD."

"Is that even a thing?"

"It is now."

"You know, there's probably a better way to help you forget it." His voice came out low and gravelly, and my legs forgot their function for a rapid heartbeat. "You need to kiss someone else. Someone who's a much better kisser."

"Do you have any suggestions who might be qualified for that task?" My voice wasn't much different than his, my breath coming in slightly faster now.

He lifted my chin with a crooked finger. "I might have someone in mind." Then he lowered his mouth to mine—and my reasons for why kissing him wasn't a good idea flew out the window and fell twenty-four stories to their demise.

I parted my lips and welcomed him in. My entire body felt like I imagined it would if I stuck a wet finger into a light socket, only better.

One of Wes's hands knotted in my hair. All I could do was moan softly at how incredible it felt. This was a kiss that outshone all others. I couldn't believe it had taken me this long to discover its existence.

"Mommy?" Everly's small voice said somewhere behind me.

14

WES

At the sound of Everly's broken voice asking for her mommy, I jerked away from Hannah and turned in time to see my niece plod into the kitchen, her bunny clutched to her pajama-clad body. Her tear-stained face instantly broke my heart.

I opened my mouth to speak but didn't get a chance. A small sob tore free from Hannah, and she crouched in front of Everly.

I did the same.

Everly looked confused about why Hannah was crying, a reflection of how I was feeling. Women didn't usually burst out into tears after I kissed them. So, having Hannah do exactly that threw me for a tailspin. Everly's appearance in the kitchen, looking for her mom, didn't help me either.

I couldn't remember the last time I'd felt so out of my element.

Hannah took a deep breath and smiled softly at Everly. "I'm going to have a baby, and sometimes that makes me cry for no reason."

Everly looked thoughtful for a moment. "You mean like Lily has a baby brother?"

"Something like that. Except I don't know yet if the baby will be a boy or a girl."

Everly tilted her head to the side. Her tears had already dried, and Hannah's, for now, had stopped flowing. "Where's the baby?"

Hannah smiled, her dark eyelashes wet with tears, and I felt a tug in my heart at how strong and beautiful she looked. She pointed to her stomach, which was still flat. "Here."

Everly nodded, although I couldn't be too sure how much she understood.

"Do you need a drink of water?" I asked her. Sometimes that was all she needed before she returned to bed, especially if she'd had a nightmare. It wasn't uncommon for her to wake up from them and want her mom.

She nodded again.

A few minutes later, Hannah and I had Everly and her stuffed bunny tucked in bed. We kissed them good-night on the forehead and left her room.

"I'll be back in a minute," Hannah said. "I want to change into something a little less dressy."

She returned a short time later in yoga pants, a pale pink T-shirt with a cartoon kitten on the front, and minus her makeup. The woman who usually came off as tough as sin suddenly had a side to her I'd never seen before—a softer side. Not the same soft side I'd witnessed when she talked to Everly and that her patients no doubt saw.

This was something different.

It was a side of her I wanted to see more of, a side that caused my heart to stir in a whole new way.

"I'm sorry about earlier." She sat next to me on the couch and gestured toward the kitchen.

That sound? It was my stomach groaning while free-falling

to the floor at her comment. I really hoped she was referring to the crying and not the kiss.

She had nothing to apologize for when it came to the kiss.

Or the crying.

"You're sorry I kissed you?" *Please say that's not what you're talking about.*

Why did I kiss her when I hadn't originally planned to go there once I found out she was pregnant?

When she told me how bad of a kisser her date had been, I couldn't help myself.

Right or wrong, all I could think about was how much I wanted to kiss her. Call it a moment of weakness.

A soft smile stretched on her face. "No, I'm definitely not sorry about that. Thank you for reminding me that not all guys kiss like my date tonight."

"I'll take that as a compliment."

"You should. He could take lessons from you." She tucked her feet under her.

"That is one thing I'll never do, teach guys how to kiss." I did see an ad once on YouTube for something like that. Some douchebag was promoting his online course on how to kiss women.

Travis, Josh, Trent, and I couldn't stop laughing for a solid ten minutes after that.

"So what are you sorry for?" Because I really couldn't see why she was apologizing.

"For breaking down when Everly asked for her mommy." She plucked at an invisible piece of lint on her yoga pants. "It brought back a bad memory, and between that and these crazy pregnancy hormones, I just kind of lost it."

I placed my hand on hers, pausing her attack on the invisible-lint invasion. "What memory?"

She shook her head, still unable to look at me.

"Hannah?" My voice was low, my tone encouraging, the way you spoke to a wounded animal you were trying not to spook.

She finally looked at me, and the sadness in her eyes almost did me in. "I told you before that I think what you're doing for Everly is a great thing. You could have just let her be put into foster care and be bounced from one home to the next. That was what happened to me.

"Unlike Everly, I didn't grow up with a loving mother. I was an accident she didn't want, but she didn't think to put me up for adoption when I was born. She didn't abuse me, but she did tend to forget to check if I had enough food, and she couldn't have cared less whether I felt loved and wanted."

A tear trailed down her face, and her gaze returned to her lap. I didn't bother to get her to look at me. I had a feeling whatever she had to tell me, it was easier to say it if she couldn't see the reaction in my eyes. The anger at her mother for neglecting Hannah as a child. Anger at her father for not being there for her.

"One day, when I was six years old, she and her boyfriend at the time ran off to Vegas for the weekend. She left me on my own in the apartment. There wasn't much food. Maybe a half-eaten box of Cap'n Crunch.

"Five days later, the cops showed up at my apartment. I had since run out of food and had missed three days of school. They had come to check on me after learning from the Vegas police that my mother and her boyfriend had died during a drug deal gone wrong."

Fuck.

I gently squeezed her hand, letting her know I was there for her. I wasn't going anywhere while she told me the rest of her story.

"The cops took me away and handed me over to social services. Everly might have been one of the lucky ones who is adopted to a nice home because they are still young and adorable. Those are the kids that parents who are looking to adopt tend to go for. Or she might have gotten lucky and ended up in good foster homes."

"But you weren't that lucky, were you?" My heart clenched hard at the thought of what could've happened to Everly if I hadn't been in the picture.

"I was luckier than Emma. That's how we met. We were both bounced from foster home to foster home. It wasn't until we were almost too old for foster care that we were transferred to the same house. Despite everything she had gone through, including an abusive foster parent, she was still sweet and hopeful that things would one day be better for her. I couldn't help but want to be her friend. She's the kind of person you would do anything for."

Hannah's tone held a fierceness that made me think of a mother bear who would karate-chop anyone threatening her clubs. I could almost imagine what Hannah had been like then —and what would she be like once her baby was born.

"While most of the foster homes I'd stayed in hadn't been as bad as what Emma experienced, I had gone through a different round of disappointment. At one point I had stayed with a nice family. I had fallen in love with them, and they eventually decided to adopt me. I was so happy. I was finally going to have parents who wanted me, who loved me as if I were their own flesh and blood. But then the adoption fell through, and I was tossed back into the system."

Shit.

The Hannah I normally knew—the one who didn't typically let this soft side of her show—suddenly made sense. She'd built a wall around her heart, impenetrable unless you were a kid.

That was why she had always kept every man interested in her—and me—at a distance, never allowing her relationships to last longer than a week, if even that long.

She was afraid of loving someone, of being loved, only for them to abandon her as everyone else had.

Hannah moved her free hand protectively to her belly. "You would think after everything I went through, I would have adopted a child instead of going the route I did to have Little Bean—especially when there are so many kids waiting for a permanent home and a loving parent." She shrugged. "There are days I feel guilty about my decision. But I have a feeling it would be like visiting an animal shelter and adopting only one pet. I'd want to save everyone." Her eyes finally found mine. "Do you think that's wrong of me?"

I removed my hand from hers and stroked my thumb against her jaw. "I don't believe there's anything wrong with that at all. And yes, I can see you trying to save everyone. Is that why you became a pediatric nurse?"

She nodded and smiled. "I knew I'd never survive being a social worker. I would burn out in no time. But by being a pediatric nurse, I'm an advocate for the kids. I'm there for them like I was there for the kids who needed someone to stand up for them in the foster homes. Now you see why I think you're amazing, Wes. You weren't planning on being a father. But now you're a single dad who would do anything for your niece." She laughed softly. "You're even prepared to give up sex and having a girlfriend because Everly comes first."

"I guess guilt works in mysterious ways."

She tilted her head to the side, her gaze studying me. "What are you talking about?"

Ladies and gentlemen, time to cut my own vein. "As you know, my company and my career were at one point the center of my universe. I wasn't looking for a long-term relationship because I already had one. I had worked so hard to make my company a success, partly because I wanted to prove to my father I wasn't the slacker he thought I was. He, unfortunately, died before he got to witness that.

"But while proving myself, I became the one person I swore I'd never be like—my father. He was a workaholic and hadn't been around as much as he should have while Eric and I were growing up. It was tough on my brother and me, and it was tough on our mom. That was part of the reason I chose to remain single.

"For the first two years of Everly's life, I was *that* uncle who visited at least once a month. When I wasn't visiting her in San Jose, she and I would FaceTime. She grew up knowing who Uncle Wes was. We were very much part of each other's lives.

"But the job started getting in the way of that about a year ago. I kept canceling on my family, always because of work. My brother even accused me once of being just like Dad. He didn't mean it as a compliment. In retrospect, if I could go back a year and do it over again, I wouldn't make my career my first priority. My family, my brother, Kristin, and Everly would have come first." I rubbed my hand down my face, wishing it was enough to rewind time. "I still have Everly in my life, thank God. But I lost two people who were important to me. I'll never get to see them again. I wasted what little time I had with them because I was too focused on my career."

I had no idea what it was like to swallow a swarm of bees, but I had a feeling it was similar to how my throat felt. Tight. Itchy. Not a lot of fun.

Hannah shifted her legs from under her and straddled mine. She gently cupped my face in her hands, and her beautiful hazel eyes studied my own for a second, enabling me to focus on the flakes of gold in them instead of how much I wanted to kiss her. "Have you talked to anyone about how you feel?"

"Does telling you count?"

"Not really. I mean a professional. You're taking Everly to see a therapist to help her deal with her parents' death. Maybe you could speak with someone who can help you deal with your own loss."

"Are *you* seeing anyone to help you deal with the guilt of having a baby instead of adopting?" I already knew the answer. *Slam dunk. Score.*

"That's not the same thing. You can't let the guilt of not being around so much for them eat you up inside. It's not good for you, and it's not good for Everly."

"I'll be fine. It's only been just over five months." A long five months with lots of ups and downs. And princess parties.

"What will it take for you to talk to someone?"

"You could kiss me. That might convince me." I winked at her.

She rolled her eyes, seeing right through my lie. "I can definitely kiss you. But only this one time, and no one can know about it."

"Not even Emma?"

"Especially not Emma. She's so determined for me to find Mr. Right because she found her own Mr. Right, that she doesn't understand I have no room in my life for that kind of complication."

"Not even for Phil the Bad Kisser?"

She laughed. "Especially not for him. So do we have a deal? One more kiss and then we move on?"

"Are you still planning to date?"

She shook her head. "I don't have the energy for that kind of drama anymore."

"What about your perpetual state of horniness?"

"How do you deal with *your* perpetual state of horniness?"

Fortunately, she was not pressed against the part of me willing to show her just how horny I was right now. She also hadn't seemed to notice my current dilemma, which wouldn't get much better once we began kissing. It was a sacrifice I was willing to make.

"The shower," I replied.

"Well, that's how I'll deal with my situation, too. Maybe not in the shower, but you get the point."

And there we had it. My cock hardened even more in my jeans. My head flopped against the back of the couch, and I groaned. "Christ, Hannah, you're killing me."

Her words and the image now in my head might have been killing me, but that was nothing compared to a second later, when Hannah's soft lips brushed against my neck.

Her kisses moved up my skin to my jaw, and every part of me buzzed with need. I moved my hands to her hips to keep her firmly in place. I didn't need her accidentally brushing her sensitive parts against my hardening length.

I only possessed so much willpower, and we were approaching its limit faster than the speed of light.

And then her mouth took mine, and I knew I was done for.

15

HANNAH

Two days after the kiss that outshone all others, Wes, Everly, and I drove to Holly and Josh's house for Thanksgiving dinner.

Wes was looking as handsome as ever, in his black trousers and a blue dress shirt. He had foregone the tie, knowing that Josh wouldn't be wearing one either.

Had Wes and I brought up again what we'd shared the night of my date with Phil?

Damn straight we hadn't. He had seen a side of me few people ever witnessed. The side that was once again locked up tight.

I was more worried about Wes, but I had a feeling getting him to talk about his guilt would come with strings attached.

So for now, I was letting it go—until I figured out how I could help him.

I turned around in my seat to see how Everly was doing. She was in her car seat, showing Snuggle Bunny the world outside her window.

"Are you looking forward to seeing Lily?" I asked her.

She grinned. "Yes!"

"Maybe you can convince Uncle Wes and Uncle Josh to play tea party with you and Lily." Because that would be utterly adorable.

Plus my phone was fully charged, ready to shoot lots of photos of Wes and Everly together.

"And maybe Uncle Wes can even borrow Lily's tiara," I added, grinning at the man in question.

He flashed me a glance that made me giggle. "Don't worry, I'm sure the members of the testosterone club won't evict you because of it."

Twenty-five minutes later, we were walking up the path to Holly and Josh's front door. My hand accidentally brushed against Wes's, and the hum that had been lingering under the surface, ever since I moved into his building, returned to the level it had been the night I straddled his legs and kissed him.

What had my lady bits thought about that? They had been chanting from the sidelines for me to rub against him. To see if it felt as good as they imagined it would, even with several layers of clothing between us.

Fortunately for all of us, my brain still had full control of my body. Okay, it still had seventy-five percent control over my body, but it was enough to overrule their demands.

For now.

Everly tried to reach the doorbell, but she was too short. So she waited for Wes to lift her so she could press the button. Westminster chimes played through the door.

Holly opened it a moment later, with three-month-old James asleep in her arms. Her long auburn hair was pulled back in a sleek ponytail. Like Everly and me, she was wearing a long-sleeved dress.

"Hannah is having a baby," were the first words that came from Everly's mouth as soon as she stepped through the doorway.

Holly's questioning gaze shot up to mine.

"Surprise!"

Her gaze shifted to Wes.

"Unless there's something I don't know, he's not the father." I placed my hand over my small bump. "Little Bean is the result of modern technology."

I didn't have a chance to explain further. Lily, who had the same long auburn hair as her mother, appeared and the two little girls started giggling and being noisy.

Thank you, God, for noisy little girls.

The perfect distraction.

Everly grabbed Wes's hand and tugged on it. Lily did the same to Josh.

"Daddy," Lily said to him, "you and Uncle Wes play tea party with us."

It wasn't a question or a request. It was a demand but in the sweetest possible voice.

The two men let the girls drag them upstairs to Lily's room.

"So when you said modern technology, you're talking about a sperm bank?" Holly asked as we followed them. Her Australian accent was still as strong as it had been two years ago when I first met her.

"That's correct." I briefly explained the hows and the whys.

She was smiling by the time I finished. "Well then congratulations, mate! You're going to be an amazing mum. And you and Wes…?"

"Are just friends. And temporary roommates while I find a new place to live." Holly already knew about my flooded apartment.

Loud giggles came from Lily's room. Holly and I went to investigate how the two men were doing.

The moment I saw them, I had to dig my teeth into my lower lip to keep from laughing out loud. And also to keep from walking over to Wes and kissing him for being so freaking adorable.

The girls had dressed up the two men in bright feather boas, tiaras, big floppy hats, scarves, and anything else they could find for hosting a royal tea party. The men weren't the only ones dressed for the occasion. The girls had on tutus and their own big floppy hats.

But the best part? Because yes, there was something even funnier than two men dressed up as eclectic, six-foot-plus princesses.

Lily's white table and matching wooden chairs were designed for preschoolers, not for full-grown men. Their butts didn't exactly fit the seats.

While the two men were busy entertaining the girls and pretending to drink their tea and talk in fake British accents belonging to old women, I took photos of the foursome—which wasn't easy to do because I was laughing so hard.

"I know he didn't set out to be a father," Holly said quietly enough so only I could hear her, "but he's going to be an amazing one."

I assumed she was talking about Wes.

I couldn't agree with her more.

It was easy to see that he would do anything for Everly, and it had nothing to do with the guilt he was struggling with. He loved her like she was his daughter.

He loved her as she deserved.

"He already is an amazing father," I said, smiling softly at him. I knew he didn't feel that way, but he really was doing a good job given the circumstances.

He looked at me and winked—and my heart melted some more toward him.

I could feel Holly watching me, but I had no idea what she was hoping to see.

So I avoided eye contact with her.

Which sounded like a good idea at the time until an unexpected question slipped into my own thoughts.

What kind of father would he be like to Little Bean?

Shit. What was I thinking?

Wes wasn't going to be Little Bean's father. He would be cool Uncle Wes, the man who would be an amazing role model, especially if Little Bean was a boy.

He would be the one teaching Little Bean to play hockey. Yes, at one point Wes had been a hockey player. Just not a professional one like Josh used to be—and Travis currently was.

He would also be the one to teach Little Bean about computer programming and help her with her math—the one subject that hadn't been my strong point at school.

That's right. Wes was going to be a great uncle to Little Bean.

Little Bean didn't need a father who would abandon us like most people I loved tended to do when it came to me.

Wes wouldn't do that...because he was nothing more than a friend.

True, he was the only friend my body got overly excited about whenever I was near him, and the only friend who caused my heart rate to spike whenever he walked into the room.

But it was temporary.

In a few weeks, my body would be over him, and everything would return to normal.

Right?

16

WES

December

Two and a half weeks after Thanksgiving—almost three weeks since Hannah and I kissed—I was in my office, signing off on some papers to do with the building I owned.

The building once belonged to my grandfather; he bequeathed it to me when he died. Only a few people actually knew I owned it, and I preferred it that way.

Despite the disappointing lack of kissing on the home front, things were going well with Hannah, Everly, and me. Everly and I had been managing okay when it was only the two of us living together, but having Hannah around made things a lot easier...and more fun.

Even though it hadn't been either of our intentions for it to happen, Hannah had slipped into the role of being Everly's mother. Whenever she could, she got Everly up in the mornings and took care of her until Hannah had to leave for work. Then Mrs. Jenkins came over to fill in until I came home.

How were things between Hannah and me? Good.

Better than good.

Other than the lack of kissing.

But I knew I needed to give her space, especially after we had revealed so much about ourselves that one evening. Not only had it left us raw, there had been a slight shift in our relationship ever since. Hannah's wall had gone back up as expected, but it wasn't as high as before.

It seemed more scalable than it had been in the past.

And damn, I suddenly wanted to scale it.

I know, I know. I was the guy who had been avoiding relationships like they were a pile of dog shit you wanted to avoid stepping in at all costs. But that was when my career and company were the number two top priorities in my life, everything else a distant third.

Becoming Everly's guardian changed all that. She helped me remember that there was more to life than my career. It was a lesson my father never learned, and I wasn't going to make the same mistake.

I had no idea if a relationship between Hannah and me would work because things were a little more complicated with her being pregnant. But I did know one thing when it came to Everly—I no longer felt like I was drowning.

When I was younger, I'd gone surfing with my brother and fallen off the board, which wouldn't have been an issue if not for the undertow.

It kept me down, and I was positive I was going to die, the air knocked from my lungs at the surprise of being tossed from my board.

Then a hand grabbed me from behind and dragged me to the surface, saving me. Allowing me to breathe again.

Hannah was like that hand. She was the one keeping me afloat.

Not because I was dependent on her to help me with Everly. I wasn't. *Much*. But having her around did make a difference.

How was her apartment hunting going? Well, that depended on whose point of view you were asking. For me, it was going great because Hannah hadn't found anywhere suitable yet.

I might have been partly at fault for that. I had insisted on joining her each time and had found issues with every apartment we visited. Truth? A number of them would have been perfect for her and her baby, but I wasn't ready for her to leave yet.

It had nothing to do with my life being simpler now because Hannah was living with Everly and me. When it came down to it, I enjoyed having her around.

A text pinged on my cell phone at the same moment that my assistant buzzed in on my line. "You have a call from a Mrs. Marylou Hitchcock," she said, and I mentally groaned.

Hannah and I had been lucky to avoid the old dragon, but according to Mrs. Jenkins yesterday, the woman had recently gotten her knickers in a twist (Mrs. Jenkins's words, not mine) about Hannah staying in my condo.

I quickly calculated the odds of making the situation worse by asking Sarah to tell Mrs. Hitchcock that I would call her back later.

Later, like when she was on her deathbed...in about twenty or so years.

Or whenever Hannah moved out.

Whichever came second.

"Okay, I'll take the call," I said on a sigh. Sarah forwarded it to my line. "Hello, Mrs. Hitchcock. What can I do for you?" My tone was friendly enough to charm, no-nonsense enough to cut her prissiness off at the pass.

"I wanted to let you know that there will be a board meeting this evening regarding your houseguest." Her uppity, I-vant-your-blood Count Dracula tone suddenly had me on edge. Well, more on edge than before.

"Specifically which houseguest are we talking about?" For all I knew, she now had an issue with Everly living with me.

"The woman."

"The woman has a name." Which she knew because it was on the form that the board had Hannah fill out, for security reasons, due to her length of stay exceeding a week.

"Right. Anyway, because of her low moral fiber, the board has issues with her staying in the building. So depending on how the vote goes, she will be asked to leave."

"What time is the meeting?" Remembering I had a text, I glanced at my phone, mostly to distract me from yelling at the old bat.

No disrespect to bats around the world intended.

I read Travis's text.

Travis: Emergency at Emma's store. She can't meet with Hannah at the ultrasound. Thought you might want to know.

"Shit," I muttered at the same time that Mrs. Hitchcock was saying, "You're not invited to it."

I guess my curse registered with her because she added, "And I don't appreciate being spoken to in that manner, young man."

I choked back a laugh. *Way to go on trying to make me feel like a five-year-old.* Too bad for her—it hadn't worked.

"I'm sorry, I don't have time to talk about this now. I'll be at the meeting tonight." I hung up on her before she could argue otherwise.

I texted Travis.

> Me: Thanks. Do you have the address?

He replied, and I packed up my office. "I have a meeting I need to go to," I told Sarah on my way out the door. "I'll be back in two or more hours."

I knew Hannah was nervous about her ultrasound appointment. A side effect of being a pediatric nurse, I guess. She had been pacing the apartment this morning to the extent that I had expected to see a deep ravine forged in the rug.

I arrived at the ultrasound clinic ten minutes before Hannah's appointment. Her car was already in the parking lot, but she wasn't in the clinic waiting room when I entered.

I strode to the front desk and asked if she was there yet. She wasn't and she hadn't canceled, so I grabbed a magazine from the waiting room table and sat in a vacant chair. Several women in various stages of pregnancy were also waiting. None were alone. They either had a man with them or another woman with whom they were chatting.

Five minutes later, the clinic door opened, and Hannah stepped into the waiting room. She walked to the front desk without noticing me, but after her check-in, she turned around, and her gaze landed on me. Her mouth dropped open, forming the perfect O.

"Hi," she said after a second. She sat in the chair next to me. "What are you doing here?"

"Travis told me Emma couldn't make it. I know how nervous you are about the ultrasound, so I came here to give you moral support."

The pre-pregnancy Hannah would have nodded and said thanks. Or more likely, told me she was fine and I could go now.

But pregnant Hannah had a different response. Her eyes filled with tears that caught me off guard.

She sniffed and smiled. "That's sweet of you. You didn't have to do that, but thanks."

"You're welcome. We're friends, and that's what friends do."

"Hannah Morrell?" a woman in a lab coat said from the doorway next to the reception desk. She scanned the room as Hannah and I stood, letting her know that Hannah was here.

She introduced herself as Jennifer, then we followed her down the hallway to a dim room with an exam table and a TV monitor. She asked Hannah to lie on the table.

"Are you the father?" Jennifer asked me.

"No, just a friend."

"I was artificially inseminated," was Hannah's immediate reply, already on the defensive.

Was she planning to do that every time she introduced her baby to someone? Making sure they knew that she had gotten pregnant by choice instead of by accident?

Or was she saying it because she was nervous?

I reached for her hand that was resting next to her on the table, and covered it with mine, threading our fingers together.

Jennifer smiled at me as if she had all the answers in the universe, then explained to us what she would be doing.

Next, she squirted a clear gel on Hannah's growing belly and placed the ultrasound wand on top of it. She moved the wand around and tapped at the keyboard every few seconds.

The entire time, her face was a study of concentration, not giving anything away, which I could tell made Hannah more nervous with each passing second. She was usually good with silence. She wasn't the kind of woman who freaked out at pregnant pauses in conversations (no pun intended). This time the silence was making her antsy.

"Do you have to be anywhere after this?" I asked her, mostly to distract her.

"I'm not on shift at the hospital until later." Which I already knew.

"I thought maybe we could go get your favorite mango ice cream and visit the Christmas store. I want to pick up a decoration for Everly." The building where the two stores were located wasn't far from the ultrasound clinic.

"You don't have to be back at work?"

"I have time before my assistant expects me." Any work I didn't finish once I returned to the office could wait until after I spoke with the residence board and Everly had gone to bed. "So what do you say we get ice cream after this?"

"I would like that. And I would love to visit the Christmas store. I'm assuming the mother of my date from over two weeks ago doesn't have issues with me shopping there. Philip introduced me to her the day I met him at the store. Which she owns."

"I'm sure she'll be fine." Although she might be surprised to see Hannah now that Hannah was obviously pregnant. Her body had changed quite a bit in such a short time.

I lightly squeezed her hand, and she smiled at me, the excitement at visiting her new favorite store reflected in her eyes.

My heart beat a little faster, echoing in my chest like several rapid bounces of a basketball against the gym floor, before executing a free throw. *That's new.*

"I'm almost done here." Jennifer turned the screen to face us. "So here's your baby." She moved the wand on Hannah's belly, and the 3-D shape of a baby came into view.

"That's Little Bean?" The awe in Hannah's voice barely hid the scratchy sound of held-back tears.

I could relate. Maybe not so much the tears part, but seeing that little human inside of her caused an unexpected raw emotion to flip on, and my throat temporarily tightened.

I had no idea why seeing her baby had that effect on me. It shouldn't have. But it did.

"Yes, that would be your baby," Jennifer said. "Do you want to know the gender?"

Hannah shook her head. "That's okay. I want to wait until the baby is born."

I returned to staring at the little bundle on the screen. That was her baby—the little individual for whom she had been prepared to turn her world upside down. No boyfriends. No husbands. No complicated relationships.

Just her and her baby.

While I fully supported her decision, because I was in the same place with Everly, a part of me deep down felt that her doing this alone was all wrong.

But hell if I was voicing that opinion.

Once the gel was wiped off Hannah's skin, she was free to go.

"I was thinking of getting Ava and Liam an ornament," Hannah said as we stepped into the Christmas store a short time later. "I already have their wedding gift, but since they're getting married right before Christmas, I thought it would be a perfect symbol of their big day."

Their wedding was in less than two weeks. Hannah, Everly, and I were driving there together. My SUV could handle the snowy conditions in Lake Tahoe better than her car.

"Wow, Hannah. I didn't know you could be such a romantic."

She laughed and lightly punched me in the arm. "I know, pretty amazing, huh? Must be the result of having a best friend who owns a store that's all about love."

Ah. Yes. The sex store.

Only don't say that to Emma's face.

She would likely karate-chop you in the nuts...or get her trusty sidekick—aka Hannah—to do it.

The store was busier than the last time we'd come here, now that more people were in the Christmas spirit and the days leading up to December twenty-fifth were rapidly dwindling. A hum of excitement filled the air, along with the familiar tune of

"I'm Dreaming of a White Christmas." Something that wasn't happening anytime soon, given this was San Francisco.

We searched the Christmas trees and displays for the perfect decorations. I found a raccoon that went with the Christmas mouse Hannah had bought there last month.

She studied the glass angels—and her fascination with the angel holding the baby the last time we were both in the store now made sense. She had known she was pregnant.

"Can I help you find something?" a woman wearing an ugly Christmas sweater, with a giant gingerbread man on the front, asked.

Her gaze jumped between Hannah and me, then dropped to Hannah's belly. Because Hannah was wearing a long-sleeved T-shirt that skimmed her growing curves, you couldn't miss that she was pregnant. "Oh, my."

If the cute blush spreading across Hannah's cheeks was anything to go by, the woman must have been Philip's mom.

"So...? You two were dating when you went out with my son?" His mother didn't seem angry—more like stuck in the confused zone.

"We're not dating," Hannah spluttered. "Wes is my friend."

The woman raised her hand. "You don't need to explain. It's none of my business. But really, is there something I can help you find?" Her tone was polite and friendly. She was putting business ahead of protecting her son's virtue.

"You had a glass angel holding a baby when I was here last," Hannah said, her cheeks still pink. "Do you have any left?"

"Sorry, we're sold out of them. We only had a few in stock. Maybe I can help you find something else?"

Without looking at Hannah, I could feel disappointment radiating from her. "I was considering buying a train set and a Christmas village to go with it," I blurted, even though I hadn't thought about it until that second.

But the moment those words came out, I knew it was the

right thing to do. To help distract Hannah from her disappointment. And to hopefully distract Everly from the reality that it would be our first Christmas together without her parents.

My insides tightened to the size of a chestnut just contemplating it.

"I bet Everly would love that," Hannah said, her eyes glowing with excitement.

"Perfect." I threaded my fingers with hers and pulled her along to the rear of the store where the miniature villages were located. "You can help me decide which set to get." I didn't care if Philip's mom was there or what she thought of me holding Hannah's hand. I just wanted to see Hannah's smile return.

"Where are you going to put it?" Hannah asked.

"How about on the coffee table? And I figure we should get a tree this weekend. I thought the three of us could go together." Especially since I was hoping a Christmas tree and a fully decorated condo might convince her to stay with Everly and me a little longer.

Hannah grinned. "I would love that."

We spent the next thirty minutes checking out the various villages and deciding which one to get. Phil's mom had left us a while ago to assist another customer, but we didn't need her help anyway. This was more about Hannah and me hanging out together. We didn't need a third wheel getting in the way.

"Everly will love this one," Hannah said after we had narrowed it to two. The one she was referring to was whimsical but not childish. It would be perfect: Everly's and my first holiday tradition without her parents—without my brother and his wife.

"You're spending Christmas with Everly and me, right?" I mentally willed her to say yes.

"You mean for the day or for dinner?"

"Both."

"You're not spending it with Emma and Travis?" she asked.

I shook my head. "They invited Everly and me, but I wasn't sure if it would be a good idea. Things might get a little overwhelming for her, what with it being Christmas. And then there's the part about it being her first Christmas without her parents. I was worried it might be too hard for her.

"So I decided that she and I would stay home and have a quiet evening. I would still make Turkey and all the Christmas fixings."

"That actually sounds nice. Are you sure you don't mind if I join you? Christmas was fun with Emma and Travis last year, but I wouldn't mind something a little less crazy this time."

By crazy, she was referring to Travis's grandmother—Fanny —and her two sidekicks. The threesome liked to think of themselves as matchmakers, taking credit for Travis and Emma falling in love.

Fanny might have been partially correct about that, but she didn't deserve full credit. Josh, Liam, Trent, and I had devised the initial scheme of Travis having a fake girlfriend to get his grandmother off his back.

How were we to know the two of them would fall in love?

"Everly and I would love it if you'd join us," I said.

We gathered the train set, the buildings, and the accessories that were part of the village we'd selected.

"Are you sure about this?" Hannah asked. "It won't exactly be cheap."

She was right. A small building alone was close to sixty dollars. And we had quite a few of them.

"I'm positive. I think it would be the perfect new Christmas tradition for Everly and me."

Her gaze flicked to the village display and she caught her lip between her teeth before quickly releasing it. "That sounds like the perfect idea."

17

WES

Everly and I exited the elevator on the second floor where the board meeting was scheduled to start in five minutes.

"I'm sorry, sweetheart, that you have to come to this boring meeting," I told her, her small hand in mine. Her other arm cuddled her bunny. "But I've got your coloring book and crayons to keep you busy."

"And my tea set?"

I patted the duffle bag containing an assortment of toys. "Check. In the bag."

"And Baby Cries a Lot?"

"Yes, she's in the bag, too."

Seriously, why the hell would anyone want a doll that cried for a minute every time you squeezed its tummy? Oh, and it peed like a real baby.

Fortunately, the creators drew a line when it came to the doll crapping its diaper.

We walked into the small conference room. Mrs. Jenkins grinned at me and waved at Everly.

Because Mrs. Jenkins was part of the board, she was unable

to look after Everly while I confronted the other members. And since I needed every vote in Hannah's favor I could get, it meant Everly had to join me.

However, thanks to Mrs. Jenkins being on Hannah's and my side, she had told me everything I needed to know about the meeting and what to expect.

Everly charged over to her for a hug, then enjoyed all the attention she got from the majority of the nine-person board. None of them could resist her dimpled smile. It didn't hurt that they all knew the sad story of why she was living with me.

And that was the real reason I'd brought her with me. I knew she would soften them up before the meeting began.

Even Mrs. Hitchcock smiled at her and asked her how her day had been.

The look she then leveled at me reminded me of the snow monster in the movie *Frozen*. She certainly wasn't Olaf, who loved warm hugs.

"This is a closed meeting," she told me, after indicating for everyone to take a seat. Everly had opened the duffle bag on the floor and was busy taking everything out to show the board members.

"The meeting isn't closed to me when it deals with my condo and my pregnant friend. I have the right to defend her staying in my place for however long she needs." And for however long I could stall her from finding an acceptable location to live.

"I agree that he should be heard," Mrs. Jenkins said. Several others seconded that.

"All right," a large bald man with a white goatee said. Mr. Chambers, who lived in the condo beneath mine. "You will be permitted to take the floor during these proceedings."

"Thank you."

Mrs. Hitchcock sat a little straighter, her chin held high. "When we agreed to let Ms. Morrell stay in your condo, while she looked for a new place to live, we didn't realize she was a woman of low moral fiber. It was bad enough that until recently you enjoyed partying, and staying out every night until the wee hours of the morning. But then to add this woman—"

"First, I'm not a partier. Those mornings you saw me coming home and looking like I'd slept in my clothes was because I had stayed late at the office most nights, working. I was a workaholic, not a partier, as you like to believe. However, since becoming Everly's guardian, I've shifted my priorities. She's now my number one priority." I smiled down at my niece. She flashed me her dimples. "Second, Ms. Morrell is a pediatric nurse who works in the ER and has saved the lives of countless kids. I don't understand how that makes her a woman of, as you put it, low moral fiber."

I kept my tone even so as not to upset Everly. She had no idea why we were there. And since she didn't know Hannah's last name, there was no reason for her to know whom we were talking about.

"The woman is pregnant."

I nod. "That is correct."

"Is the baby yours?" she asked.

I felt a frown form on my face. *Think happy thoughts. Go to your happy place. Do whatever you can to not let the old bat provoke you.* "What difference does it make if it's mine or not? And for the record, who fathered the baby is none of your business."

Happy. Thoughts. Those thoughts flicked to this afternoon in the ultrasound clinic when I saw Hannah's baby on the computer screen.

That was enough to erase the frown from my face.

"I have to agree with him there," one of the women, whom I didn't know very well, said. She glanced down the table to everyone seated there. "And to be honest, I still don't understand the problem with Ms. Morrell staying with Mr. Chiasson.

If they were married or getting married, there wouldn't be an issue."

She turned her gaze to me. "You're not by any chance getting married to Ms. Morrell, are you?"

Mrs. Jenkins was the next to sit up straighter, her face glowing with excitement.

"No, we're just friends," I replied.

"Are you sure?" Mrs. Jenkins asked. "Friends always make the best lovers and husbands."

I almost laughed at the horrified expression on Mrs. Hitchcock's face. But I wasn't sure which part scandalized her more: best lovers or husbands.

Or maybe it was both.

"I'm sure," I confirmed, ignoring the image that flashed in my head of making love to the woman in question.

"What about the baby's father?" another woman asked. "Is he not man enough to take care of his own responsibilities?"

Fortunately, Everly was too young to understand what anyone was talking about. As long as she didn't repeat any of this to Hannah or anyone else, we were doing good.

"Again, that isn't any of the board's business. However, since I don't want anyone besmirching Ms. Morrell's reputation, I hope she won't be too angry at me for betraying her confidence."

Okay, I was laying it on a little thick, but I was beginning to feel like I was dealing with a group of individuals bored with their regular lives, and who needed the excitement of a little daytime drama to get them through their day.

"She chose to conceive a baby through artificial insemination because she has a lot of love to give a child, but she hadn't found someone worthy enough to settle down with. She knew she wasn't living in a fairy tale, waiting for her Prince Charming to sweep her off her feet. She was ready to have a child in her life, and she didn't want to wait around for this mystery man any longer."

Did anyone else think I went into the wrong career? Maybe I should have become a lawyer for a bunch of fairy-tale creatures.

Note to self: No more watching *Shrek* with Everly. The movie was doing crazy things to my brain.

"So if you believe Ms. Morrell is of low moral fiber because she's pregnant," I said to Mrs. Hitchcock, "you couldn't be more wrong. Her pregnancy was planned, and her child will receive nothing but love from her. And I'm sorry that you believe it's wrong for her to be staying with me while she's looking for a new home after her apartment flooded, leaving her temporarily homeless. I was hardly letting my pregnant friend fend for herself. I wanted to make sure her pregnancy is stress-free. Plus she's helping me with Everly, and Everly absolutely adores her."

The members of the board exchanged glances and nodded among themselves. My closing argument even appeased Mrs. Hitchcock. A satisfied smile broke out on her face.

She high-fived Mrs. Jenkins, who looked equally pleased.

Huh?

Mr. Chambers spoke first. "By unanimous vote, Ms. Morrell is permitted to stay for as long as you wish her to remain under your proverbial roof. Though I do have to ask on behalf of everyone in this room, are you sure there isn't a little more behind your desire for her to stay in your home?" Their eager expressions all zeroed in on me. "Perhaps an unrequited love?"

Oh, Christ.

18

HANNAH

Grinning, Everly jumped up and down numerous times on the dirt path and pointed toward the multiple rows of pine trees. Wes, Everly, and I were spending the morning at Knott's Christmas tree farm, searching for the perfect tree.

The air was chilly, but that didn't seem to bother her. Her festive red coat, woolen mittens and hat, and thick tights kept her warm. All the jumping and running around wasn't hurting either.

It had been five days since the ultrasound. Five days since things between Wes and me had shifted. I couldn't explain what exactly had changed or even what it meant. I just knew that it put me at ease and at the same time scared me.

I chalked it up to another pregnancy-related symptom, like swollen ankles and frequent trips to the restroom.

"This way," Everly said before taking off on us. Wes gave her a short head start; then his long legs quickly ate up the distance between them.

"I think you need to be higher up to see the trees better." He scooped up the giggling preschooler and set her on his shoulders. "Is that better?"

I wasn't sure if he was asking Everly or me. He winked at me, and I laughed. "Yes, much better."

"All right, let's go find our tree. Which way should we go?" he asked her.

She bounced on his shoulders. I told him in which direction she was pointing.

Not far behind us, the sound of sleigh bells drew closer. This resulted in more bouncing from Everly.

"Do you want to go on a sleigh ride after we find our tree?" Wes's question was mostly for Everly, but he was looking at me when he said it.

"That sounds like fun." How many sleigh rides had I been on in my life? Zero.

But I was certain it was somewhere on my bucket list.

He grinned at me. "Then it's set. After we find our tree, we'll go on a sleigh ride, followed by a trip to the elves' workshop and a visit with Santa."

That's right, the Christmas tree farm offered all those things...and more. It was everything a little girl and a Christmas-loving big girl could want. The heavy scent of pine didn't hurt either. If this place didn't get you into the Christmas spirit, well then, bah humbug to you.

"That tree," Everly said after we'd been walking for about five minutes. She was pointing at a tree that was taller than Wes.

Wes removed her from his shoulders and made a show of examining the tree; then he declared that Everly was right. It was the best tree on the farm.

He held his hand out to me. "My saw, lassie."

Everly giggled at his terrible Scottish accent.

I handed him the long saw I'd been carefully carrying. The

blade was covered, but you could never be too cautious—something I was familiar with from working in the ER.

He lowered himself to his knees. "Are my assistants at the ready?"

"What are you now? A Scottish pirate?" A sexy Scottish pirate with a god-awful accent.

He winked at me again; only this time heat rushed to my core. "Aye, if that's what ye need me to be, lassie."

Was anyone else feeling hot?

I knew why he was doing it. And it had nothing to do with me. He loved to make Everly laugh. A smiling, laughing Everly was better than the one who cried because she missed her mommy and daddy and couldn't understand why they hadn't yet come back for her.

That was the other reason why we were here.

Wes was creating new Christmas traditions for Everly, for them both. Her parents had never taken her to a Christmas tree farm. Their old tree was a fake one they had bought a few years ago.

Because of that, Wes had insisted on a real tree this year.

I grabbed the trunk of the Chosen One, and Wes began sawing the base. Everly supervised. Which was another way of saying she ran up and down the dirt path, dancing and singing. And as always, Snuggle Bunny was joining in with her antics.

"Mommy and Daddy will love the tree," she said once Wes had cut it down. The tree was lying on the ground, waiting for us to carry it to his SUV.

My breath caught; my heart ached. Not just for Everly but for Wes. He had been smiling a few seconds ago, but now sadness hung around him like a storm cloud.

Without thinking, I wrapped my arms around him and rested my head on his shoulder. His arms immediate went around me and held me tight. Everly was too busy examining something on the ground to notice what we were doing.

"It's going to be okay, Wes. You just have to trust that things will get better. It won't always be like this for her." I shifted my head away from his shoulder and went to kiss him lightly on the jaw.

But as my lips were about to brush against his day-old facial hair, his head moved slightly, and my mouth made contact with his lips instead.

And just like that, we were kissing.

The kiss was tentative, nothing more. But it was enough to ignite a fire inside me.

Oh, no. Not a good idea.

I stepped away from him. The last thing the farm needed was for me to spark a forest fire, and somehow I didn't think Smokey the Bear would be too impressed either.

But if I continued standing this close to Wes, that was precisely what would happen.

"So, Everly," I said, my voice sounding a little off. "You ready for a sleigh ride?"

Whatever had held her interest before didn't even register on the excitement Richter scale compared to my question. She went back to bouncing around like a bunny, barely able to contain herself.

We walked to the main entrance. Everly held my hand while Wes half carried, half dragged the tree.

After he paid for it and fastened it to the roof of his SUV, we headed to the sleigh ride. Wes helped Everly and me into the open wagon and joined us on the crowded bench. He lifted Everly onto his lap so she could see better, and we snuggled under the blankets covering everyone's laps.

Because we were so close together, due to the limited space in the wagon, Wes's leg rested against mine. I did everything in my power not to focus on it. *Good luck with that!*

It helped when the horses began walking—the perfect distraction. Wes and I spent the entire twenty-minute ride pointing out different things to Everly. The chubby little birds chirping from the pine and leaf-bare trees. The brook bubbling alongside the path. A squirrel running up a tree.

"It's so beautiful out here," I said, more to myself than for anyone else's benefit.

"It is." Wes's hand moved to my knee, still under the blanket. I tensed for a second but allowed myself to relax. It didn't mean anything. Wes was merely thanking me for what I had said to him earlier about Everly.

After the sleigh ride, the three of us had hot chocolate and made craft-stick elves in the workshop with colored pipe cleaners, buttons, bits of ribbon, and googly eyes.

"These will look great in the tree," I told Everly after she'd finished creating hers. I carefully gathered them up, the glue still drying, and we continued to the final hut: Santa's workshop.

"Do you want to sit on Santa's lap again?" Holly and I had already taken Lily and Everly to see him at the mall.

She nodded. But as soon as the nodding stopped, the chewing of her lower lip started.

I crouched, which was getting more awkward with my growing belly. "Would you like me to come with you?"

She nodded once more but this time with a smile.

"Ho, ho, ho," Santa said as we approached, holding hands. His voice was deep and merry, and Everly relaxed a little more. He was sitting on what looked like the back seat of a sleigh, but it was roomy enough for several people to sit on.

"Santa!" she squealed and pulled me over to see him.

Her excitement was infectious, and I suddenly felt like a three-year-old getting to see the one person I had waited all year to visit. In reality, that couldn't have been further from the truth. My mother had never taken me to see Santa when I was a kid.

Maybe that was why I was so excited about it now.

I had a lot of lost time to make up for.

His gaze landed on my growing stomach, which was hard to miss because I wasn't wearing my coat. I had taken it off in the elves' workshop. "I see you're going to be a big sister," he said to Everly.

Her smile widened, and she nodded some more. I opened my mouth to correct him but then realized she probably had no idea what he was talking about and would agree to anything at this point. I also realized that I didn't have to constantly explain why I was pregnant to every stranger who commented on my obvious state.

I shut my mouth and waited while Santa helped Everly onto his lap.

"Okay, Mommy, you can sit here." He patted the space next to him on the seat. "And Daddy, you sit on the other side of me for your baby's first photo with Santa. Well, more like the prequel photo." He laughed with a deep "Ho, ho, ho," his free hand on his ample belly.

And now I knew what it felt like to be a deer caught in sleigh lights.

A warm hand settled on my lower back. I didn't even have to glance over my shoulder to know it was Wes. "I think a photo with Santa wouldn't be a bad idea, even if he has gotten everything wrong." His voice was low and husky in my ear, soothing and also stoking the lust-fire.

Oh, damn.

To it all.

Wes and I did as Santa suggested and sat next to him on the cozy seat. As soon as the elf took our photo, I jumped up from the seat faster than if I had sat on hot coal.

Everly's shyness at seeing Santa vanished, and she got to work telling him what she wanted for Christmas. Again.

"Here you go," the elf said to Wes, handing him the printed picture.

"And I want my mommy and daddy home," Everly said to Santa. "They were in an accident." She continued listing the toys she was hoping to find under the tree.

Wes stiffened next to me. Santa's gaze darted to me, and I gave a sad, barely perceptible shake of the head. Santa nodded, understanding what I was telling him.

A pesky tear made its presence known. I wiped it away before Everly noticed it.

Not knowing what to do for Wes, I threaded my fingers with his and gave his hand a light squeeze.

He squeezed back in gratitude.

19

WES

The following Sunday, I stepped out of my bathroom, freshly showered, and headed to my drawers for clean clothes.

A framed photo sat on top of the dresser—the picture from the day at the Christmas tree farm, with Everly sitting on Santa's lap. Hannah's hand rested protectively on her stomach, her pregnant form visible through her body-skimming sweater. She, Everly, and I were smiling at the camera.

Like a family.

The pinch in my chest now was nothing like the one that happened shortly after the photo was taken, when Everly had said she wanted her parents home for Christmas.

That pain had left me struggling to catch my breath, as if I had once again been pulled down by a rogue wave.

This sensation felt different. Better.

But I couldn't explain it.

I quickly changed and went to check on Hannah and Everly. The moment I left my room, the delicious smell of pancakes greeted me.

The smell wasn't the only thing coming from the kitchen.

Everly's *Moana* soundtrack was playing, and the two of them were standing near the stove, pretending their wooden spoons were microphones, and they were singing enthusiastically to the lyrics of "How Far I'll Go."

Well, attempting to sing the lyrics when it came to Everly. She didn't care if she didn't know the actual words. She was beaming and bouncing around as they performed the song. Neither of them noticed me standing there watching them.

I wouldn't say that Hannah was a great singer. She missed a few notes. But neither of them cared about that either. They were too busy giggling and dancing and singing. I couldn't help the big grin on my face.

They finished the song with a flourish of arm movements, still not noticing me. The light shining from the living-room windows highlighted them like a spotlight and gleamed off the stainless-steel appliances.

Clapping, I walked toward them. "Nice job. I'm impressed."

They turned to me. Hannah's face flushed. Everly rushed over to me.

"We're making pancakes, Uncle Wes."

"Morning, Princess." I picked her up, hugged her, and kissed her cheek. She hugged me back. "They look and smell delicious. Can I help?"

Hannah traded her wooden-spoon microphone for the spatula. "What do you think, Everly? Should we let your uncle help us?" She grinned at the little girl in my arms.

Who was still in her favorite bunny pajamas.

Hannah was in her black yoga pants and a red long-sleeved maternity T-shirt. Her hair was pulled up in a messy bun, and she had a streak of flour on her cheek. I'd never seen anyone look sexier and as fucking adorable as the woman in front of me.

"Yes!" was Everly's emphatic reply.

Hannah passed me the spatula, and I got to work flipping the pancakes.

She walked over to the fridge and opened it. "I bought some breakfast sausages. Do you guys want some?"

Everly started bouncing around the kitchen again like a kangaroo hyped-up on sugary cereal.

"I think that would be a yes," I said with a chuckle.

Hannah brought them over, heated up a frying pan, and put the sausages into it. Then she and Everly set the table while I watched over the cooking food.

She handed Everly a plate. "This is for Uncle Wes."

Everly put it in my place. Her Winnie-the-Pooh plate and Hannah's plate followed. The playlist that I'd created with Everly's favorite Disney soundtracks began to play "Be Our Guest" from *Beauty and the Beast*.

I grabbed a tea towel hanging from the oven door and started singing and dancing along with Lumière. I wasn't much better at singing than Hannah, but that didn't seem to bother Everly. She giggled her head off and danced on the spot.

I took hold of Hannah's hands and twirled her around the room. I couldn't remember the last time I'd had this much fun. Hannah and I were laughing so hard, it made singing more challenging, but that didn't stop me from doing it.

Then Mrs. Potts started singing the lyrics, and Hannah took over her part. When she sang, "Heaven's sakes, is that a spot?" I couldn't resist it. I wiped my thumb across her cheek, removing the smear of flour, and mouthed, *You had flour there*. My body crackled like a live wire just from touching her.

She mouthed back, *Thank you*, and curtsied.

That was when it hit me like a bull charging after a red cape.

Ever since she moved in with Everly and me, Hannah had been showing a side of herself that I'd hadn't seen before, but lately, I'd been witnessing more and more of it every day. It was the fun Hannah, the woman who had an ocean's worth of love to share.

It was the Hannah I could easily spend every day of the rest of my life with.

Just the thought of that had my heart beating fast and proud, rattling on my ribs, eager to declare its intentions for the entire world to hear.

That's right. Without realizing it, I'd been falling in love with Hannah day-by-day for the past month.

This silly, strong, beautiful woman in front of me had sneaked her way into my heart.

And not just her. From the moment I saw her baby on the computer screen, the idea of us being a family didn't scare me as much as I thought it would. No more than it would scare most guys my age whose girlfriend or wife had a baby for the first time.

However, I didn't feel that way because things would be so much easier when it came to Everly if Hannah permanently took over the role of being her mother.

Even if Everly wasn't living with me, I would still want to be with Hannah...assuming the stars all lined up the way they had. The big one being Hannah as my short-term roommate, allowing us to get to know each other better.

Allowing her to open up to me the way she had.

I'm falling for you.

My heart urged me to say out loud the words balanced precariously on the tip of my tongue. It also whispered, *Go ahead and kiss the girl.*

My brain had a different plan.

With most women, having a man declare that he's in love with her wouldn't be a problem (assuming she was actually into him). But that wasn't the case with Hannah. She would be more like a skittish animal, afraid to trust me and once again be let down, a common theme in her past.

With Hannah, I needed to bide my time, fully gain her trust. Show her how I felt about her.

My plan?

I had no fucking idea when it came to the specifics. All this was foreign to me. I'd never been in love before. I needed time to formulate my strategy. My game plan.

"Are you excited about going to the mountains next week for the wedding?" Hannah asked Everly.

The little girl nodded. "We'll see snow?"

"Definitely," I told her.

Hannah crouched to her level. "I'm picking up my dress this afternoon for the wedding. I thought maybe you'd like to come with me, and then we can get you a special party dress, too."

"I think that's a great idea," I said.

Judging from the rapid nodding of Everly's head, she agreed with me.

And while they were doing that, I would be working on Liam's project and working on my own project: figuring out how to get Hannah to open her heart to me.

20

HANNAH

I entered my bedroom at the inn where Ava and Liam's wedding was taking place. It was the same location where they had found themselves stranded a year ago due to a blizzard two days before Christmas.

Ten years before that, they had been engaged, but then for some reason, Liam had called off the engagement. They never saw each other again until that fateful night last December.

However, according to legend, less than twenty-four hours later, they realized they had never stopped loving each other, hence their friends and family gathering at the inn for the next two days to celebrate their long-awaited wedding.

A knock at the door pulled my attention from the quaint bedroom with the king-sized bed—a king-sized bed that reminded me just how alone I was because I had no one to share it with.

I mean, other than Little Bean.

The knocking came again from the door linking my room with the one next to it. I unlocked and opened it.

Wes was standing on the other side, grinning that sexy one-sided smile of his that turned my knees liquid, which was happening more and more with each passing day.

This was especially true after I found out he had confronted the condo board so I could stay in the building for as long as I needed. I only found out about it two days after it happened, when Mrs. Jenkins and three other board members bumped into me on the elevator. They were all in a twitter over what had happened.

Wes had channeled an inner-defense-lawyer he hadn't known lurked beneath the surface. No one—other than Emma—had ever stood up for me the way Wes had.

I smiled back at him. "Hi, neighbor."

Right on cue, my horny hormones flared up. From the way Wes was looking at me, I suspected he knew they were up to no good, my no-doubt heated gaze giving them away.

His own eyes changed into a mirror image of mine. "Hey." His voice came out low and rough, and everything inside me quivered.

"Look. Look, it's snowing," a rather excited three-year-old called out from Wes's room. The same excited three-year-old who had been bouncing in her car booster seat from the moment she had witnessed the snow on our drive here.

"Do you want to build a snowman?" she began singing. Except it was the only line she remembered from the *Frozen* song, so she kept singing it again and again and again.

I laughed. "I think she wants to build a snowman."

Wes chuckled. "Yes, I get that impression." He took a step backward into his room. "What do you say the three of us go outside and build our own Olaf?" he asked her. "We still have a few hours before the wedding."

Stepping forward again, he returned his attention to me. "Or would you prefer to stay here and rest?" His gaze dropped to my growing belly, and his hand gently cupped Little Bean.

He'd been doing that a lot ever since the ultrasound. For some reason, I didn't mind. I wasn't fond of it when strangers touched my stomach—like it was a lamp they were hoping to free the genie from—but it didn't bother me when my friends did the same. Although they usually asked first.

And they did it less frequently than Wes.

That's because you're not living with them, I reminded myself. *He has more opportunities to touch my belly.*

I promptly ignored the voice in the back of my head asking if maybe there was another reason Wes kept touching Little Bean.

"Are you kidding me?" I said, grinning. "Do you know how long I've waited to finally make a snowman?"

Little Bean kicked me in agreement. My hand went to the spot where she had poked me, and my smile widened. The kicking never grew old...even when my bladder was the main target.

"She's kicking you?" Wes asked, recognizing the Oh-Little-Bean-is-kicking-me-again expression on my face. He'd witnessed it enough times.

I grabbed his hand and set it against the spot. "Do you feel anything?"

He shook his head, shoulders drooping.

"That doesn't surprise me," I said, feeling the sudden need to chase away his obvious disappointment. "It would be hard to feel anything through all these clothes." I gave him a quick kiss on the cheek. "Let's go build Everly her snowman before we have to get ready for the wedding."

A few minutes later, the three of us were outside, fully dressed for the cold climate, and traipsing through the lightly falling snow to an open area.

"So, other than using Elsa's magical ability to make a snowman—which is cheating if you ask me—do either of you know how to build one?" It wasn't like I had experienced any snow days while growing up in San Francisco.

"I've made a few before," Wes volunteered, then got to work, showing us how to create our own Olaf. Minus the legs and the ability to walk and talk and sing—which, if you asked me, was kind of a bummer.

Everly helped Wes roll the giant snowball across the open stretch of snow. At one point she paused and opened her arms wide. "He's going to be a big snowman."

"I think you're right," I said. "We might need a ladder to hoist his head onto his body." I was exaggerating. Slightly.

"Will you be able to pick that up to put on his lower half?" I asked Wes. "It looks heavy."

Wes stopped pushing the oversized snowball and stood up. "Are you saying I'm not strong?" He flexed his arms. Arms that were definitely strong—not that you could tell through his winter coat.

I laughed. "Definitely not. Everly, do you think Uncle Wes is the strongest man we know?"

"Yes! Uncle Wes and Daddy both strong," she said, and I cringed at the second part.

She jumped up, landed with her legs separated, and flexed her arms, imitating Wes...other than the jumping part. He hadn't done that. "Look, I'm strong, too."

Laughing, Wes scooped her up and carried her over to where I was standing. "Yes, you are." He kissed her cheek and lowered her to the ground, flashing me a defeated glance.

Not wanting him to dwell on her comment, I surprised us both by kissing him. It was a quick kiss. It was also the first time we had done that since the Christmas tree farm. And like that day, my entire body buzzed with pent-up need.

"I've been wanting to do that again for a while," Wes said, his voice low and gravelly.

"Technically, *I* was the one who kissed *you*."

His arms enveloped me, and he pulled me to him. "How about we fix that?" His mouth was on mine before I could respond.

My body replied instead, and I leaned into him, my expanding belly pressing against him. We kept it PG-rated, but that didn't dull the craving to get closer to him...even when I was pretty much as close as I could get.

"Ewww," a little voice said behind me.

Chuckling, Wes and I broke apart.

"You're right; kissing *is* gross." I made a disgusted face, like I'd licked a grapefruit, and Everly giggled. "We should get back to building our snowman."

Fifty minutes later, we were the proud parents of a snowman and his two snow-kids. Everly had been having so much fun making the first snowman, she decided we needed to create an army of them. However, due to lack of time, we compromised with the two much smaller ones.

"How's your back?" I asked Wes as the three of us returned to the inn.

"Why? Are you offering to give me a massage later?" He winked at me, and I blushed.

Which was probably hard to tell, given the cold air had already turned my cheeks and nose rosy. "Sorry, that option isn't available from the spa."

"Would the spa like a foot massage?"

"No, she's good." And no, he hadn't given me one before, in case that was what you were wondering.

We entered the inn. Ava's mother and Betsy (the inn owner's wife) were busy decorating for the wedding. Betsy was dressed in a similar style to her husband. Both reminded me of paintings I'd seen of an old-fashioned Santa and Mrs. Claus. Everly was convinced Harold was the real Santa.

But she also believed the ones we had visited at the mall and the farm were the real deal.

"Do you need any help?" I asked the two women, who had been laughing and chatting when we entered the lobby.

"No, dear," Ava's mom said. "We've got it covered. You three go enjoy yourselves until the wedding begins."

"There's hot chocolate in the dining room," Betsy added. "Help yourself." To Everly, she said, "And we have fresh-baked chocolate chip cookies that are especially yummy after an afternoon of building snowmen." She winked at the little girl.

Everly grabbed Wes's hand, his dwarfing hers, and tugged him toward the dining room. "C'mon, Uncle Wes. You need a cookie."

"Is that your way of saying *you* want a cookie?"

She flashed him what could be described as a no-duh expression, which caused the two older women to laugh.

The dining room was empty when we entered. Harold and Betsy had closed the inn for two days so Liam and Ava could have their wedding there. They had taken full credit for getting the pair back together. And because of that, they had offered to host the wedding.

Wes, Everly, and I grabbed some hot chocolate and a couple of cookies, then sat at a table near the window.

"Do you think you have enough marshmallows?" I asked Everly on a laugh. She had insisted on filling her mug half-full with them before Wes added the hot chocolate.

Her lips squished into an adorable pout. "No."

Wes had only given her half of what she wanted. When she argued that her mommy always gave her that many marshmallows, he had reminded her about the discussion the three of them had last spring on FaceTime. He knew Everly was exaggerating the truth. Her mom had only let her have a few marshmallows, but since today was a special occasion, Wes allowed her to have slightly more than usual.

"But it's still yummy, right?" I asked.

She nodded enthusiastically, the pout falling away.

We finished our treats and headed upstairs to get ready for the wedding.

"I'm going to have a shower and get dressed; then I can help you with your pretty dress," I told her.

I showered, moisturized my body, and blow-dried my hair, leaving it loose about my shoulders. Next, I slipped on my knee-length maternity party dress. The sapphire blue fabric, with the same color lace overlay, skimmed my body. The narrow lace sleeves stopped just below my elbows, and the blue satin ribbon, attached below my breasts with the bow to the side, draped against my baby bump.

I'd need Wes's help with the zipper in the back, but other than that, the dress was perfect. I quickly applied my makeup and put on a pair of simple silver earrings and a silver bracelet.

"Are you ready to put on your dress?" I asked Everly as I stepped through the open doorway between our rooms.

They both looked up from the Candy Land board game they were playing on her bed.

Everly scrambled down and beamed up at me. "You look pretty. I want to look pretty like you."

"With your gorgeous dress, you'll be even more beautiful than me."

That made her happy, and she performed a funny little dance.

I looked over at Wes, who was silently watching us, his mouth slightly ajar. "Could you do up my zipper? I can't quite reach it."

He gave a single nod but still didn't say anything. I turned my back to him and waited for him to help me. Everly had already left the room, and I could hear her in my bathroom, probably searching through my makeup bag. That wouldn't have been the first time.

Wes's fingertips lightly traced my skin as he dragged the

zipper up. My breath hitched, and a humming sensation tingled through my body.

He stopped partway and swept my hair to one side so he could finish zipping up the dress. His fingertips continued their path of torment, setting off my horny hormones like a match to a stick of dynamite.

His warm breath brushed against my exposed neck, then the shell of my ear. "Christ, you look fucking gorgeous and hot in this dress." His voice was low and heated, causing my body to shiver with excitement, quiver with need.

Stop it, I told my body. It didn't listen.

Wes planted a sizzling kiss on my neck.

That dynamite he just lit? It went *kaboom*.

I was surprised I didn't go up in flames along with it.

"You can shower now if you want," was all I was capable of saying, and even that was a miracle. "I'll get Everly ready in my bathroom."

But instead of doing that, he slowly moved his hand down my shoulder, down my arm, down to my baby bump. He covered the growing expanse with his hand, and his thumb gently caressed the top of my belly.

The gesture felt more intimate than if he had been stroking the sensitive part between my legs, but I didn't know why. The one thing I did know was that it spooked me, and I stiffened.

I wasn't positive, but I thought I heard a faint, exasperated sigh. He dropped his hand from my belly and walked away, leaving me to wish I could snatch back my reaction.

It was too late. His bathroom door clicked shut.

You're such an idiot, my heart said. My body echoed its sentiment—but for different reasons.

What do you *know?* my brain replied, tone full-on snark.

I ignored their bickering, removed Everly's dress from her closet, and returned to my bathroom.

As I had suspected, she was playing with my makeup and now had red lipstick smeared on her face.

I bit back a grin. "I see you've been busy. We should probably clean that off your face and get you dressed. But if you want, I bought you some special lip gloss we can put on you." It was meant for little girls.

Even though I'd never met Kristin—Everly's mom—I had a feeling she would be okay with it. I also liked to believe she was watching from heaven, silently guiding me when it came to taking care of her precious daughter.

The thought of that sent me reeling. What was I thinking? I wasn't taking over Kristin's role as Everly's mother. I was only temporarily living with Wes and Everly. As soon as I found a new home for Little Bean and me, I would be moving away.

I wasn't a permanent fixture in Everly's life.

I mentally nodded to myself, happy to have gotten that straightened out, and ignored the voice in the back of my head eager to argue against my plan.

After I cleaned the lipstick off Everly's face, I helped her into her sleeveless, princess-style satin dress, which was the same color as mine. A band of silver sequins—like diamonds in a tiara—decorated the simple neckline.

I braided a thick strand of her blonde hair and fashioned a hairband out of it. Then I finished off the look with the colorless, shimmery lip gloss.

"There you go. You look like a princess. Are you ready to show Uncle Wes?"

Wes was waiting for us when we entered their bedroom. He had changed into a medium-gray suit, a white shirt, and a royal blue tie. I had seen him in suits before, but I'd never gotten over how hot he looked in them. He had also applied the aftershave that I always had a hard time resisting every time he wore it.

Which to my detriment was regularly.

And this time was no exception.

He flashed Everly a big smile. "Wow, don't you two ladies look beautiful."

"Hannah and I have the same dress," Everly proudly declared.

"Which is why you both look like princesses. And I hope you'll both save me at least one dance tonight." His gaze flicked up to mine.

At the raw, unnamed emotion in his eyes, my pulse fluttered, a butterfly taking flight from its cocoon.

21

WES

What do you get when you mix Christmas and a wedding? You get the most decorated inn lobby known to humankind.

That was the sight greeting my two Christmas-loving girls as we walked downstairs to join the wedding guests already milling about the lobby. Pine boughs, pinecones, tiny fairy lights, and small, rustic hurricane lamps decorated every available surface.

The wooden dining-room chairs had been set up in rows facing the altar. White, tulle ribbons with sprigs of evergreen and white-tipped pinecones hung at the end of each row. The huge Christmas tree—also abundant with rustic-themed decorations—stood to one side of the altar. In the background, a fire burned in the large hearth, the low flames adding a soft glow to the scene without barbecuing the bride and the groom.

Josh and Holly were talking to Kelsey, both women holding their infant sons in their arms. Lily was with them, but as soon as she saw Everly, she raced over. The pair quickly became two giggling girls who were happy to entertain the guests until the wedding commenced.

Kelsey and Holly hugged Hannah as best as they could. Between the babies in their arms and Hannah's growing bump, it was amazing they could hug at all.

Immediately, the threesome began talking about all things baby- and pregnancy-related. This gave Josh and me a chance to escape. Travis and Emma weren't down yet, and Trent was Liam's best man, so he was currently busy.

Josh's mouth curled up to one side. "That was an ingenious plan."

"What plan?" I honestly had no idea what he was talking about.

"Making it look like you, Hannah, and Everly are a family, so any mothers here hoping to marry their daughters off will immediately cross you off their list. And nice touch with the matching color." He flicked his finger against my tie, referring to the blue that matched Hannah's and Everly's dresses.

"First, the matching color was an accident. I only saw their dresses shortly before we came downstairs. They've been secretive about them."

"What's the second thing?"

"I don't think I have to worry about any mothers hoping to marry off their daughters to the next eligible bachelor who shows up at the wedding. It's not like Liam and Ava invited a lot of guests."

"Which means there aren't any opportunities for you to get lucky tonight. But that doesn't matter, does it? Because there's only one woman you're interested in."

"Is that a question or a statement?"

"So what's really going on between you two?" Josh gave a chin-nod in Hannah's direction. She didn't see it because her back was to us.

"Honestly? Nothing."

"But you want there to be. Something has changed, and

now the idea of being with a woman who isn't Hannah doesn't sound too appealing. Am I right?"

"Sounds like someone has been spending too much time reading Emma's Dr. Lovejoy sex column." All right, it wasn't so much a sex column as a relationship column, and no, I hadn't read it. Much.

"You're deflecting."

"And you work in the marketing department for the Rock. What's with all the psychological mumbo jumbo?"

"A large part of marketing involves psychology."

"Not relationship psychology."

A smug grin appeared on his face. *Uh, oh.* That couldn't be good. "How about we ask for a second opinion?" He redirected the smile to something over my shoulder.

I didn't have a chance to see what he was talking about— the *what* slapped me on the back.

"Second opinion about what?" Travis asked.

"What Wes should do about his feelings for Hannah," Josh said.

I groaned. "C'mon, guys. Please don't tell me that being married has converted your nuts to ovaries, because that's not going to be a selling feature for most single guys. And as a single guy, I speak on behalf of my tribe."

"All right, let's put it this way. You've liked Hannah for almost two years."

"Right—as a *friend*." Hell if I was admitting anything to them—yet—when it came to how I felt about Hannah.

"And now you're a single father raising a three-year-old on your own, and your single friend is pregnant. Haven't you even considered for a moment that maybe it's time to settle down? You guys could raise your niece and Hannah's baby as a family. You've already applied to adopt Everly. Why not take things a step further?"

For a second, all I could do was stare at Josh. Then I turned to Travis. "And you feel the same way?"

He didn't have to answer. I could tell what he was thinking. His eyes gave it away.

I let out a hard breath and checked that no one else was within hearing range. "I'll admit I have been considering that possibility. But not because it would be a convenient solution to suddenly becoming Everly's guardian. I care for Hannah. A lot. But she's not like your wives. Well, she's more like Emma, given they both grew up in foster care."

Yes, I had turned into a rambling fool, but neither guy noticed or cared. It was official. They had become presiding members of the Ovary Club—established in 1907.

And maybe so had I...in a thoroughly manly way, of course.

"But unlike Emma," I explained, "Hannah is terrified of loving someone and then having them abandon her like everyone else in her life has. She has serious trust issues. The only person she really trusts is Emma. So I'm taking things slow with her so that she's not spooked away. And proving to her that she can depend on me—I'm not going to be a repeat of everyone else."

Now I was talking about her like she was an injured animal found on the roadside, wary of strangers. Although when I thought about it, the analogy was still apt, even if she was one of the strongest women I knew.

"So you are interested in her as more than a friend?" Travis asked.

"Yes, but don't tell Emma that. I don't want to risk her saying something to Hannah and freaking her out. This is going to take time."

"How much time?" This question came from Josh.

"You tell me. Your childhood was similar to hers, no thanks to your parents. The only difference was that she ended up in the system and was abandoned time after time. Your grandparents raised you. Your scars might be different from hers, but they're still there."

I knew what it was like to lose someone I loved. And don't get me wrong, the thought of going through that again scared me. But I couldn't imagine how Hannah felt, always expecting the worst. Always on edge, waiting for someone she loved to give up on her.

"You have a good point," Josh said. "How can we help?"

"He means other than lie to our wives about your feelings for Hannah and what you're doing." Travis's expression betrayed both his amusement at the situation and his less-than-happy thoughts at keeping the truth from his wife.

"If you have any suggestions on how I can win Hannah over sooner rather than in ten or so years, I'm all ears." All ears. Eyes. Telepathy. Any which way they could relay the advice to me was fine.

Both appeared to be at a loss for suggestions.

The situation required Dr. Lovejoy's level of expertise, but hell if I was asking Emma for her advice.

To their obvious relief, Trent's father picked that moment to join us. "Thank you all for making it to the wedding."

Confused why he was acting like the father of the groom when Liam was the one getting married and not Trent?

Let me bring you up to speed. Liam and his sister Kelsey lost their parents in a car accident over thirteen years ago. Liam was serving in the military at the time, and Kelsey was only eighteen years old.

Trent's mother and father had been close friends of Kelsey and Liam's parents. Kelsey and Liam had grown up with them, so they were already like second parents to the pair even before Kelsey and Liam's mother and father died. Hence Trent's dad filling in for the role of the groom's father. He was also the one who had given Kelsey away when she married Trent.

"You've had a great marriage," Josh said, having known

Trent's father the longest of the three of us. He flashed me a quick I've-got-this glance. "Do you have any advice on winning over a girl when you have a bad reputation for being a love 'em and leave 'em kind of guy? One of the guys on the team is falling in love with a girl he's known for a while, but she sees him as nothing more than a playboy. Any suggestions on what he can do?"

I could feel my eyebrow quirk up. *Seriously? You're asking him for advice about* my *love life?* Luckily for me, John Salway was too busy paying attention to Josh to notice my reaction.

But Josh certainly noticed it. His gaze flicked briefly to me, and the corner of his mouth twitched up slightly.

I am not *a playboy*, I mouthed. Josh ignored me.

"He needs to earn her trust," was John's unhelpful advice. I'd already determined that much for myself.

"But how can he do that?" I blurted. *Play it cool, dude.*

"First and foremost, be her friend," he said directly to me. Shit, had he caught on that I was the player Josh was referring to, even though I didn't play hockey for the San Francisco Rock?

"But while he is being her friend," John continued, oblivious to my inner freak-out, "he needs to romance her. Let her know his feelings for her."

"What if she doesn't trust his feelings for her?" I asked.

Neither Josh nor Travis said anything. They were too busy glancing over at their wives, who were heading our way. Both men flashed me a We'll-head-them-off-at-the-pass expression, and peeled away from our little group, leaving John to give me the advice supposedly meant for a player on Josh's team.

"If she really means everything to him," John continued, "then he needs to show her that. He can't give up on her just because she's not ready to give him a chance yet. He needs to fight for her. Some women love big gestures. To others, the little things mean the most. They aren't flashy, but they come from the heart all the same." He glanced at the front of the room, where Liam was standing with Trent, talking to Harold, the inn owner. "Excuse me. I'm being summoned. Good luck with the lucky woman. Remember, if she's worth it, patience will go a long way." He winked at me and walked away.

And there you had it. Josh and I would be crossing "being actors" off our list of future careers. Neither of us had fooled him.

I still had a few minutes before the ceremony began. Everly was busy with Lily, and Hannah was distracted with her friends. I slipped into the dining room and called my brilliant assistant. I might have promised her a big Christmas bonus if she succeeded with my request—the request that was the first of many to show Hannah that I was falling for her. Hard.

The guests were taking their seats when I returned. Hannah and Everly were sitting with our friends, saving a chair for me. I joined them.

Harold, now wearing a dark-gray suit and green tie, nodded for the keyboardist to begin. Classical music filled the room.

The matron of honor stepped through the doorway to the dining room, wearing a long navy dress with short sleeves. In her hands was a bouquet of cream-colored roses, with small red roses and bright-green leaves mixed in.

She walked to where Trent and Liam stood near the fireplace. The music changed, and everyone stood.

Ava entered holding her father's arm. And for a second the blonde bride was replaced in my mind with the image of someone with soft brown hair. I could almost imagine Hannah walking down the aisle toward me, leaving me breathless at the sight of her, like when I first saw her upstairs in her new dress.

"Who is giving the bride away?" Harold, the marriage officiant for today, asked.

"Her mother and I are," her father replied. And so began

the wedding ceremony that should have taken place over ten years ago.

A hiccupped sob came from the direction of Trent's mom after Liam said his vows to his bride. I heard a few other sniffles around me. Hannah pretended she had an itch in the corner of her eye.

Liam slid the ring onto Ava's finger, lifted her hand to his mouth, and kissed it. The sniffles switched to dreamy sighs. It was a good thing Everly and Lily weren't sitting together. I was positive those two would be giggling with mischief if they were.

"With the power vested in me by the State of California," Harold said, "I now pronounce you husband and wife. You may kiss the bride."

He glanced upward in an obvious way that made Liam and Ava do the same. Above their heads was a sprig of mistletoe hanging high from the ceiling.

They kissed, keeping things PG-rated, while I contemplated the chances of getting Hannah under the mistletoe to kiss *her*. Would she see it as a romantic gesture...or just an opportunity for me to kiss her?

Which I did want to do, desperately.

Once the wedding party left for photos—with Kelsey as the award-winning photographer—the rest of us waited in the lobby for their return. Betsy and Harold gathered all the young kids and entertained them with stories. Josh was holding his infant son. Holly had Trent and Kelsey's son in her arms.

"So when are you joining me for prenatal yoga?" Emma asked Hannah.

"You should come, too," Travis said to me, the corner of his mouth twitching.

Huh? "What are you talking about?"

"When Holly was pregnant with Lily," Josh said, "I hired a yoga instructor to come to the house twice a week to work with us. Some of the guys on the team swore by yoga when it came to their performance on the ice. We hired her again when Holly was pregnant with James."

"Because these two"—Travis gestured to Holly and Josh—"highly recommended her, we hired her for while Emma is pregnant. I don't know how much it's helped my game, but it's great for flexibility and relaxation."

"Suzanne is amazing," Emma added. "Kelsey and Trent also hired her when Kelsey was pregnant. I can send you our schedule, which varies from week to week due to Travis's away games. And then you can figure out which days work with your schedule. They're typically in the morning because that was the best for all of us."

"We'll do it," I said. A little too enthusiastically, perhaps?

If the funny look Hannah flashed me was anything to go by, I'd say that was a yes.

"So, this is something that requires a yoga partner?" she asked Emma.

Emma cringed. Not a lot, but enough for me to notice. "No, but we did it together because...because..." She squirmed.

"Because Travis, Trent, and Josh are your husbands and the fathers of your babies?" Hannah filled in for her.

"Well, technically, Josh and I weren't married at the time when I was pregnant with Lily," Holly said, also joining the cringing club.

"But he was still her father," Hannah pointed out, and Holly reluctantly nodded.

"So in summation." Hannah shifted her attention to Emma. "You're inviting me to join you and Travis for your biweekly yoga session with the instructor, but I don't need a partner to be able to participate?"

"Yes—that's pretty much it."

"But it does help to have your birthing partner there..." Holly started to say but left the rest of the sentence dangling precariously.

This time it was Hannah's turn to cringe.

"What's a birthing partner?" I asked, because hell if I knew.

"It's the person who is with the pregnant mother, giving emotional support, during labor and delivery," Holly explained. "Usually it's the baby's father, or the mother-to-be's sister or mum. Or even a close female friend who can help out."

Great—except Hannah's sperm donor wasn't in the picture. Her close friends all had babies of their own, or in Emma's case, would have a baby by then. And Hannah didn't have a sister or a mother.

I took a breath and asked Hannah, "Who's your birthing partner?"

22

HANNAH

"Who's your birthing partner?" Wes asked me, and I could have sworn the inn lobby suddenly went silent, everyone waiting for me to answer his question.

Someone shoot me now!

The truth? I had avoided thinking about who to ask ever since the positive pregnancy test.

I couldn't ask my close female friends to help me out. It was one thing for Emma to come with me to the OB appointments and the ultrasound (which she couldn't go to in the end). It would be impossible for her to help me when she had her own baby waiting at home.

This wasn't the first time Emma had brought up the topic of a birthing partner, but I had brushed it off every time.

Until now.

"I haven't finalized that yet. Oh, look, Everly needs me." I speed-walked toward her even though she and Lily were doing just fine. They were socializing with a grandmother who was fussing over them.

She needed me as much as I needed the Q&A about my nonexistent birthing partner.

"I'm gonna have a little brother like Lily." Everly proudly told the woman.

The woman flashed her a toothy grin. "Then you're a very lucky girl because little brothers are the best."

I had no idea what to say. As far as I knew, Kristin hadn't been pregnant at the time of the accident.

Everly's comment couldn't be because of what Santa had said to her at the tree farm, could it? She wasn't talking about Little Bean?

"What are you two troublemakers up to?" I asked the little girls, smiling. They giggled in reply.

"You must be this little cutie's mommy." The woman parked her hand on my belly as if it were a crystal ball.

I glanced down, double-checking if I had a Please Touch Here sign glued to my dress.

Nope, no sign.

"Everly isn't my daughter. She's the niece of my friend." *Please don't ask any more questions. Please don't ask any more...*

The woman's gaze scanned the room, but the only other visibly pregnant woman here was Emma, and it wasn't hard to guess who her husband was. Travis's arms were around her waist.

Emma had curly red hair. Travis had dark hair like mine.

And Everly? Her hair was pale blonde.

Like her mother's had been.

The grandmother must have been able to read my mind, because she didn't ask any more questions. *Phew.* One potential catastrophe diverted.

Wes was staring at me, a crease between his eyes. I didn't need super mind-reading powers to know what he was thinking. I was almost tempted to ask the woman what she was doing around April fifteenth, my due date. Maybe she was available to be my birthing partner. Then I could tell him that she was going to do it, and he could wipe the frown off his face.

Besides, I had no idea why he was worried. I still had sixteen weeks left to decide—give or take a week or two.

That was plenty of time.

Wes peeled away from the group and joined us.

"This is Uncle Wes," Everly said, introducing him to the woman.

"So you must be the friend of our lovely mother-to-be here." The woman gestured at me with a sideward tilt of her head. From the way her eyes were glowing knowingly, I had a feeling she believed that Wes was Little Bean's sperm daddy.

He settled his hand on my lower back, firmly cementing that idea in her head.

And like always, the familiar electrical hum spread throughout my body at his touch.

Quit doing that, I reprimanded my body. It didn't listen.

What's new?

What was my body expecting me to do? Drag him under the mistletoe and kiss him like our lives depended on it?

It didn't help that I was still dealing with horny hormones. Luckily for me, in a few months, they would be a thing of the past, and my fantasies about banging Wes would finally end.

"That's right," Wes said, answering the woman's question. "Do you mind if I steal the lovely mother-to-be from you for a few minutes?"

"Steal away. I can entertain these two while you're gone."

Wes thanked her, and with his hand still on my back, guided me toward the dining room. We entered it to discover we were the only ones there.

"Are you okay?" he asked. "You look like someone just announced a pop quiz, and you have to name all the presidents in order of their presidency."

A very apt analogy. Could I name them? Not on your life.

"Was Everly's mom pregnant when she died?"

He shook his head. "I know they were planning to try again soon, but as far as I know, she wasn't. Why?"

"Because Everly believes she's going to have a brother like Lily. You don't think it has something to do with what Santa said at the Christmas tree farm, do you, and she thinks my baby is going to be her brother?"

"Maybe. She and Lily have been spending a lot of time together. They're the same age. She might not understand what a brother is and could be projecting what Lily has to her own situation. I can talk to her about it though, if that makes you feel better."

I nodded. "It would."

"So about the birthing partner Emma and Holly were talking about…"

I looked up at the ceiling as if the answer to my prayers was there.

And it was.

Without warning, I pressed my lips up against Wes's. All right, we could mostly blame my body for that.

Wes certainly didn't complain. He possessed my mouth as much as I possessed his.

And my horny hormones? They were busy chanting, *Push him up against the wall. Make him hot and heavy.*

Not very helpful, if you asked me.

Our tongues teased and tangoed, stoking the fire inside me.

My hormones kept up the chanting, pleased that I was listening to them.

I moaned softly and ran my fingers through Wes's hair. All that did was add gasoline to the flames.

I was so going to hell.

Wes rested his forehead against mine, his breath coming in fast, mirroring my own. "What was that for? Not that I'm complaining. And I'm more than happy to go back to kissing you after you answer my question."

I assumed he meant the question about why I kissed him and not the one about my nonexistent birthing partner.

I pointed up. To the mistletoe hanging from the ceiling. It turns out the piece Harold had hung up for the wedding ceremony wasn't the only sprig he owned.

Wes laughed. "I've been wondering how to get you to kiss me under the mistletoe in the other room. I knew you wouldn't want to do that in front of everyone."

I mentally rubbed my fingernails against the lace covering my chest and blew on them. Yep, I was better at creating a distraction than I had realized.

Go me.

"We've got a few minutes before everyone wonders where we disappeared to," I said coyly. "We could get in some more kissing under the mistletoe if you want?"

"I'd be game for that, but first you have to answer one question."

"If it's naming the presidents in order, you're out of luck. With my pregnancy brain, you'll be lucky if I can name the last five."

"That wasn't the question I had in mind. What are we doing?" His arms were still around my waist, and he wasn't in a rush to remove them from their current position.

"Doing? If I had to venture a guess, I'd go with practicing the fine art of kissing under the mistletoe."

"No, I mean us. You and me. If we're going to kiss under the mistletoe, it has to be for reasons other than you trying to distract me from my question about your birthing partner."

Damn, the man was perceptive.

I shrugged—mostly because I was clueless where he was going with this. I just wanted to kiss him again. But really, could you blame me?

He was one super-hot kisser.

As my lips and my body and my hormones could attest.

"What other reasons could there be?" I asked.

"Are you going to give us a chance? You and me?"

"So you want to have sex with me?"

That noise? My lady bits hooting and cheering.

"I'm all for that. However, that's not what I meant. I want you to give me a chance to be your boyfriend. And so there's no confusion, this means you'll be my girlfriend."

Forget naming the damn presidents. I was positive that the expression on my face had upgraded to something else.

Something more freaked-out.

"We can't do that," I said, working on keeping my tone from matching my expression. "Things are more complex between us than two single people who are attracted to each other."

Wes's mouth quirked to one side. "So you admit you're attracted to me?"

I threw him a *What-do-you-think?* look. "You have Everly, and I have Little Bean. Our priorities aren't the same as with other couples just starting out. If this doesn't work out between us, there are more people involved than just you and me. And you've got the adoption process to think about."

"So you're saying you're not interested in being my girlfriend?"

Don't listen to her, my body screamed, forgetting that he couldn't hear it.

"That's exactly what I'm saying. You and I can only be friends, Wes. Maybe things would have been different if you weren't suddenly a father and I wasn't going to be a mom. But that's not the case, and we can't change things."

"You do realize there's a name for that? It's called a family."

"Yes, well, in my world that doesn't mean a whole lot."

"Then maybe it's time we change that."

I shook my head. "I can go for a casual, fun friendship with benefits until I move out. But that's as far as it can go."

23

WES

A few months ago, if Hannah had offered me the option of a friends-with-benefits arrangement, I would have been ecstatic. It was my kind of relationship—the type with no strings attached.

But she was right. Now that I had taken over the role of Everly's father, things were more complicated. And Hannah's impending motherhood didn't make it any less so.

What about fighting for her? Prove to her you're worth taking a chance on, my inner critic said to the *Rocky* theme music playing in my head. *You might have better luck doing that if you agree to her demands, but treat her like she's something special, something more...something like, oh, I don't know, her* boyfriend, *dumbass.*

As you can tell, my inner critic was always the supportive one.

"All right," I told her. "If you want to keep the relationship casual, I can do that."

"Good. And we should have rules."

"Rules?" I was familiar with the standard ones for casual flings, but I had a feeling we were beyond those.

"Yes, rules. The first one is a biggie. Our friends can't know about this."

"You mean the friends who are obviously rooting for something to happen between us?" I did get the general gist of that when Emma and Travis suggested we join them for their regular prenatal yoga sessions.

She rolled her eyes. "Yes, those would be the ones."

"Fine, no one will find out about it."

"And that includes Everly."

"That *especially* includes Everly. Which means if we're having sex, it will have to be in my room because it's the farthest from hers."

"And there are no stay-overs."

I gave her a simple nod. "That's fine." I tended to avoid them when it came to one-night stands and short-term relationships, so that rule was second-nature for me. "Anything else?"

"Once I find a new place to live, this thing between us"—she gestured between our chests with her finger—"ends. It's convenient while I'm living with you. It won't be once I move away. And neither of us will have time for it."

"Okay. You have a point there." However, since I was doing my best to keep her from finding a new apartment, for now, her rule wasn't a concern.

Satisfied with our agreed-upon terms, Hannah offered her hand for me to shake and seal the deal.

Fuck that.

I looked pointedly up at the ceiling, to the mistletoe. Then I cradled the back of her head with one hand and kissed her. Deeply. It was firm like a handshake, but also tender, a taste of what she could expect from our newly forged relationship.

The version of our relationship she wasn't counting on.

But here lay my first problem: her friends. If they pushed too hard for our friendship to be something more, it might break down the initial parts of the bridge I was constructing between Hannah and myself. Any inroads I'd made so far could easily crumble if we weren't careful.

The guys were aware of my plans, but I didn't know how to broach the topic with their wives. Women could be so goddamn stubborn when they set their minds to something.

Case in point, the woman I was kissing.

Reluctantly, I ended the kiss and stepped away from her, all too aware that at any moment someone could enter the dining room. "We should probably return to the lobby, so no one gets suspicious about what we're doing," I said.

Hannah nodded, and I won't claim that the slightly dazed look in her eyes didn't give my pride a high five. My kiss had done that to her. She wasn't immune to me.

We returned to the lobby, and easily joined our friends' conversation as if we hadn't just been in the other room kissing and planning our secretive arrangement.

The wedding party entered the inn a short time later, once Kelsey had finished photographing them. They all gathered around the fireplace to warm up.

Once the group had defrosted, we headed to the dining room, which mirrored the rustic-Christmas-wedding theme of the lobby.

Because Trent was the best man, he had to sit at the wedding party table. He spent the next few minutes throwing longing looks at Kelsey, who was sitting with us.

"Is it just me," Hannah murmured to me on a soft laugh, "or does Trent look ready to give Liam and Ava all his money so he can sit with Kelsey?"

I chuckled. "That's exactly how he looks."

After dinner was over and the brief wedding-party speeches had come to a close, they were free to escape their table. It was time for the bride and groom's first dance together.

"I'm kind of disappointed he didn't vault over the table,"

Hannah said as Trent strode rather quickly to where his wife was seated.

"That would have definitely been more interesting," I said, laughing.

The music started, and Liam and Ava began dancing. Everly scrambled down from her booster seat, to be joined by Lily, her partner in crime.

"What are you two up to?" I asked them.

"Dancing." Everly pointed to the floor.

Before I could say anything, the two of them were giggling and bouncing to the music...which was quite the feat given that it was a slow song, and there was nothing slow about those two girls.

During dinner, I'd been good and kept my hands to myself when it came to Hannah. However, now that she was busy talking to Emma and Travis, I decided to have a little fun. My hand slipped under the table and moved to Hannah's thigh. Surprisingly, she didn't move it.

Her skirt had risen slightly, allowing me to touch her soft skin. The downside? Her skirt was narrow, which made it more challenging to do what I'd hoped to accomplish.

All I could do was stroke her skin and hope she was getting more turned-on by the second.

Which was a stupid plan, now that I thought about it. Because while I had no idea if I was accomplishing my goal when it came to Hannah, the same couldn't be said about me.

My cock lengthened in my pants, making me see the fallacy in my plan. The only thing I had achieved was my own sexual frustration. *Way to go, idiot.*

My second accomplishment of the evening? I was stuck in my chair until my below-the-belt situation subsided—which wouldn't happen with my hand on Hannah's leg.

I shifted it off her.

As if sensing my dilemma, which was no one's fault but my

own, Hannah turned her head to me and smirked. She then returned her attention to Emma and Travis.

The slow song ended, but instead of playing a faster one, the DJ—also known as Jayden—started a song that was no less romantic than the last one.

Travis said something to Emma. She nodded and stood.

She wasn't the only one. The two other married couples at the table headed for the dance floor. Ethan and James had both fallen asleep during dinner and were passed out in their infant car seats. Kelsey and Holly were keeping an eye on them from the dance floor while in their husbands' arms.

"I seem to remember you promised me a dance," I said to Hannah.

"Is that a good idea now that we're secretly involved?"

"I don't think us being secretly involved makes a difference. I mean, if you think you can't keep your hands off me..." I left the rest of the sentence hanging with a smug smile.

"I'm sure I'll be perfectly capable of controlling myself against all temptation." She didn't roll her eyes, but it was there in her tone.

She pushed herself to her feet and held out her hand to me.

We walked to the dance floor, still holding hands. Yes, this violated Hannah's rule of keeping our relationship a secret from our friends, but hell if I was pointing that out to her.

I wrapped my arms around her waist and pulled her to me, as close as her baby bump would allow. She placed her hands on my shoulders.

What I wanted was to kiss her neck, her jaw, her mouth, but that was hardly the normal behavior of two friends. Plus I valued my package. If I crossed the friend-zone line in public— even though we had already done that—my package's safety would be at risk.

A few hours later, Hannah and I returned to our rooms. Everly had fallen asleep on my shoulder while I carried her upstairs.

I laid my sleeping niece, who was still clutching her bunny, on her bed. Hannah removed Everly's shoes, and I pulled up the bedding to cover her.

Hannah gently kissed the sleeping princess on her forehead. The actions were that of a mother—a mother that Hannah never really had. And from the sounds of it, except for the one couple who almost adopted her, Hannah hadn't been on the receiving end of any form of motherly love during her childhood.

Yet here she was, gifting Everly the love that Hannah had missed out on growing up, even though the little girl wasn't her daughter.

It made me want to gather Hannah in my arms and show her how much I appreciated what she was doing for Everly... and for me.

To show her that I was falling for her.

Hannah lifted her hand to her mouth, covering her yawn. She had already yawned several times in the past twenty minutes, her exhaustion hard to hide.

"I'm going to bed," she said, "but if you want to go downstairs and enjoy the rest of the reception, leave the adjoining doors open. I'll stay here with Everly."

"No, I'm good." All of our friends had retired for the night. Little girls were tired. Babies needed to be put to bed. Mothers were exhausted...and their husbands had no intention of being downstairs without them.

The only exception was Liam's colleagues. But since there were no single women at the reception for them to get lucky with tonight, I suspected they would be heading into Lake Tahoe to see what they could find there.

And that included Isabelle.

"Okay, well, good night." Hannah leaned in to kiss my cheek.

However, I had other plans.

I turned my head at the last moment, her lips brushing against mine. She had clearly not planned for things to go beyond a brief kiss, but everything changed in that second.

Her mouth was on mine again, and our kisses moved from testing the waters to jumping off the rock face into the oasis below.

Hannah released a stuttering sigh and swayed slightly in my arms. Both had my heart launching up, recognizing her reaction for what it was. My kisses were at least getting to her—good news for my long-term plans.

She pulled away after a few minutes, her breathing ragged like mine. "Good night, Wes."

She yawned once more and staggered into her room, shutting the door behind her.

Why aren't you going after her? my heart asked. *Get your ass moving.*

Because she shut the door, I reminded it.

What? And your arms don't work anymore?

I ignored its crazy-ass comment and went to have a shower.

A brutally cold shower.

24

HANNAH

Even though Everly would have loved to stay in the Lake Tahoe area for longer, we returned to San Francisco late the following morning.

Christmas Eve morning.

The most exciting day of the year...other than Christmas Day itself.

My Christmases when I was a kid were disappointing. I'd learned at a young age that Santa didn't exist.

Or more like, he didn't exist for girls like me—according to one of my mother's delightful deadbeat boyfriends.

I was five years old at the time. The kids in kindergarten had been excited because Santa was coming soon. That was when I first learned that a man, with a big belly and dressed in a red suit, visited the homes of all the boys and girls and left them presents while they slept.

I couldn't remember him doing that, but it didn't stop me from being hopeful. Maybe he had just forgotten me in the past, I'd reasoned.

That year, the old lady from across the hallway helped me

mail my letter to Santa. I was so excited. This would be the year Santa remembered me.

But he didn't.

I woke up Christmas morning to find nothing from him. We didn't even have a tree. My mom couldn't afford one, and her boyfriend wasn't going to waste his money on something like that. Not when it was earmarked for his beer.

Needless to say, I was disappointed.

I began to worry that maybe I wasn't on Santa's Good List. Somehow I'd gotten on his Naughty List.

The neighbor who mailed my letter to Santa knocked on the apartment door and asked to see me. "Santa accidentally left this gift at the wrong apartment. This is for you." She handed it to me. The box was wrapped in paper with cartoon Santas on it, and it had the biggest red bow I'd ever seen.

But before I could get too excited about it, my mom's douchebag boyfriend snatched it from me. "Oh, *please*." He hit the last word with enough sarcasm to down Santa's sleigh from the sky. "Santa doesn't exist, and she's too old to believe in that crap."

He handed it back to Mrs. Stephensen.

Mrs. Stephensen glared at him. "Santa exists. He lives in our hearts."

"Well, given that Hailey is a bad girl who no one wants, I can say without a doubt he doesn't live in her heart."

It hadn't escaped my notice that he didn't even remember my name...only proving to five-year-old me that I really had been unwanted.

"So what do you think?" I asked Natalie, pulling myself out of the past to the here-and-now. To the reason I was at the hospital on my day off.

Natalie was a nurse I worked with in the ER who was helping with Operation Christmas Cheer. I gestured at my elf outfit. Fortunately, volunteer services had a dress that fit my pregnant belly.

That's right. Like I had for the past five Christmases, I was helping to hand out presents to the kids who were stuck in the hospital over Christmas. It was one of the ways that I had regained the Christmases stolen from me for all those years when I was a kid.

Emma did something similar at the youth center for unprivileged kids where she regularly volunteered. Travis also participated in their event every Christmas, along with some of the other Rock players.

"You look adorable. Like a pregnant elf. Do you have plans tonight?" Natalie asked, knowing that I was single. She also knew how Little Bean came to be.

"I'm just spending it with my roommate and his three-year-old niece."

"This would be the hot roommate, right?"

Yes, Natalie had met Wes when he came to visit me one day at work. That was when I explained that he was my platonic friend and roommate.

"That would be the one."

"I don't suppose you could pass on my phone number to him, could you?" She laughed at whatever emotion she saw flash on my face. "That's what I thought. When are you going to admit to yourself you have the hots for him?"

Well, that was where she got things wrong. I *had* admitted it to myself, which was why I'd agreed to take Wes's and my friendship to the next level. The next level being where our platonic friendship involved earthquake-inducing kisses and sex.

Of course, I wasn't going to admit *that* to Natalie.

Fortunately, I didn't have to...at least for now. The leader of the elves announced we were ready to commence Operation Christmas Cheer.

Our group of ten people—nine elves and Santa—made our way from unit to unit, spreading holiday cheer to the kids, their siblings, their parents, and the staff who were working tonight.

I teared up a few times due to the reaction of several kids when they saw Santa. And it had nothing to do with my pregnancy hormones, although they weren't completely guilt-free either.

Witnessing the happy faces of the kids who had believed that Santa would forget about them, because they were in the hospital instead of at home, always did that to me. I knew what it felt like to believe that Santa didn't care about you. I never wanted another kid to feel the way I had growing up.

By the time we were finished three hours later, I was physically and emotionally drained and ready to take a long nap.

But I didn't have time for that. I still had lots to do to ensure Christmas was perfect for Everly and Wes. He had worked hard to make sure tonight and tomorrow were magical for Everly, but I knew he would be hurting, too. This was his first Christmas without his brother and sister-in-law.

At the condo building, I parked my car and walked through the damp, chilly air into the lobby, which was decorated for Christmas.

By decorated, I meant it was the dream place for anyone who lived for the holiday season. There was even a giant Christmas tree.

The elevator door opened as I approached, and Mrs. Jenkins and Mrs. Hitchcock stepped out. Both were grinning— a look I was familiar with when it came to Mrs. Jenkins. Not so much with Mrs. Hitchcock.

"Merry Christmas," I said, smiling. It didn't matter how tired I was, the Christmas-themed lobby always left me feeling happy.

"And a Merry Christmas to you and your little one." Mrs. Hitchcock's words slurred slightly, and she gestured to my belly.

Mrs. Jenkins giggled. "We were just enjoying a little eggnog."

"You know," Mrs. Hitchcock continued, "you're good for him."

"Him?" I asked.

"And for the little cutie, too," she added, ignoring my question.

"You mean Wes and Everly?"

She nodded a little too enthusiastically for her to be sober. But that didn't mean her words didn't fill me with warmth. A bonus after the wet chill I'd experience walking from my car to the building entrance.

"I was wrong about him, thinking he was a partying womanizer just because he worked late at the office. But some of the members of the board told me about all the wonderful things he has done for people here. They had the idea of the—"

"Oh, heavens." Mrs. Jenkins threw Mrs. Hitchcock an exasperated look. "We don't want to bore her with those details. Everything turns out as predicted in the end, and all will be good in due time."

She returned her attention to me. "But she's right about Wes and Everly. I've seen the difference in her with you in her life. With both of them. He's smiling more than he was before."

"Wes smiles all the time." *I should know. He and I have known each other for almost two years.*

Mrs. Hitchcock shook her head. "Not the in same way he has been lately, ever since you moved in to help with Everly. Like I said, you're good for both of them." She threw her arms around me and gave me a big hug.

Which also felt good. Because she smelled like a grandmother, all sugar and vanilla.

Mrs. Hitchcock wasn't the only one who was in a hugging mood. Mrs. Jenkins also smothered me with a big hug, which wasn't new—she tended to be a hugger.

I OPENED THE APARTMENT DOOR, AND THE DELICIOUS SMELL OF sugar cookies instantly greeted me. I sat on the chair that Wes had recently put in the hallway and removed my sneakers.

Everly came rushing around the corner. "Hannah! We're baking cookies. Uncle Wes let me help. And we were decorating them. And they're yummy."

I grinned at her excitement and the pink icing on her face. "I can see that. Did you save me any?"

Practically vibrating like a bumblebee after finding the pollen mother lode, she nodded so hard I was surprised her head didn't fall off.

As soon as I'd set my second shoe on the floor, she was dragging me down the hallway to the kitchen. Wes was standing there in his jeans and T-shirt, looking sexier than ever.

My heart rate picked up, urging me to kiss him like there was no tomorrow.

Urging me to kiss him like he was the best Christmas gift ever.

Clearly, being an elf for the afternoon had fried my brain.

However, that realization wasn't enough to stop me from walking to him and kissing him on the cheek.

While the air might have smelled of sugar cookies, Wes certainly didn't. He smelled of sexy man and pheromones and whatever scent he liked to wear that always made him smell so amazing.

"They look sooo good," I said, gazing past his shoulder to the cooling racks spread across the counters. Dozens of sugar cookies shaped like stars, Christmas trees, and teddy bears filled every available surface. Thick blobs of bright-pink icing oozed over the edges and onto the counters.

"Everly picked the color for the icing," he said.

"You don't say. You guys did a great job."

"And that's not all we did while you were busy volunteering. I made dinner. So go rest up on the couch, and I'll clean up here so we can eat."

Everly jumped up and down. "Then we watch a Christmas movie while we wait for Santa."

"That sounds like a plan, but I'm going to shower first." *And go to the bathroom.* Little Bean had decided my bladder needed kicking again. Repeatedly.

After dinner, Everly played with the train and the little village that Wes had set up on the coffee table. She loved watching it go around and around and around the track. While she did that, he and I placed the dirty dishes in the dishwasher and tidied up the kitchen. And finally, we settled on the couch to watch *Elf*.

Or rather, Wes and I sat on the couch. Everly lay on her stomach with a cushion on the floor in front of the TV.

Wes and I weren't sitting next to each other. I was sitting at one end of the couch, my feet tucked under me. Wes was sitting a few cushions over. With Everly engrossed in the movie, Wes gestured for me to put my feet on his lap.

"I'm good where I am," I whispered.

"You've been on your feet all day, volunteering at the hospital, bringing Christmas joy. Massaging your feet is the least I can do."

I grinned. "Did Travis, Josh, or Trent tell you to do that?"

He shook his head. "Jayden."

That got a raised eyebrow from me. "What does he know about giving pregnant women foot massages?"

"He has three sisters."

"And they taught him how to give foot massages?"

"No, but their husbands told him that if he ever knocks up a woman, he'll get a lot further in life if he massages her feet."

My grin widened, and I moved my feet to Wes's lap. "Remind me the next time I see him to give him a big kiss."

"Right. I'll be sure to do that." His tone suggested the opposite.

And the winner for the best foot massages went to...

How I kept from groaning out loud while he massaged the soles of my feet, my ankles, and my lower legs is beyond me. Maybe *I* deserved an award for remaining quiet so not to alert Everly as to what he was doing.

What was he doing...beyond chasing away my achy feet? Turning me on.

Big-time.

I couldn't remember the last time a man had touched me that way...or in any way. It had probably been just before dinosaurs went extinct.

Or at least it felt that way.

I was putty in his hands, which was why I didn't balk when he patted the couch next to him. I hadn't been that close to him since the night I told him about my mom.

I curled into him, his arm around me, and we watched the rest of the movie.

Which was incredible in itself, given how much more turned-on I was getting as the minutes ticked by. It didn't help that all I wanted to do was twist around in his arms and straddle him, kiss him, taste him.

Devour him.

I really was a lost cause.

25

HANNAH

"I think she's finally fallen asleep," Wes said a few hours later, rejoining me on the couch after checking on Everly.

When you grew up knowing Santa didn't exist, falling asleep on Christmas Eve wasn't a problem. You knew he wouldn't be leaving you a present while you slept. There was nothing to be overly excited about.

Christmas Day was just another day.

Later, when I was a ward of the state, most of the foster parents I stayed with couldn't be bothered to keep up with the Santa lie. The only one who did was the family who had come close to adopting me, but the damage had already been done, and they too stopped pretending Santa existed.

They were also the only foster parents who had given me toys for Christmas. Everyone else simply gave me a bag of potato chips or a candy bar or something of similar value.

None of this was the case for Everly. Which meant getting her to fall asleep had been a challenge. She had kept sneaking out of her room to check if Santa had been here yet.

"Were you that bad as a kid?" I asked Wes.

"I was probably worse. You?"

I told him about my Christmases growing up. About my mother. About her boyfriend at the time who had spoiled Santa for me. About the foster families. And about the one person who tried to make my Christmas magical when I was five years old.

He stroked my cheek with his thumb once I'd finished, brushing away an imaginary tear. "You're amazing, do you realize that?"

"Because I had crappy Christmases as a kid?"

"Because you had crappy Christmases as a kid, but it didn't turn you into a cynic. Every time we visit the Christmas store and every time you see anything related to the holiday season, you're as excited about it as a little kid. And today, despite being five months pregnant, you spent your day off helping the kids at the hospital keep believing in Santa. That's why you're amazing."

He didn't give me a chance to reply. He tenderly kissed me.

I didn't know what the original intent was behind his kiss. All I knew was that it wasn't enough for me.

My lips parted, and I deepened it.

Except that still wasn't enough. Wes cupped my face and kissed me like I was the air he was starving for.

Or maybe that was just how I felt about the kiss.

It was possessive.

It was soul-searching.

It was divine.

I moved my hands under the hem of his Henley, needing to soak in the feel of his skin, and moaned softly against his mouth.

We kissed for a minute or two; then he rested his forehead against mine. Our breaths came in fast and ragged. "Before we take this where I think we're headed, I want you to open one of your presents from me first."

"Isn't tomorrow Christmas Day?"

"Yes, but I want you to open it tonight."

"Okay." I didn't mind exchanging gifts a day early. Did we normally exchange gifts with each other? Not at all. But none of the previous Christmases had involved me living with him, so there was always that.

Semi-reluctantly, I removed my hands from under his top. He walked to the tree and selected a present that hadn't been there earlier. Not that I had been snooping under the tree. That had been all Everly. But at some point this evening, he had slipped the gift there without me noticing.

I directed him to the present I wanted to give him now, and he brought them to the couch. His expression was a mix of warmth and excitement and nervousness, which had me all the more curious. I didn't think his nervousness was related to what *I* had given him.

He handed me a box with shiny gold paper and a shiny gold bow. "Open mine first." His voice was low and rough, and every part of me tingled at the sound of it.

I ran the tip of my tongue along my lower lip, my mouth suddenly dry, and slowly unwrapped the paper from a square blue box. I removed the lid and the thin piece of Styrofoam protecting whatever was inside, revealing a delicate tree orna-ment—the glass angel with the baby in her arms.

She was gazing down at the infant. You couldn't see her expression, but I imagined if she had been real, it would have held the same look I knew I often wore whenever I caught sight of my growing belly: wonder and love and a fierce protec-tiveness.

My eyes misted and I blinked away the tears. "It's perfect," I whispered, unable to talk any louder around the ornament-sized lump in my throat. I looked up at Wes. "I love it. Thank you."

I leaned into him and gave him a light kiss. "Now your turn." I nodded at his gift on the table.

He smiled softly. "I've got a different present in mind." His voice wasn't much different from mine, and his eyes held a raw emotion I couldn't quite place. Lust was there, but so was something else.

He pushed himself to his feet and offered me his hand. It didn't take much to guess where he was going with this. We had been heading in this direction for several weeks now.

I let him help me to my feet and made a move to put the angel on the table.

"You might want to bring that with you, in case Everly is up before us. It might not fare too well if she gets to it first."

"Good point." I carefully returned the angel to the box and carried it to his room.

His bedroom blinds were still open, and the moon was peeking from behind the clouds, gently lighting the space. I set the box on his dresser.

Despite what we were about to do, I couldn't help but walk over to the window to look out at the bay and the part of Downtown that was visible. Tiny dots of light from the buildings lit up the dark skyline. "It's so beautiful," I murmured.

Wes wrapped his arms around me from behind and rested his hands on my stomach. "Yes, it is," he said in my ear. My legs quivered at the huskiness in his voice.

I turned around and kissed him. It wasn't a tender kiss like he had given me a short while ago. This kiss spoke of desire, of impatience, of let's-get-down-and-dirty.

Or at least that *had* been my goal.

At the feel of his kisses and the way his hands worshiped my body, something inside me shifted. Suddenly, this wasn't about satisfying my horny hormones. It was about satisfying another part of me—a deeper yearning. Only I couldn't puzzle out what it was.

I pushed the hem of his Henley up, revealing taut abs and pecs. His body no longer resembled that of a fitness model, as it had a year ago when he had time to spend over an hour a day in the gym. Now his body was a combination of hard and soft.

It was perfect.

"I haven't had a chance to hit the gym as often as I used to before Everly moved in with me," he murmured.

I placed my finger against his mouth. "And I have a baby in my belly and stretch marks. Does that mean you don't find me desirable?"

God, I hoped he still found me desirable after I'd just admitted to the stretch marks. I didn't like them. I would have been happier without them. But they didn't change who I was, so I put up with them.

His eyes heated several more degrees. "Not at all. I find you desirable regardless of those."

"You're still working out to stay healthy, for Everly's sake. For your sake. That's more important than if you're a guy who cares more about his muscles than his child. I still think you're sexy, Wes—more so because I know how important Everly is to you. Besides, haven't you heard? The dad-bod is in style."

I didn't have a chance to say anything else. Wes's mouth was on mine again, making my legs weak in a way few other guys had ever succeeded.

He stopped to yank his top over his head. I planted a kiss on his pecs and removed my maternity T-shirt. I was standing in only a black lacy bra and maternity yoga pants. He was still in his jeans.

Wes dropped to his knees and peeled the soft fabric of my pants over my stomach and down my legs.

Despite what I'd said to him a few moments ago, a shot of self-consciousness built up inside me. My body no longer looked like it belonged to me. It no longer felt like it belonged to me either.

Wes didn't have the same qualms about my body. He reverently kissed my stomach—and the wall around my heart crumbled slightly.

But it wasn't enough to allow him to hurt me. Not enough to allow myself to become more attached to him than was wise.

Why? Because at the end of the day, I couldn't risk him walking away from Little Bean and me. If history had taught me one thing, it was that the people I loved always abandoned me and it would happen again.

Trust me. Give it time and you'll see.

Wes stood up and led me to his bed. Even in the dim light of the room, there was no mistaking he was turned-on. I could see it in the outline of his jeans.

I reached for the top button and flicked it open. Wes's breath caught. Next, I unzipped his jeans while my fingers brushed against his cock. Teasing him was a lot of fun...for me anyway.

Before he could say anything—if there was anything to say—I slipped my hand past the opening of his jeans and found what I'd been looking for.

This time it was *my* breath that caught. Truth? I had wondered a few times what his cock was like. Don't look at me that way. I could guarantee I wasn't the only woman in San Francisco who had wondered the same.

I carefully peeled Wes's jeans down his legs. Which I might add was a little awkward now that I was pregnant. Once I got to his ankles, he kicked them off the rest of the way.

And helped me to my feet.

"I always figured you were a briefs man," I said before realizing: (a) how stupid that sounded, and (b) how I had just admitted that I'd been thinking about him and his underwear before now.

Smooth move, Hannah.

That got a smirk out of him.

So I did what any smart woman would do: I smacked him on the chest.

That only made him laugh. "Don't worry, I've been wondering what your bra and panties look like. And now I know."

I rolled my eyes.

And decided enough was enough. I slipped my hand under the waistband of his briefs and almost groaned at how hard his length felt at my touch. I wanted him inside me so badly, I wasn't sure how much longer I could last.

I swirled my thumb against his tip, spreading the moisture there. Based on his groan, I had a feeling we shared the same sentiment when it came to him being inside me.

Wes reached behind me and unhooked my bra. He dropped it to the ground and palmed my breasts in his large hands.

"Kind of wish I got to keep those," I said. My breasts weren't usually that big. The increased size was one of the perks of being pregnant.

Did that mean I would get implants once they returned to their normal size?

Hell, no.

"I think you're perfect either way," he said, "but I'm certainly making the most of them while I can." He brushed his thumbs across the super-sensitive buds, and I almost came right then with a groan. Liquid heat rushed to my core, and I arched my back slightly, pushing my flesh against his palms.

Now that he knew the secret to making me lose control, Wes had his fun with my breasts, squeezing them, sucking them, licking them, until my knees came close to buckling under me.

The next thing I knew, he had pulled me to the bed.

He glanced at it and at my belly. "Any suggestions on how

we do this? I didn't exactly ask Travis or Josh or Trent how to have sex with a pregnant woman."

I laughed softly. "Can't say that I asked the girls the same question either. But that was because if I *did* bring it up with them, they'd be interrogating me to find out who I was planning to sleep with."

"Yes, I can see why that would be a problem. Especially since we're keeping this a secret from them."

"Exactly. Although in your case, if you asked the guys the question about having sex with a pregnant woman, they'd probably guess it was me even if it wasn't."

"So now you see why I didn't ask them."

"Smart move. Of course, that doesn't solve our dilemma. I'll admit that even though I've been horny for months, I never really gave it any thought as to *how* to have sex once I found a willing victim."

Wes ran his lips along my jaw to my ear. "I'm definitely willing, but I'm hardly a victim." His voice was even huskier than last time. If he kept that up, I wouldn't have time to figure out *how* to do it with him. It would be firework city for my lady bits, with or without him.

"We could try with me straddling you." I pointed to the bed, hinting where I wanted him. *Now.*

"Not so fast. You've still got too many layers on." He reached out and ran the tip of his finger along the edge of my panties. I shivered at his touch.

"I can see where that would be a problem. And you do too, in case you haven't noticed." I gestured at his briefs.

Wes slipped his fingers under the waistband of my panties and dragged them down my legs, his fingertips leaving a fiery path.

I stepped out of them and went to help him with his underwear. He didn't have the patience for that. He had them off in record time.

I expected him to climb onto the bed, but he didn't. He kissed me thoroughly again, leaving me breathless. The kiss wasn't demanding or possessive. It held the same tenderness from earlier.

And it completely threw me.

I couldn't even identify the emotion in his eyes—the same raw emotion in his gaze from earlier. No other man had ever looked at me that way.

The idea of that both thrilled me and scared me.

I pushed away all thoughts of it and grinned at Wes. "Maybe we should do this now before Santa shows up. We don't want to scar him for life."

"Something tells me he and Mrs. Claus know a thing or two about getting it on. At least they did in their younger days," Wes said with a laugh, then scooted onto the bed.

I crawled to where he was sitting in the middle. "Are you sure about this?" Because once we did this, there was no going back.

I mean, eventually, things would return to normal once I moved into my apartment, but we could never ignore that we'd had sex.

"I'm positive," he said. "But if you've changed your mind…"

"I haven't." I looked at his nightstand. "I don't suppose you have condoms in there? I know I can't get pregnant, but I'd rather not take any risks."

I was clean. It was part of the testing I'd undergone before I became pregnant. Plus I'd never had sex without condoms. However, when it came to Wes, I had no idea if he had always practiced safe sex. The discussion hadn't exactly come up during our conversations as friends.

"Understandable. I was tested not long ago and I'm clean, but the condoms are in that drawer if you want to use them." He pointed to the drawer in question.

I pulled it open and my breath hitched. Next to the box of

condoms was the condolence card I'd sent him after I heard about his brother's and sister-in-law's deaths. An odd sense of giddiness pulsated through my veins, and I removed the card from the drawer.

"You saved it?" I showed him what I was talking about.

"Why wouldn't I? It meant a lot to me." He shrugged as though it were no big deal, but that obviously wasn't true.

I smiled softly at him, returned the card to the drawer, and removed the string of condoms.

Wes chuckled. "Planning to keep me busy tonight, are you?"

"I have a lot of sex to make up for from the past few years." I winked at him.

His mouth curled to one side. "In that case, we'd better get started."

I tore off a square package, ripped it open, and unrolled the condom onto Wes's very hard, very ready cock. Then I slowly lowered myself down his length, allowing myself time to adjust to his width.

Wes swore under his breath.

"Are you okay?"

"More than okay. You're incredibly tight." He pulled my head down to his and kissed me one more time. "*You're* incredible." The last part came out as a whisper, husky and all-male.

Once he was fully seated inside me, I moved my hips. Wes's hands guided the pace. It wasn't fast like most guys would prefer. To them, it was a race to see who came first—with them usually the victors.

Not Wes. He was moving me slowly and deliberately, his gaze locked on mine. The intensity in his eyes caused something deep inside me to tighten.

And that caused something else farther south to also tighten. A familiar something that would take me to a happy place.

"Oh, God," I breathed, "I'm not going to last much longer."

Usually, I didn't come that fast. But when you combined my horny hormones, my lust-driven body, and that intense gaze of his, the ticking bomb had a very short fuse.

"I'll be right with you."

That, and his husky voice, was all it took.

I tumbled into happy land, bringing Wes along with me.

26

WES

Several hours—and multiple orgasms—later, Hannah was asleep in my arms...and violating one of her relationship rules. The rule about no overnighters.

What she hadn't counted on when she came up with it was that between being pregnant and having sex several times in a row, she would be too tired to return to her own bed.

By the time I'd returned to my bed after dealing with the condom, she was already asleep. She didn't even stir when I'd climbed under the covers with her and settled my hand on her stomach.

I stroked the soft skin with my thumb, marveling at how there was a mini Hannah in there. A baby that I'd seen during her ultrasound and for whom I was developing feelings.

Which didn't make sense.

The baby wasn't mine. It belonged to a stranger.

It's because you're in love with its mother, a voice in my head reminded me.

I had been attracted to Hannah from the moment I'd met her. Granted, some of that might have been the thrill of the chase. I'd known she was unobtainable, which made her fascinating to me. That was no different to how it was for a lot of guys. Once they got laid, they moved on to the next emotionally unobtainable girl who got their dick hard.

But before that happened, they pursued her. I don't mean in a creepy, serial killer way. They got the girl to drop her guard, and in turn, they screwed her brains out and moved on.

Except even from the beginning that hadn't been my plan with Hannah. I hadn't known it at the time, but even from the first moment I saw her with Emma, I had been interested in more than just the chase. I had been interested in the woman behind the mask.

And now the same woman was asleep in my bed, but I still didn't know how to take the next step with her—beyond the suggestion Trent's father had given me.

Eventually, she would be moving out. I could only stall her for so long before she found a new apartment. And as much as I wanted to keep seeing her once that happened, she was right when she said it would be more challenging. We would have to balance dating along with meeting the needs of a preschooler, a newborn, and our careers.

I could tell her I loved her, but what if she wasn't ready to hear it?

I couldn't risk scaring her away before she was ready to give me a chance with her heart.

Yep, call me a coward if you must, but there was so much at stake here. So much more than if we had been in the usual boy-meets-girl type of scenario.

I kissed Hannah's shoulder. She didn't stir. "I love you," I murmured.

You need to say it to her when she's awake, you idiot, my heart grumbled, not thinking things through like my brain was.

Her breath didn't so much as hitch or do anything else to indicate she'd heard me.

I needed more time. It was as simple as that.

But thanks to my assistant, I had taken the first step in proving my love to Hannah. The glass angel had been the perfect gift. Sarah deserved a massive pay raise after managing to find it with less than twenty-four-hours' notice.

Now I just needed to determine my next steps for winning Hannah's heart and for proving that I would never abandon her—the thing she feared the most when it came to loving someone.

Or maybe I could just pray for a Christmas miracle.

27

WES

February

The Christmas miracle I had hoped for? It never materialized.

Seven weeks later, I was no closer to winning Hannah's heart than I had been the night we made love. The first of many nights we made love.

And like that time, Hannah kept ignoring (or forgetting) her rule about staying in my room afterward. We'd fall asleep with her back against my chest, my arm wrapped around her.

Did she sneak out of my room while I was sleeping? Not at all. Each morning, she would still be in my bed when I woke up, which was convenient when it came to dealing with my morning wood.

And a lot of fun.

Now seven weeks later, I was kicking things up a notch.

It was Valentine's Day.

Unfortunately, the State of California didn't understand the significance of the day. A social worker involved with my adoption application was scheduled to visit my condo.

It was the first of four interviews I would have to happily endure.

And she was already twenty minutes late.

Because Everly didn't have to be there for it this time, she and Hannah were shopping with Emma. I was home cooking a romantic dinner—for three.

The sweet smell of slow-roasting vegetables and maple chicken breasts filled the air.

So far, so good.

The intercom announced that Judith Suede, the social worker, had finally arrived, and I buzzed her in. She knocked on my condo door five minutes later.

Only she wasn't alone.

Mrs. Hitchcock and Mrs. Jenkins flanked her and were merrily chatting at the slightly flustered social worker.

"Everyone in this building absolutely adores Everly," Mrs. Jenkins said. "She and Wes magically brighten everyone's day."

"I'm sure they do," Judith, who looked to be in her midthirties, said even though she had yet to meet my niece. She was clasping her leather bag to her side, a shield against the two overly zealous women.

Mrs. Jenkins had known about my meeting today with the social worker. She must have shared that tidbit with Mrs. Hitchcock.

Was I worried about what they were up to?

Not really.

Did I think it made a difference?

Not at all.

I opened the door wider to let Judith in, and when she turned her back to the three of us, I raised my eyebrows at the two older women in a *What-the-hell-are-you-up-to?* gesture.

They ignored me.

"I'd be delighted to answer any other questions you might have," Mrs. Jenkins said. "I live in apartment 2201. I love Everly like she's my granddaughter."

"Mrs. Jenkins looks after Everly while I'm at work," I explained to Judith.

She nodded. "She already explained that to me."

I mentally cringed at what else Mrs. Hitchcock and Mrs. Jenkins might have told her in the elevator.

Especially about Hannah.

I said good-bye to the two older women and shut the door. But not before they both grinned and gave me double thumbs up.

I released a hard breath. *Oh, Christ.*

Judith removed her dress shoes and followed me into the living room.

"Sorry I'm late." She sniffed the air. "Whatever you're cooking smells delicious. What is it?"

"Maple roasted chicken and roasted vegetables."

"And Everly eats that? I'm impressed. My kids are stubborn when it comes to vegetables."

"Everly isn't much different. I have no idea if she will like it."

Judith glanced around the area, taking in the scenic view, the high-quality furniture, the cleanliness of the space. It wasn't hard to tell that she was impressed with what she saw, but the first two shouldn't have surprised her. The adoption application listed my annual income.

"You have a very nice home."

"Thank you. Would you like to see Everly's bedroom?"

"I would."

I led her down the hallway to Everly's and Hannah's rooms.

Everly's bedroom was in slight disarray, but it was an improvement to what it had been like before I started picking up her toys an hour ago. I was aiming for the happy, lived-in look.

The room drew the same reaction it always did whenever women saw it—which I hoped was a positive sign when it came to adopting Everly. Judith's eyes were round with awe and the little girl desire still buried deep inside her.

"Did you paint the mural?" she asked.

"No, a friend of mine did that for Everly. I wanted to make sure she felt special and a part of my life. I wanted her to feel like this room belonged to her and no one else."

"It's a very nice room. Do you have much experience with little girls?"

"Not really. Other than with Everly. And even then, every day is a learning experience. But it helps that I've known my niece her entire life. We weren't strangers before I became her guardian." I had no idea if that was a good enough answer. The family lawyer I'd hired to help me with the adoption told me to be truthful. Other than my being a single parent, there was no reason why the courts wouldn't grant my request to adopt my niece.

She had explained that my single-parent status wouldn't be an issue, especially because I had a strong support system outside the home.

I could only hope that Judith and the courts agreed with that sentiment. I didn't know what I would do if they said no.

Everly was the only immediate family I had left.

She was everything to me.

As we walked back to the living area, Judith noticed Hannah's bedroom door and paused. The door was partly opened, and it was clear that someone was staying in the room.

"Your bedroom?"

"No, mine's on the other side of the living room. This is a guest room. A friend of mine is staying here while she finds a new apartment. Hers was flooded."

"This would be the friend that the two women in the elevator mentioned?"

Oh, Christ.

28

HANNAH

Everly stopped walking a few feet ahead of Emma and me, then took a hop forward. She landed on the next tile of the mall floor. As usual, Snuggle Bunny was with her, in dire need of a bath.

But getting Everly to part with her beloved stuffed rabbit long enough for me to wash it was always a challenge. Her parents had given it to her a few weeks before the accident that claimed their lives. It was her lifeline to them.

"Do you and Wes have plans for tonight?" Emma asked me. Everly shuffled forward to the next square and jumped into it.

Emma and I waddled behind her. I was due in about two months. Emma only had a few weeks before she would be busy with her newborn. So neither of us cared that we weren't moving at more than a pregnant snail's pace.

"I'm not working today. That's the only plans I have—other than shopping with you and Everly while Wes is meeting with the social worker." Which Emma knew about.

"So no big plans?"

"Maybe read a book or watch TV after Everly goes to bed." Or have sex.

Okay, that part was a given. So far I hadn't grown tired of having sex with Wes.

Just the opposite.

"It's Valentine's Day," Emma said, "and the best answer you can come up with is 'read a book or watch TV'?"

"Pretty much. I'm not dating anyone and I'm not married. Valentine's Day is just another day for me...like it is for every other single person."

"But what about Wes?"

"Same deal with him. I guess. He's not dating anyone." *Truth.* "So today is just like any other day to him, too." I already knew that Emma and Travis were going out tonight. He was taking her to her favorite restaurant.

Emma made an I-don't-believe-that-for-a-second grunt. "You two are practically dating each other."

"I'd hardly call being roommates the same thing as dating. You and I were roommates at one point, and we weren't, as you put it, practically dating."

"Yes, but that was different."

I snorted a laugh. "Why? Because you and I are both females and neither of us is a lesbian?"

"Well, partly that, but—"

"So you're saying that roommates of the opposite gender who are straight are really dating...even when they don't actually go out on dates?"

"Not exactly—"

"Good. That's a relief."

"Yes, but we're not talking about just anyone here. We're talking about you and Wes."

"He and I are just friends. I mean, sure, our situation is a little different than it is for most friends of the opposite gender. We're temporarily living together, and he's a single father and I'm pregnant."

She flashed me *that* look. The one that said: *Exactly. Which is why you two should be a couple.* "So you're telling me you two aren't—"

Everly paused her jumping from tile to tile and turned to face us.

"Fire-trucking?" A big grin slid onto Emma's face.

I open my mouth to...lie.

I didn't get that far.

"I knew it! And don't even try to deny it, Hannah. You've got that post-fire-trucking glow."

"That's because I'm pregnant. That's why they call it a pregnant glow."

Everly resumed her jumping game.

"True. But that's not the kind of glow you have going on." She waved at my face like her hand was a magic wand, and she was about to turn me into Cinderella.

A pregnant Cinderella.

"No one looks that satisfied all the time," she said, "unless they're getting regular service of the old fire-truck engine."

I giggle-snorted. "Is that what you call it in your Dr. Lovejoy column?"

I knew for a fact, as a regular reader of the column, that it wasn't.

"C'mon, Hannah, you're my best friend. Plus I kept your pregnancy a secret until you were ready to announce it to everyone. I even lied to my husband so that it would remain a secret. So in my books, you owe me."

"And by owing you, you mean...?"

"Tell me the truth. True or false, you are fire-trucking Wes?"

I let out a hard breath, knowing Emma as well as I did. She wasn't going to drop this, and I did hate lying to her. Period. "Okay, he and I are fire-trucking on a regular basis. But it's only temporary. While I live with him. Which I guess makes us fire-truck buddies." I smirked at her—mostly so she didn't get the wrong idea about my arrangement with Wes.

We weren't dating.

We weren't girlfriend and boyfriend.

"Why can't you and he be something more?" she asked. "You guys are great together....Do you love him?"

I shook my head—even though I had no idea what the answer to that was. I was falling for him. Sure. But how much of that was real, and how much of it was because of my wacky hormones?

"I care for him. A lot," I finally admitted to her. "But it doesn't matter. I can't trust him with my heart and risk him walking away and crushing it. It's as simple as that."

"Why not? Love is about taking risks."

"I know, but it's easier to say it than to actually follow through on it. I'm probably being an idiot, but that's just the way it is. Besides, you're talking about him like he's in love with me. He's not. We're just friends."

"Who are both parents. Or in your case, will be one soon."

"Yes, but that doesn't mean anything. In a few months, you and I will be mothers, but we will still be best friends. We're not going to have a romantic relationship."

Emma looked like she was going to say something but just shook her head. I couldn't tell if she was shaking it at my response or to an unspoken question she had just posed to herself.

She grabbed hold of my arm. "C'mon, Everly," she called out to the hopping girl. "We're going to get Hannah some sexy underwear—so she can have a very special night tonight." That last part was said in a low murmur so that Everly couldn't hear her.

Everly stopped pretending to be a bunny and took hold of my hand as we walked into Victoria's Secret.

"I'm pregnant," I needlessly reminded Emma. "I'm not going to be able to fit any of this."

"Sure you will. It's just a matter of finding the right style that can accommodate your growing belly. Trust me. I'm a pro at this."

Given that I had once a upon a time born auditory witness to what went on between Emma and her husband in their bedroom, I had no doubts that she was a pro when it came to sexy underwear and the pregnant form.

"All right. I put my lingerie needs in your capable hands. But this is for me and no one else."

And possibly for Wes, but she didn't need that confirmed.

Emma led us to a table of low-cut lace panties, removed a bright-pink pair, and held them up. "What about these? They're sexy."

"Pretty," Everly said, reaching for them. I assumed she thought they were pretty because pink was her favorite color.

Emma handed them to her to inspect. I picked up a lavender pair. "I like these better."

"Good choice. They'll look great with your dark hair. And I bet the store has matching bras."

She was right about that. We found a matching demi bra a few minutes later that fit me perfectly.

"Wes is going to love that," Emma said, pretending to fight off a grin. "It's perfect for him."

I rolled my eyes but didn't bother to lie that he wouldn't see the panties and bra that night or any other night.

I paid for my purchases, and then the three of us continued with our shopping. Fortunately, Emma decided not to bring up our previous discussion about Wes and me.

Once we were finished, Everly and I got into Wes's SUV, and I drove us to his condo. Emma had met us at the mall in her own vehicle.

About halfway back home, Little Bean started kicking my bladder. I was beginning to think my baby's sperm daddy was an Olympic-level soccer player.

My bladder seconded that.

Everly and I had been busy shopping, and because of that, my hands were full when we approached the door to Wes's condo. So when I went to put the key into the lock, I accidentally dropped the Victoria's Secret bag.

Before I had a chance to pick it up, Everly grabbed it and pretended that Snuggle Bunny was carrying it.

I opened the door and let her in. She quickly slipped her shoes off, flinging them halfway across the foyer, and rushed down the short hallway, the Victoria's Secret bag still in her hands.

I sat on the chair that Wes had placed there, so I could easily remove my shoes now that Little Bean was a lot bigger.

"Look what Hannah bought you, Uncle Wes." The rustling of a paper bag being opened came from the direction of the living room.

And that was when I noticed the women's shoes on the floor.

Women's shoes that didn't belong to me.

Oh, crap.

29

WES

One minute Judith, the social worker, and I were seated at the dinner table, discussing the mandatory adoption classes I'd been attending over the past few weeks.

The next, Everly was showing us the lacy lavender bra and panties that Hannah had supposedly bought me from—according to the bag in Everly's hand—Victoria's Secret.

Fuck.

Before either Judith or I could react, Hannah speed-waddled into the living room. Her face was as red as the hearts associated with the day.

"S-sorry about that," she stammered. "She didn't mean they are Wes's...because obviously Wes doesn't wear women's..." Her voice trailed off, panic rolling off her in tsunami-sized waves.

Everly didn't seem to notice the odd tension crackling in the air. She was busy showing her stuffed bunny the bra and panties.

"Judith, this is my...my friend, Hannah." I had no idea what to call her. I wanted to say "my girlfriend," but I sensed Hannah wasn't ready to go there yet, and I didn't want to make the situation worse by putting her on the spot.

Especially during something as important as the adoption interview.

"Are you by any chance the roommate with the flooded apartment?" Judith asked.

"That would be me. Wes is letting me stay here while I look for a new place to live." Hannah began caressing her stomach in a distracted, maternal way. She looked down at it and paused. "I was artificially inseminated," she blurted.

The need to wrap her in my arms and kiss away her embarrassment overwhelmed me. But since I wasn't sure how either Judith or Hannah would react if I gave in to the impulse, I temporarily smothered it.

"I'm sorry," Hannah said, "but I really need to go to the bathroom. The baby has been kicking my bladder since Everly and I left the mall." She turned to Everly. "Can I have *my* underwear?"

The little girl happily gave them to her and went off to play with her kitchen set, located next to the real kitchen. Hannah waddled off as fast as her mortification could carry her.

"Your friend is a pediatric nurse?" Judith asked.

"Mrs. Jenkins and Mrs. Hitchcock mentioned that in the elevator?" My words held a ghost of a chuckle. I would be surprised if Judith hadn't already known that Hannah was pregnant, and that she had opted to go the sperm-donor route.

"They did. They also mentioned that she has taken on the role of Everly's surrogate mother."

Shit, how did I answer that?

"It's more like her maternal instincts are coming out— thanks to her pregnancy and because of her job. She's great with kids, and she enjoys spending time with Everly, and Everly loves spending time with Hannah."

That made two of us.

But I wasn't going to share that with Judith.

The truth? Hannah and I had been spending the past few weeks acting more like a couple than anything else.

I didn't mean because we had sex on an almost daily basis. It was those little things. Like the way she curled up next to me on the couch when we watched TV together.

The way we often cooked dinner together.

The way we flirted with each other the way couples did—or at least the way our friends, who were couples, did.

We even went for walks to the playground with Everly.

So why hadn't I told her yet that I loved her? Why hadn't I taken our relationship to the next level and pushed for it to be public, for her to admit to herself and everyone else that she was my girlfriend?

Because every time someone commented on us being a couple, she would stiffen and emotionally pull away from me for the next day or two.

But despite that, I hadn't given up on her. Why not?

Hope. Because every time it happened, things always returned to normal between us a few days later.

Judith concluded the interview several minutes later and left.

The condo door clicked shut behind her. Two minutes passed, but there was still no sign of Hannah. Everly had moved on from playing with her kitchen to playing with her doctor's set and stuffed animals on the couch.

I walked down the hallway to Hannah's room. She was busy pacing the length of the hardwood floor. Her curtains were still open, the sky a washed-out blue from the soon-to-be setting sun.

I entered and watched her for a moment. She didn't notice me, too deep in thought.

"Loved the new bra and panties," I said, and she startled. "I hope you're planning to wear them tonight."

She paused her pacing, and I narrowed the distance between us.

"I'm so sorry about what happened," she said. "I had no idea Everly was going to show them to you. And I hadn't realized the social worker was still here until it was too late."

"Don't worry about it. I doubt Judith thought they were mine. For one, they're not my size." I pulled her into my arms like I had wanted to do a short time ago. "And lavender doesn't look good on me. But it will look hot on you."

I leaned down and brushed my lips against hers. Just a tease. "Dinner will be ready in a few minutes."

A slight frown creased her forehead. "Aren't you even the tiniest bit worried that the underwear incident will hurt your chances of adopting Everly?"

"I doubt it will make a difference. Judith might, though, think that you and I are involved."

I carefully watched Hannah's reaction to that little insight.

Her eyes widened just enough for me to notice. "Why would she think that you're involved with a pregnant woman, especially when I made it clear that it's not your baby?"

"Is it that mind-boggling to you that a man might be interested in a pregnant woman even though the child isn't his? That he can't love another man's child? That he's only capable of loving kids that came from *his* sperm?"

"Of course not. You wouldn't be adopting Everly if that were true."

"What about the first part, about the pregnant woman? Do you really think it's that crazy for me to be into you even though you're pregnant with another man's child?"

Her mouth tilted to one side, my favorite spark in her eye. "Obviously not, given our roommates-with-benefits arrangement. If you weren't into me, we wouldn't have sex practically every day."

She had a point there.

However, she was also missing *my* point.

"Do you think it will cause you problems with the adoption process if she thinks we're...?" Hannah gestured between us.

"Having sex?" I laughed. "I'm pretty sure that even though I want to adopt, I'm still allowed to date and have sex. I don't remember any of the documentation stating it was forbidden. I chose *not* to do either of those things with another woman because I didn't want to confuse Everly."

"That's my sentiments exactly when it comes to my dating life once Little Bean is born. Not that I have a dating life. But if I did..."

"You have a dating life."

She chuckled. "I've been on one date in the past year. I'd hardly call that a dating life. Now, if you're referring to our sex life, then I guess I've been experiencing a very rich dating life."

"That's not what I was referring to." I kissed her briefly and walked out of the room, not giving her a chance to respond.

I returned to the kitchen to execute the next step in my Valentine's Day dinner plans. Everly helped me. She and I had made place-setting cards yesterday while Hannah was at work, with heart cutouts that Everly had helped to glue onto the stock paper. We also covered them with red and white glitter.

We placed them at our usual spots at the table, and she helped me arrange the assortment of pink roses I had ordered for the occasion.

"What do you think?" I asked Everly, my Valentine's Day adviser.

"Pretty."

"What about candles? Should we put a few on the table?"

Her face brightened. "Birthday candles?"

"No, these aren't for blowing out until *after* dinner."

She helped me set up three crystal candleholders of various heights that had belonged to my brother and sister-in-law. I added the white taper candles and lit them. "Remember, no blowing them out until we have finished dinner," I told Everly.

Hannah joined us as I was removing the food from the warm oven.

"We made you dinner," Everly said, taking full credit even though she hadn't been here while I was cooking it.

Hannah made a production of sniffing the air. "Mmm. It smells yummy. And I love what you two did to the table. It looks very...festive."

I pulled Everly's chair away from the table and helped her into her booster seat. Then I did the same for Hannah—minus the booster seat part.

I leaned down, my mouth close to her ear. "You're wrong about not having a dating life," I murmured so that Everly couldn't hear me. "This a date. Our first date. Happy Valentine's Day."

I kissed her on the cheek.

30

HANNAH

What did I think of Wes's comment? The one about Valentine's Day dinner being our first date?

I had no idea. We'd already had "the talk" the day of Ava and Liam's wedding. He had agreed that our relationship would only be sexual, and no one would know about it.

Except Emma now knew about it—and had possibly suspected it for a while.

How many of our other friends had also figured out that something was going on between Wes and me?

I cut up Everly's chicken and vegetables into preschooler-sized pieces, then took a bit of my chicken. "Mmm. This tastes amazing," I told Wes. Everly took a tentative bite of hers and agreed with me.

I wouldn't have considered our dinner a date—given that it included a three-year-old chaperone—but it was a lot of fun. There was none of that uncertain, *What-the-hell-was-I-thinking?* tension often seen with first dates. It was nothing like my last date, with Philip.

Of course, that might have also had something to do with

the lack of two spies tonight by the name of Isabelle and Jayden, who had been asked to keep an eye on me during my date with Phil.

I already knew Wes was a fantastic kisser, and there would be no awkward *Will-he-kiss-me-or-not?* deliberation once the date was over.

There was no question we would be kissing at the end of it.

There was no question that he and I would be having great sex later.

The real question was: Did I want to take a risk and see where this thing between us could go?

Or did I want to return to my typical pattern of ending the date with no plans for another?

I was a pro at the latter—and an amateur at the former.

After dinner, the three of us played Candy Land. This was followed by us reading to Everly, bathing her, and putting her to bed.

Once she was settled under the covers, Wes and I kissed her good-night on the forehead and shut her bedroom door partway behind us as we left. She didn't like it fully closed.

Wes reached for my hand and led me to the living room. "Just so you know, our date isn't over yet."

"I kind of figured that. We haven't had sex."

"That's not what I'm talking about." He walked over to his speakers and selected a slow song. He then took me in his arms. My arms automatically went around his neck, and we swayed on the spot.

"I'm hoping you like me enough for a second date," he said.

"I'll know in a minute."

"A minute? Why what's going to happen in a minute?"

"This." I reached up and lightly pressed my lips against his.

He kissed me back. I parted my lips and let him in.

Our kiss continued, slowly teasing, tasting, worshiping, the sway of our bodies momentarily paused.

In time, I pulled away slightly and smiled softly at him. "You passed. We can see how date number two goes."

A gorgeous smile spread on his face. "Thank God for that." He grabbed my face between his hands and this time the kiss was more heated, yet it still possessed the gentleness of our last kiss.

It wasn't the kind of kiss that said I want to have sex now.

It was the kind that made you weak and trembling in all the right places.

You're making a mistake, a voice deep down grumbled. *You're trying to turn your life into a fairy tale.*

Except real life wasn't a fairy tale.

Real life was filled with ups and downs and disappointments.

Happily ever after was a fantasy.

You're currently living that fantasy—nothing more, the annoying, party-pooper voice pointed out.

I ignored it.

Or at least, that had been the plan....

31

HANNAH

Two weeks later, I waddled through the doorway to Quade Security and Investigations. The comfy leather armchairs and the couch were empty. The only person in the waiting area, other than a snoozing Mojo, was...

Isabelle jumped up from her desk. The blue in her dark hair shone under the artificial lighting. "Wow, look at you. You look gorgeous. If I knew pregnancy would do that to me, I'd get knocked up in a heartbeat."

"You do realize that at some point you would have to give birth to the baby?" Jayden asked, exiting from his office. Mojo's head popped up at the sound of his owner's voice. "And then you'd have a kid to look after. You can't stay pregnant forever." He mussed up Isabelle's hair.

She batted his hand away.

"But she's right," he said to me. "You do look great. Are you looking for Wes?"

"Yes, he was supposed to meet me here. I'm running out of time before I need to move into a new apartment." I rested my hand on top of my rather large belly. "Assuming this baby waits until his or her due date, I've got less than six weeks to find an apartment, buy the furniture, and set up the baby's room."

I had procrastinated long enough.

It was shocking how fast time had flown once Christmas was over. I'd been busy with work, taking care of Everly, having toe-curling sex with Wes, and before I knew it, I was in my final trimester.

"So I have a question for you," I said to Jayden. "When I met your grandmother back in November, she mentioned you own a store in this building." The building Wes owned, worked out of and pretended he didn't know who owned it. "Which store does she think is yours?"

"The computer repair shop."

"There's no computer repair shop in the building."

"You know that and I know that, but she doesn't know it. My grandmother is allergic to computers and doesn't own one. So she has no reason to actually go to my mythological store."

"But why tell her you own a store? You could have told her you were a doctor or an accountant if you were going to lie to her."

He shook his head. "I had to come up with something mundane so there was no risk of her telling people what I do for a living. Or what she thinks I do for a living. With my job, I need to be as low key as possible."

Isabelle laughed. "What he means is he got caught in a lie. Someone he was watching, for a client, knew his cover as a computer repairman. This was the same person who happened to meet Jayden's grandmother one day. She had no idea what Jayden was doing after he'd left the military, and the person told her he repaired computers for a living. He couldn't very well tell her the truth after that."

Jayden lifted his shoulders in a shrug. "What can I say? I

was new at the job, and my grandmother had been stressed every time I was deployed to dangerous territory. While this job isn't as dangerous, it still comes with a lot more risk than your average job. I knew it would stress her out like my old career had, so I let her continue to believe what she already thought to be the truth."

Did anyone else notice how Isabelle squirmed whenever he mentioned danger?

Or maybe it was a pregnancy-induced hallucination. Even if I couldn't get past my fear of someone I loved walking away from me, that didn't stop me from hoping for a happily ever after for someone else.

And I truly believed that Jayden and Isabelle would be a great couple.

Even if they didn't agree with me.

No, I don't mean I had actually discussed it with them. Because that would be crazy. Plus Isabelle and I had come to an agreement—an unspoken mutual agreement—that we didn't discuss each other's love lives.

"So what exactly is going on with you and Wes?" Isabelle asked me.

Okay, so much for our mutual agreement.

"We're just friends. And for a little longer, roommates." Friends who'd had a date two weeks ago—on Valentine's Day— but hadn't had a chance yet to go on a second one.

A real date.

A date that didn't include a three-year-old.

She made a disbelieving sound.

"What? We are."

Jayden shot her a look I couldn't decipher. She didn't see it. She was too busy studying me. Now I understood how bacteria felt under a microscope.

"You guys are more than just friends and roommates. I've seen how he looks at you and how you look at him." She kept her gaze steady on me, and I returned it without so much as a flinch.

"Isn't there an optometrist office downstairs?" I asked. "Maybe you should book an appointment to get your eyes checked."

Jayden chuckled.

Isabelle simply looked smug. "I notice you didn't deny it."

"Sure, I just did. Hence my suggestion to go make nice with the optometrist."

She crossed her arms and flashed a warning look: *Don't bother trying to BS me. I'm an expert at your game.* "So you're telling me that you haven't considered settling down with Wes? Having a family with him, which if you ask me, you two already have going between your baby and his niece? Why not? You guys are perfect together."

"We're not a family."

"Really? Because I've seen how that little girl is with you. She's under your spell as much as Wes is."

"You make me sound like a witch."

That got a snorted laugh from Jayden.

But the truth was, Everly wasn't the one who was under anyone's so-called spell. It was me. I had inadvertently fallen in love with her even though she wasn't my daughter. We had shopped together, made cookies together. I'd given her baths and tucked her in bed whenever I wasn't working at the hospital. I'd been there for her when she was having a nightmare. I had even gone with Wes last month to check out preschools for the fall.

And Everly had voted for Little Bean's official name: James, the name of Lily's baby brother.

Day by day, I had slipped into the unofficial role of being her mother. I hadn't seen it coming, and then I had ignored the truth...until now.

Without realizing what was going on, I had also fallen so easily into the role of being part of a family.

And that scared me.

Why?

Because being part of their family came with a ticking time clock. As soon as I found an apartment, I would be moving away and that illusion of a family would come to an end. The only family after that would be the one consisting of two people: Little Bean and me.

Don't look at me that way. Sure, Wes and I had agreed to date, but that didn't spell a long-term relationship.

What we had between us wasn't real. At least not in the way that counted the most.

It was convenient. For him. For me. For Everly.

But once reality bit us in the butt, we would be faced with the problem of how to make our relationship work once I moved away. We would be too busy being parents and with our careers to have time to nurture the early bud of what we had between us.

And if it wasn't real, if it didn't have time to flourish, then it would be easy for Wes to walk away—and take my heart with him.

"You're wrong about everything," I said to Isabelle, with as much conviction as a toddler who wanted a candy bar.

Minus the meltdown.

"Are you sure about that?"

"Absolutely. We're just roommates, but you did make a valid point."

"She did?" Jayden asked, not sounding at all convinced.

"It's about time I find a new apartment." I didn't want to confuse Everly more than I already had.

Wes and I knew our arrangement wouldn't last forever.

I would definitely miss the sex.

And waking up in his arms...because I'd been too lazy to go back to my room afterward.

Oh. God. How could I have been such an idiot? I had taken a giant leap over the line I had drawn in the sand. And the worst part? I had convinced myself our little family situation wasn't real, but now it felt more real than ever.

The problem?

I wanted a relationship built on solid ground—not one that was convenient because we were living together. As long as I lived with Wes, we would never know for sure if what we had was real, if it could stand the test of time and everything else we threw at it.

And let's not forget how history could be a bitch. It was good at repeating itself and all its errors, as it had already done several times for me.

But knowing all that didn't stop the memory of how great it had felt waking up in Wes's arms and curling up with him on the couch while we watched a movie together.

It had been nice pretending to be a couple.

But our living together had to end.

For Everly's sake.

And for my own sake.

My body booed the decision.

And then it tried another tactic. The negotiation tactic that involved begging for one more night with Wes—because who knew when I would get to have sex again?

Apparently, after months of looking for an apartment with no success, my body thought I'd be able to find one this afternoon...just like that.

Though it did have a valid point.

My sex life was about to go on another long hiatus because once Little Bean was born, I would no longer have time for Wes.

Oh. Joy.

I started toward the entrance. "When Wes shows up, tell him I couldn't wait any longer for him. I'm meeting up with the realtor, and I'll see him tonight."

And with that, I left on my mission to find a new apartment...today.

32

___

WES

y phone pinged in my jeans pocket. I ignored it while I watched Everly and Lily walk across the balance beam in Wonder Play, the gym for little kids.

Beneath them was the blue mat they were pretending was the ocean. Around us, other three-year-olds were laughing, playing, and exploring while their parents helped them navigate the equipment. The lyrics to "The Wheels on the Bus" played in the background.

"So when exactly are you planning to tell Hannah you love her?" Josh asked me.

"I'm still waiting for the right moment."

He snorted a laugh. "And what moment is that exactly? After she's had her baby? After Everly graduates from high school?"

"Aren't you jumping ahead of yourself there? She hasn't even started preschool yet."

"You get the picture. You need to hurry up and find the right moment before Hannah moves out of your apartment."

"One, she hasn't found anything yet, and I doubt she'll find anything soon." No thanks to me finding fault with every location we had looked at so far. "I've still got time."

"You do realize she's due in a month and a half, right? She's not an elephant with a twenty-two-month gestation period."

I felt my eyebrows leap halfway up my forehead. "How do you even know how long an elephant's gestation period is?"

"Holly told me when she was pregnant with James. She was kind of cranky at the time, and the fact just stuck in my head for useful moments like this." He flashed me a wry smile. "So what's your second reason for stalling when it comes to telling Hannah you love her?"

"There's a chance I might be waiting for a sign that she loves me, so I don't tell her prematurely and scare her off. I'm slowly gaining her trust, and things are good between us." Better than good actually. "But I'm not sure she's ready yet for me to tell her how I feel about her. For any other woman, it wouldn't be an issue. But most other women don't struggle with abandonment issues."

"What kind of sign are you looking for? A neon one on her forehead?" The wry smile was back for an encore.

"That would be helpful. How did you know when it was the right time to tell Holly how you felt about her?"

"I didn't. I took a risk. Except I did have one advantage you don't have."

I helped Everly down from the balance beam. She had been so focused on walking across it and giggling with Lily, she wasn't paying attention to what I was saying to Josh. "What's that?" I asked him.

He nodded at his daughter. Point taken. Josh had been the father of Holly's child. I didn't have that kind of connection with Hannah's baby, at least not in the same sense.

But while I might not have contributed to its gene pool, I did have an emotional connection to Little Bean. I had felt the baby kick numerous times, which was up there on the coolness scale. I had talked to the baby every day, telling him or her all the cool things they'd get to do once they were born. I had accompanied Hannah to her OB appointments. I had done all the things Travis and Josh and Trent had done when their wives were pregnant.

I had even hired Travis and Emma's yoga instructor to come to my condo three times a week, to do prenatal yoga with Hannah and Everly and me.

In our own way, the three of us had become a family.

Hannah had to have seen it, too. It was what she had wanted all those years when her own mother had been alive, and then when Hannah had been stuck in the system. It was why she had gotten pregnant thanks to an anonymous donor.

She had wanted a family.

"Look, I'm just saying, don't waste time waiting for the right moment," Josh said, helping Lily down. "You might miss it if you're not careful, or you might miss out on something even better because you were too busy walking on eggshells to take a chance sooner."

"You're right. I'll tell her tonight."

The class finished a short time later, and Josh wished me luck. "I don't think you'll need it, though. You're a great guy, wealthy, and not bad looking. How can she say no?" He chuckled. Not because it wasn't true—because it was. Hannah was nothing like the women I had dated in the past. They had been attracted to me partly because it was obvious from my clothes and my pre-Everly BMW that I had money.

Hannah had never come off like she gave a damn about my net worth. That was one of the things I loved about her.

Everly and I still had to do one more thing before we could return home. While I drove us to the store, I tried coming up with the best way to tell Hannah that I loved her.

She was the type of woman who preferred simple gestures. Like when I gave her the angel tree-ornament for Christmas.

Or I could tell her while watching a movie.

Definitely not after sex. Even I knew that was a big no-no.

Somewhere in the back of my head, a voice told me spontaneity was the way to go with Hannah. She was less likely to feel cornered when she wasn't ready yet to hear the three words. I didn't want her to feel like the woman at a professional sports game, whose boyfriend proposed to her on the Jumbotron and she wasn't interested in going there with him... and now the entire world knew about it because the video went viral.

While Everly and I were in line at the grocery store, I checked my texts, which I had forgotten to do after we left Wonder Play. Everly was busy examining the different candy bars.

Jayden had texted me.

Jayden: Heads up.

Jayden: Your woman dropped by looking for you at the office. Isabelle might have asked her about your relationship and pointed out that between you, Everly, Hannah, and her baby, you're a family.

This was followed by:

Jayden: Your woman looked freaked at the suggestion.

Jayden: Also, Isabelle might have mentioned how it's obvious you and Hannah have a thing for each other. Hannah also looked pretty freaked out at that suggestion.

Fucking Christ. Why the hell did Isabelle have to do that? Now I had no idea what to do.

I texted Jayden right back.

> Me: Thanks for letting me know.

> Jayden: And just so you know, you made plans to go apartment hunting with her for today. That's why she showed up at the office. She went without you.

I did? I honestly couldn't remember having plans to go today. Tomorrow, yes. But not today because Everly and I had the play class with Lily and Josh. The four of us had been going there for the past two months.

Hannah knew that.

But that was okay. The chance of her finding something today was next to slim.

My bigger problem had to do with Isabelle's conversation with her.

Or so I thought....

33

WES

Hannah wasn't home yet when Everly and I arrived at my condo.

I had already sent her a text, apologizing for standing her up, and telling her that I confused the day we were meeting with the realtor. I had it written down for the next day.

By the time we arrived home, I still hadn't heard from her.

"He needs a Band-Aid." I handed Everly one for her teddy bear, who was lying on her bed.

She ripped open the package, revealing the Disney Princesses. She pulled off the backing and attempted to stick the Band-Aid on the bear's arm, even though she'd told me his leg had the owie.

"How's his heart rate doing?" I asked.

She picked up the toy stethoscope, pretended to listen to his heart—which seemed to be located in his belly—and gave me a thumbs-up.

I studied the pile of stuffed animals on the bed. "Okay, who's next?"

She pointed to a giraffe whose neck made me think of a horse more than it did a giraffe. I passed it to her.

"Hey, what are you two up to?" Hannah asked from behind us.

Everly ran to her and threw her arms around Hannah's legs. "I'm being a doctor and Uncle Wes is the nurse and he loves you."

Hannah's expression flickered through several emotions. None of them were what I was hoping for. The most predominant one being disbelief—as in, she believed that Everly had made up the last part.

Her expression ended with the lack of any emotion.

Which was the worst of them all. I had no idea what she was thinking.

Oh, who was I kidding? I was a male. I didn't know what she was thinking most of the time.

Everly let go of Hannah's legs and returned to the bed. "Mr. Giraffe needs a Band-Aid, too," she told me.

From the corner of my eye, I could tell she was holding her hand out to me, but I wasn't one hundred percent certain. My attention was focused on Hannah and her reaction to Everly's news.

Her gaze jumped from Everly to me and then back to Everly.

Hannah lifted her shoulders, the move so subtle I might have missed it if I weren't watching her intently. "I have some big news," she said, waddling over to us. "I finally found a new apartment. It's perfect. It's not near the hospital, but it's really nice. And I get to move in this weekend, which means I need to go shopping for baby furniture tonight." She was talking so fast, I had a hard time following what she was saying.

She removed a Band-Aid from the box on the bed and handed it to Everly. The three-year-old happily accepted it, Hannah's words having gone right over her head.

"How did you end up getting it so quickly?" I asked. "You just saw it this afternoon." What kind of dive was it for her to be approved so soon? Was it that bad no one else had wanted it?

"The building manager showed Janice and me around the place. She remembered I was the nurse who took care of her young son when he had been in the ER due to a skateboard accident a few weeks ago. That was enough for her to quickly approve my application. I got lucky because the apartment was listed this morning and would have been snatched up in no time."

She smiled at my niece. "You're doing a great job, Dr. Everly."

"He's all better now." Everly hugged the giraffe.

I wanted to talk to Hannah about Everly blurting that I loved her. However, I figured it wouldn't be a smart idea to do that in front of the three-year-old.

You know what else wasn't a smart idea? Talking to your friend in front of said three-year-old about how you loved someone, while assuming she wasn't paying attention.

I should have known better.

But even though I wanted to talk to Hannah about it now, I had to wait until Everly was in bed first. Damned if I was letting my niece drop that bombshell on Hannah without me talking to her about it.

My phone pinged to let me know the delivery guy was here. "I'll be back in a minute," I told them. "I ordered Chinese food for dinner."

It wasn't the romantic dinner I had originally considered. Everly was joining us because she also loved Chinese food.

"Sounds great," Hannah said. "But I really can't stay. If there's any left when I return, I'll have it then."

My heart told me not to let her walk out the door without talking to her first. But really, what was it expecting me to do? Kidnap her?

"We can go with you." I had no idea where the words came from. They simply steamrolled out of my mouth. But now that I'd said them, it didn't seem like a bad idea.

I wanted her to be a permanent part of our lives and not a train passing through. And what could be more permanent than shopping together for baby furniture?

She shook her head. "I don't know how long I'll be. I might not be finished until after Everly's bedtime."

"It's not like she has to go to work or school tomorrow. I'm sure going to bed a little later than normal won't hurt her this one time. Think about it for a moment while I get the food."

"Okay."

Was I the only one who hoped that she meant *Okay, you guys can come shopping with me* instead of *Okay, I'll think about it while you get the food*?

By the time I returned, Hannah and Everly had set out the dinner plates and cutlery. Relief rushed through me like Speedy Gonzales at seeing them in Hannah's spot. "Does this mean you're at least staying for dinner?"

And permanently?

"Everly did a great job convincing me why I should stay for dinner. I mean, how can I walk away from ginger beef?" Hannah's favorite.

I sat in my seat. "So Everly. Do you want to go shopping with Hannah after dinner to help her find furniture for the baby?"

"Yes!" was her emphatic reply. She beamed at Hannah, who smiled back at her.

"Where were you thinking of going?" I asked her as I spooned steamed rice into Everly's Winnie-the-Pooh bowl.

She named the store where Travis and Emma had bought their baby furniture. "They have a sale that ends tomorrow," Hannah said.

We ate our dinner. The odd tension from when Everly

announced to Hannah that I loved her had diminished slightly, but it was still thick enough to cut with one of Everly's toy knives.

But while I might have noticed it, Everly was fortunately oblivious to the tension. She was happily eating her food and telling Hannah about her afternoon.

"Lily and I were walking over the ocean and Uncle Wes said he loves you," Everly told her.

"The ocean?"

"It's a huge blue mat," I explained, "but the girls like to call it the ocean."

Hannah nodded like it made perfect sense. "So, he told you he loves me?" While her tone might have been candy-apple sweet for Everly's sake, the undertow was as calm as a cow caught in a tornado.

Everly shook her head. "No, Uncle Josh."

"Uncle Wes told Uncle Josh that he loves me?"

Everly nodded and shoveled a spoonful of rice into her mouth.

Sure, you couldn't have done that a minute ago, could you?

Maybe now was a good time to change topics...while Everly was still up.

"Have you decided yet who's going to be your birthing partner?" Okay, clearly my mouth and my brain weren't on speaking terms. That was no better than when I had blurted that Everly and I could go shopping with Hannah. Although in that case, I had wanted to go furniture shopping with her.

Hannah squirmed in her seat, which told me everything I needed to know.

"I can do it." This time my mouth and brain were in synch. "You can't do this alone, and right now you don't have any other options."

All right, I take it back about my mouth and my brain. What the hell was that?

"I have someone."

"You do? Who?"

"Mrs. Hitchcock."

"The dragon lady?" Oops. Hadn't meant to let that one slip in front of Everly.

"She's not all that bad once you get to know her. Plus she used to be a midwife when she was younger, so she knows what she's doing."

"But haven't things changed since those days? They no longer put sticks in the mother's mouth when she's pushing the baby out." I might have seen that in a movie once. I had no idea if it was true or not, but I figured it proved my point.

What was my point?

That *I* should be the one to help Hannah while she was in labor. I loved her and wanted to be there for her.

But again, this wasn't the time to bring that up.

It would have to wait until Everly was in bed.

HANNAH LOVINGLY TRACED HER HAND ALONG THE RAILING OF THE dark, cherrywood crib. I was clueless when it came to baby furniture, but even I could tell the nursery set—with the matching change table and drawers—was from a high-end designer. I also could tell it was love at first sight for Hannah when she saw it.

She looked at the price, gave a little oh-well shrug, and moved on to the next set.

Everly was enthralled with the cribs, too, mostly because each one had a stuffed animal in it.

She pointed at the floppy, gray-blue bunny in the one crib. "Can I see?"

I took it out and handed it to her. She hugged it and declared it was perfect.

"I don't think you need any more stuffed animals," I told her. "You already have more animals than the San Francisco Zoo." Or close enough.

By the way, never tell a little girl that she has enough stuffed animals. She will never agree with you. Hannah smirked a good-luck-with-that smile and waddled to the next crib.

"It's not for me," Everly declared.

"Then who's it for?"

"My new brother." She pointed in Hannah's direction.

Everly and I had already talked about how Hannah's baby wasn't her brother. Clearly, it had zero impact.

She now wore the stubborn expression I had become quite familiar with, ever since she had moved in with me. Whatever I was going to say on the subject of Little Bean was going to be ignored. Again.

"You want to get it as a gift for the baby?" I asked instead.

She nodded.

"Do you want it to be a surprise?"

She nodded once more.

"You won't tell Hannah until the baby is born?"

Another nod.

Somehow, I had a hard time believing that. Everly had a tough time keeping secrets. However, I couldn't blame her for telling Hannah that I loved her. She didn't know she wasn't supposed to repeat what she had overheard at Wonder Play.

"All right. Let's return this one to the crib, and I'll come back tomorrow to buy it. Is that okay?" I held up my hand for her to high-five.

Everly did that, then tossed the bunny over the crib railing. It landed in a heap on the mattress. I fixed it to how it was before, and she and I joined Hannah by another crib.

Now that Everly had found the perfect gift for the baby, she gave her not-so-expert opinion about each crib.

Or maybe it *was* her expert opinion. She was judging each one based on how easy they looked to escape from. Even though there were a few that Hannah liked, none resulted in the same excited glow on her face as the first nursery set.

After deciding which nursery set she wanted—dark wood like the first one—Hannah headed for the bedding section. Everly and I joined her.

"This one." Everly pointed at a quilt on the wall with cute woodland critters on it. The border was a smoky dark blue.

"That's adorable," Hannah said. "But I was considering something in a more neutral color, in case the baby is a girl. What do you think of this one?" She pointed at another quilt of similar design, but it was more on the side of gray and green.

With her head tilted to the side, Everly inspected the quilt, tapping her finger against her chin as if deep in thought. She nodded. "Yes, that one."

Both looked at me, and I agreed it was the perfect choice. "Are you asking Travis to paint a mural on the baby's wall?"

I already knew he would be happy to do it. It had become almost standard protocol for him to paint bedroom murals for his friends' babies and little kids.

"I can't," Hannah said. "I'm not allowed to paint the apartment walls."

"That's too bad." *I don't suppose I can include it as a bonus for staying with me when I have the talk with her tonight? Stay with Everly and me, and I'll throw in a mural painted by our very own Travis.*

I grabbed the bedding set so that Hannah didn't have to carry it. By the time we were finished, she had selected a few other items for the baby's room. All shared the same woodland critter theme.

I wanted to pay for it, but I knew she would never let me. The woman had too much goddamn pride.

Usually, that would have been a turn-on.

Not so much this time.

But that didn't matter. I knew exactly what I needed to do to sidestep it....

34

HANNAH

The best part about driving home with a three-year-old when you didn't feel like talking to the man sitting next to you?

You could sing along to her favorite kiddie playlist—the best distraction ever. For one, it entertained Everly, because she was happy to sing along with me. And singing to "Puff the Magic Dragon" was the best way to avoid the white elephant (or maybe that was the white dragon) squished next to her in the SUV.

Yes, I'll admit it. Inside, I was a freaking mess. But could you blame me for feeling that way? As if what Isabelle had told me about Wes, Everly, and I being a family hadn't been enough, there was Everly blurting that Wes loved me.

And not only that, he had told Josh that he loved me.

But Wes didn't *actually* feel that way about me. He had confused love with the need for a surrogate mother for his niece and thought I was the perfect choice.

But that wasn't what I wanted.

I wanted a love that was real.

A love that was impossible to walk away from.

Did I love Wes? I had no idea. My pregnancy hormones had been messing with me. I had no idea what was true and what was them simply being assholes.

One thing I did know was that I cared for him—a lot.

However, that didn't mean anything. I'd been burned in the past by the people I loved.

But their love hadn't been real.

You know the quote "Fool me once, shame on you. Fool me twice, shame on me"?

I wasn't quite as quick a study. It had taken two additional times before the lesson finally sunk in.

But now I was wiser.

I was just surprised Holly hadn't texted or phoned me after Josh mentioned to her what Wes had told him at Wonder Play. Or maybe he never said anything to her about it.

Maybe his lips were sealed tighter than Everly's—which wouldn't take much. If you didn't want any part of your conversation repeated in public, then you needed to make sure she wasn't within hearing range when you said it.

Yep, that was another lesson I had learned the hard way.

But I'm sure the old lady who got an earful about some of my more embarrassing pregnancy-related issues (that I had shared with Emma while with Everly) had gotten over it.

Eventually.

After downing a bottle of wine.

By the time we arrived at Wes's condo, Everly was fast asleep in her car seat. She didn't even stir when Wes scooped her up and carried her upstairs. She also didn't stir when he laid her on her bed, removed her shoes, and covered her.

Even though I knew I shouldn't, I kissed her forehead. Not having her in my life every day would be hard, but Little Bean would help me get over it soon enough.

I was one hundred percent positive about that.

Okay, eighty percent positive.

Wes and I left her room. I made a move to return downstairs to retrieve the rest of the things I'd bought at the store. The furniture was scheduled to be delivered to my new apartment on Saturday.

Wes took hold of my hand, stopping me from going anywhere. "We need to talk."

Uh. Oh. Nothing ever good came from those words.

Maybe he had realized things would never work out between us. That we needed to rethink his initial plan for us to date.

My heart shrunk two sizes at that thought and slumped in my chest.

It's okay, I reminded myself. *Most parents struggle to go on dates with their spouse once they have kids.* We would be no different.

I followed him into the living room. Not that I had much choice. He was still holding my hand. He gestured for me to sit on the couch and I did, happy to get off my feet again.

What I didn't expect was for Wes to begin pacing. He rubbed the back of his neck, but the pacing didn't stop.

"So..." I began, unsure of what to say. "Are you still planning to talk or is this part of your new exercise plan?" The plan that involved him wearing a path into the area rug.

He finally stopped pacing. "Right. Look, I had this planned to go differently. I spent the afternoon coming up with the best way to tell you I love you. Having Everly blurt the news wasn't part of the plan. I knew, because of what happened in your past, you would freak out if I told you I love you."

"I don't know, you look pretty freaked out yourself." Which didn't bode well for his declaration. Love wasn't supposed to scare you.

Right?

"I'm not freaked out over my feelings for you, Hannah. I'm

in love with you, and nothing you say or do will change that. But I need you to give me a chance to prove it to you."

Okay, not quite what I had expected him to say.

He has been proving his feelings for you and more, my heart implored. I ignored it, doing what I did best when it came to that particular organ.

He sat next to me and covered my hand with his. My pulse rushed, my breath turned ragged, and my mouth put the Sahara Desert to shame.

Little Bean must have sensed this because she gave me a swift kick in the side. I had no idea if that was her way of saying to give Wes a chance, not to give him a chance, or *I need to stretch, so please just ignore me.*

His hand on mine was warm and comforting, but I wasn't ready to let that sway me. "Are you sure that you're in love with me? Or are you in love with the idea of having someone around who can fill in for Everly's mother?"

"Everly has nothing to do with this. I cared about you even before I became her legal guardian. I would have still fallen in love with you, even if she hadn't been living here while you were my roommate."

I gave him a small nod because I didn't know what to believe. He might have *thought* he loved me now, but what about later on, when he got bored of me like everyone else in my life tended to do?

"I'm asking for more time to prove that I'm worth giving your heart to, and to prove that I'm not going to hurt you or abandon you like people in your past have. I'm here for as long as you want me in your life, Hannah...which I'm hoping is a very long time."

"I'm still planning to move into my new apartment this weekend." I needed the space from him and Everly so that I could think clearly.

He nodded, no doubt already suspecting as much.

Honestly, I had no idea how he was planning to make things work once I moved away. I was going to be busy soon enough with my baby, and he was already busy with Everly. What we had between us wouldn't be a long-distance relationship, but over time, it would feel like it was.

In time he would realize it wasn't worth the effort.

Oh, well. At least our fizzled relationship wouldn't be a shocker.

No pity parties would be required. No streamers or noisy kazoos needed to apply.

But unlike in the past, I wouldn't be alone. I'd have Little Bean.

I could live with that.

Do you know what else you can live with? my heart asked. *Kissing him.*

My lips thoroughly agreed.

Of course, they would. Traitors.

As if reading my mind, Wes leaned in slightly, and his gaze dropped to my mouth. "Is it okay if I kiss you?" His own mouth wore a hopeful grin.

I nodded, and his smile widened.

One thing that hadn't changed in the months I'd been living with him was the way my body responded the moment our lips touched. Despite being almost seven and half months pregnant, my body still hummed at his touch and craved him.

Needing to keep him close, I knotted my fingers through his hair. He groaned against my mouth, firing me up some more.

I really was going to miss kissing him on a daily basis.

"I need you..." I panted against his lips. "I need you inside me." In so many different ways, but hell if was I admitting that to him.

He pulled back. Only an inch separated our mouths. "Are you sure?"

I nodded, all ability to speak having taken a hiatus for now.

He helped me up, and I awkwardly got to my feet.

The one benefit about having sex for the past two months was that we had discovered several positions that worked for us. All right, the topic had also come up during one girls' night with Holly, Emma, and Kelsey. This was a few weeks ago, when Ava announced that she and Liam were now expecting their own little bundle of joy.

And so began The Mommies Club, where virgin daiquiris and girl talk were part of the weekly menu.

In Wes's room, neither he nor I spoke. Our mouths and our tongues and our hands were busy conveying everything there was to say.

We took our time removing each other's clothes, savoring every moment, knowing that it would soon be our last time together this way.

Kissing me deeply, Wes guided me backward until my thighs hit the bed. I moved onto it and lay on my side, waiting for Wes to wrap himself around me from behind. He leaned over and we resumed kissing. Welcome to the pregnant woman's version of Twister-meets-sex.

His fingers found my clit. Mine found his hard length pressed against my butt cheek. He tenderly kissed my shoulder. My neck. The shell of my ear. "I love you, Hannah. Nothing will change that." His words came out as a rough whisper that did all kinds of amazing things to me.

Once he had me panting and wet with need, he entered me from behind. Filling me down to my soul, to the one place I didn't want to feel vulnerable. But that was exactly what was happening.

I didn't know what to think—so I didn't. I just let the moment engulf us.

35

HANNAH

Three days later, I was standing in the middle of the living room of my new apartment, directing Wes, Travis, Josh, Trent, and Liam where to put my stuff. Emma, Holly, Kelsey, and Ava were helping supervise the men.

And believe me, it wasn't easy.

I don't mean the supervising part. I was referring to the part where the ten of us were in an apartment that wasn't designed for large crowds.

And ten people in an apartment this size was considered a crowd.

"We have a delivery here for a Hannah Morrell," a burly man said from the open doorway.

"Yes. Go down the hallway, and it's the room on the right." I pointed in the direction the two men needed to go.

"Hannah," Wes said from the kitchen, "where do you want these?" He nodded at Trent, who was standing in the living room. Trent returned the nod.

Welcome to the society of cavemen, where they communicated with single gestures and grunts. But at least they knew what the heck they were talking about, so who was I to complain?

I waddled to where Wes was standing in my too-small kitchen. It wasn't any different from the kitchen in my old apartment, but after staying in Wes's condo for the past four months, it felt mouse-sized.

All right, my big belly wasn't helping the situation any.

"So, what do you think of the place?" I asked him.

"It's…how did you phrase it? Oh, that's right. It's nice. Great view, by the way." He chucked his chin toward the living room window and the lovely view of the apartment building next door.

Sooo, pretty much the same view that I'd had with my old apartment, except this building-next-door was slightly more interesting to look at.

"All right, I'll admit the view isn't as great as yours. And the apartment isn't as nice as your condo either."

"Or as big."

"That too. But it's Little Bean's and my new home, and at least it's not a dive."

"That is true. But you gave up a great place to live here." Wes nodded toward my living room.

"I couldn't live as your guest indefinitely."

"I wasn't asking you to live there indefinitely as my guest. But I did want you to live there as my girlfriend."

I opened my mouth to explain why I couldn't keep living with him.

"Sorry to interrupt," Burly Delivery Guy said before I could get out a word. "I need you to sign this to say that we've delivered your order." He handed me his electronic device.

"I need to check that it's all there and is okay first," I said.

Trent appeared over the guy's shoulder. "I just checked it, Hannah. Everything is in order. Great choice, by the way." Instead of looking at me when he said it, he was looking at Wes.

"Okay, thanks." I signed the form on Burly Guy's device and thanked him. He and his companion left. I took a step toward Little Bean's bedroom.

"Where are you going?" Wes asked, still in the kitchen.

I turned in time to catch his gaze flick to Trent. "I'm going to Little Bean's room."

"You can't do that," Kelsey said from the couch. The new couch that had been delivered an hour ago.

Both she and Emma were sitting there. Kelsey had a sleeping baby in her arms. Holly was walking toward the kitchen, carrying...a blender filled with virgin strawberry daiquiris mix? Josh's hands were also full, but with a six-pack of beer in one hand and three pizza boxes perched on the other.

Now that I thought about it, those two had disappeared at one point. I'd just figured they were enjoying their temporary child-free status while making out somewhere. Everly, Lily, and James were staying with Mrs. Jenkins at Wes's condo.

"We wanted to give you a surprise house-warming party," Holly said.

She and Josh set the food and drinks on the dining room table. Boxes, which still needed to be emptied, currently overloaded the kitchen counters. I opened one marked "plates."

"I've got these," Wes said, shooing me to the side.

"Okay. I'll get the glasses."

"Sorry, not happening. You're pregnant and are supposed to take it easy. That's why we're here to help out."

A few minutes later, Wes had the plates and glasses on the table. Travis, Liam, Trent, and Ava joined us from wherever they had vanished to, and the ten of us stopped to have lunch.

We were spread all over the apartment: the dining room table, the couch, the lonely armchair.

"This is great," I said to my friends. "Thanks for helping out."

"We wouldn't have missed it for the world." For some odd

reason, Emma's expression reminded me of the day she received her college admission's acceptance letter and when the bank approved her loan for Aphrodite's Boutique. She really needed to get out more if she found my moving into a new apartment exciting.

She wasn't the only one acting that way. The four women were grinning, their gazes every so often flicking to Wes, who was standing near me.

And that made me squirm in my seat like I'd sat on a huge ant nest.

We finished our pizza, and everyone got back to helping me unpack.

"So when are you showing us Little Bean's room?" Emma asked. The last of the boxes had just been emptied.

I hadn't been in the room yet. I was waiting until everything else was organized before I arranged the nursery.

"I still have to set everything up, but I can show you what I bought, if you want."

The girls all eagerly agreed to that; the guys wore knowing grins on their faces. I had no idea what to make of the latter.

They followed me down the short hallway. I opened the door and stepped into the room.

And froze.

Someone had already set it up. The furniture was assembled; the bedding and accessories were in their proper place. Even the woodland mobile Everly had helped me pick out was ready for action, attached to the side of the crib, looking down where in two months Little Bean would be sleeping.

But that wasn't the only reason I'd stopped in the doorway.

"This isn't the furniture I ordered." My voice was not much more than a croaked whisper. I was one hundred percent positive I hadn't accidentally bought it. Even with all the accessories, the amount I paid hadn't come close to what this would have cost. Plus there was also a light-gray armchair in the corner, which hadn't been part of the purchase.

A hand on my lower back nudged me into the room. "I knew this was the furniture you really wanted," Wes said. "So I returned to the store the next day and changed the order. It's my baby gift to you and Little Bean." He settled his hand protectively on my baby bump.

I didn't know what to say. The tears welled up again. *Damn hormones.*

"Do you like it?" Ava asked.

And now I understood why Trent had been quick to tell me everything looked fine. It was so I would sign the delivery form without going into the room first. They had all known what Wes had been up to. Ava had been the one to tell the men how to set up the room while I'd been distracted in the kitchen.

Part of me said I should be annoyed at Wes for changing my order and paying so much for the baby gift. However, a larger part of me knew I couldn't do that. Not in front of our friends. They had all been in on this, especially Emma. They just wanted to see me happy.

Which would have been a lot easier to do if the damn tears hadn't gone rogue and rolled down my face.

I sniffed. "It's perfect. Thank you."

My friends all hugged me. All except for Wes. While they were saying good-bye to me, he hung back.

He finally spoke after the last person had left the room and the apartment door clicked shut. "How are you doing?"

"Good. You know, you really didn't have to do this. But thank you."

"I know, but I wanted to." He lowered his lips to mine and gently kissed me. My body shouldn't have responded, but it still did.

He didn't deepen the kiss, much to my body's dismay. He

stepped away and smiled. "So, when's our second date going to be?"

"Second date?"

"You know, when a boy likes a girl, and he takes her out for dinner. And if he doesn't come off as a douchebag, she agrees to go out with him again."

The corners of my mouth twitched. "Yes, I do seem to remember that's how it works. It might have been a few months since I last went out on a date, but I do remember the general concept."

"Glad we've clarified that. Are you free tomorrow night?"

I shook my head. "I'm on shift at the hospital for the next five days."

"So Thursday night it is."

"You don't have to take me out on a date." We'd already been to third base. Several times. The idea of going on a date after that seemed ridiculous.

Truth? I was still scared that things wouldn't work out between us.

Wes would finally realize, now that I was no longer living with him and Everly, he didn't love me like he thought he had.

But you couldn't blame me for feeling that way. I was doing my best to protect my heart.

Unlike the rest of me, it wasn't as street smart.

"But I do." He winked at me; then his expression grew serious. "I've already told you I'm not giving up on you, Hannah. I love you, and I'm planning to do whatever it takes to prove it to you. I also plan to do whatever it takes to prove I won't abandon you like you suspect I will."

I nodded, mostly because his delicious smell was making it difficult for me to think.

"Okay, then. I'll pick you up on Thursday at six p.m." He lowered his mouth to mine with a searing kiss I wouldn't forget anytime soon.

36

WES

March

I walked out of my bedroom, dressed in a business suit.

Everly was still in her pajamas, sitting on the couch, and watching her favorite preschooler-friendly kid's show.

Hannah was sitting next to her, also watching the show.

"Hey, I wasn't expecting to see you for a few more hours," I said, striding over to her.

We had an early date planned for that night. Mrs. Jenkins would be babysitting Everly.

It was Hannah's and my third date. The second one after Valentine's Day.

So far we hadn't had much luck with actually going out on dates together. First, there was her work schedule. She mostly worked afternoons. By the time she was finished, it was too late to go out for dinner. The only thing she had energy for was to go to bed.

Her bed. Not mine.

Once we had finally managed to lock down some dates, we were forced to cancel the last two attempts to actually go out together.

The first time was because Everly had been dealing with a terrible cold, and I wanted to be there for her, to make sure nothing happened to her.

Mrs. Jenkins had chuckled and told me that Everly wasn't dying from the plague. She would be okay.

I didn't want to chance it.

The second time was because Mrs. Jenkins did have the plague.

All right. It was more like a bad cold, but it still knocked her out of commission for a week.

Hannah struggled to get to her feet, her swollen belly making things awkward.

I held my hand out to her and helped her up.

"Thanks. I just came by to see Everly and to tell you that I have to cancel tonight. One of the ER nurses called in sick, and I said I would cover for her. I figured I might as well get in as many shifts as possible before I start maternity leave."

Christ. Since when did dating become this tough?

"I'm really sorry, Wes." She took my hand and led me to the front door so that Everly couldn't hear us. "I had a feeling this wasn't going to work out between us. And this is before Little Bean is born. Can you imagine how difficult things will be soon enough? Who knows when we'll have time to see each other?"

"Is this your way of breaking up with me?"

"No. It's just me being practical."

I grunted, more at myself than for any other reason.

When I was a kid, my family owned a small black dog. I loved him more than anything. Ninja was my best friend. My confidant. My sidekick.

One day my parents gave him away to a new home. There wasn't a day that went by after that when I didn't miss him.

But what I had felt back then with the loss of Ninja was nothing compared to Hannah no longer living with me.

With her no longer being part of my everyday life.

"Do you miss me?" I blurted. "When we're not together...do you miss me? Or is Everly the only reason you come here?"

"I miss her. More than I realized I would."

"But what about me?"

She hesitated for a moment, then nodded. "Yes, I miss you." Her tone was soft, almost as if afraid to put a voice to her words.

"Enough to move in with me again?"

She winced. "Us living together won't change anything, Wes. I want a relationship that is real."

"And what are we? A fake couple?" That was news to me.

"No. I mean, I don't know. I just know that things were very convenient when I was living with you and Everly. But I didn't know how much of it was real and how much of it was a fantasy, to replace the family I never had growing up, to replace the family Everly lost."

"So your moving out was because you want to see if what we have is real?"

"Yes, exactly that."

That made sense, as much as I hated to admit it. But it still didn't solve the problem that was preventing our relationship from having a chance. "But how do we make this work between us when our schedules don't coincide often enough, or because of the billion other reasons that seem to keep us apart that are out of our control?"

She released a hard exhalation. "Maybe that's the point."

"Screw 'that's the point.' " I stepped closer to her and gently cupped her face in my hands. "What I feel for you, Hannah, is very real. I wish you would see that."

I lowered my head to hers and demonstrated just how real it was.

Everly's giggles could be heard coming from the living room, along with the upbeat music from the TV show. At least for now, she was entertained, and I didn't have to leave for work just yet.

I continued kissing Hannah, her tongue and lips meeting mine stroke by hungry stroke.

She eventually pulled away and rested her forehead against mine, our breaths coming in as ragged pants. "I definitely missed that."

"That's all? You only missed me kissing you?"

She chuckled softly. "I'm pretty sure that's not the only thing I miss."

I felt the corners of my mouth twitch slowly up. "Promise me we'll keep trying to make this work?"

"If that's what you want, then I promise. We'll keep trying. At least until Little Bean is born."

At this point, I was willing to take whatever she could give me.

I just had to hope that it would be enough.

37

HANNAH

I opened my apartment door. What my yoga pants and floral T-shirt lacked in glamor, they more than made up for in comfort. The top wasn't as loose as it had once been. Now it hugged the curves of my pregnant body, which was in its thirty-seventh week.

To complete my non-glamorous look, my hair was pulled up in a messy ponytail.

Emma had called earlier, saying that the girls wanted to visit me before my afternoon shift at the hospital. It was one of my few remaining shifts before my maternity leave commenced.

I moved to the side to let Emma inside—not that there was much room with my big belly in the way. Her daughter's car seat was in one hand, the baby fast asleep.

That's right. Daughter. Katherine had come into the world less than three weeks ago. Fortunately, she'd timed her arrival for when her daddy had a series of home games.

In her other hand, Emma was holding a paper bag. And as a finishing touch to the mommy ensemble, her diaper-bag strap hung across her body.

Pretty much the same look Holly and Kelsey were sporting behind her.

"Ava would have joined us," Holly explained, "but she's at work."

Ava was an elementary school teacher. The other three were on maternity leave, although that was a stretch when it came to Emma. She had decided to cut back the hours she worked in her store until Katherine was a year old, which she could do thanks to her husband being a well-paid professional hockey player. She had promoted one of the girls who worked in the store to full-time manager while Emma took the year "off."

"So what's the special occasion?" I asked once I had served everyone their drinks and we were seated in the living room.

Emma had told me when she called that the three of them wanted to meet with me due to a special occasion. She had even brought my favorite mini muffins from The Coffee Nut, which we were currently enjoying. The babies remained asleep in their car seats.

I couldn't for the life of me fathom what the special occasion could be. They had already thrown me a baby shower last weekend.

Emma shrugged. "I might have exaggerated why we wanted to talk to you. I didn't think you would be too excited about it if I told you we're here to stage an intervention."

"An intervention? For what?"

"You and Wes."

That had me even more confused. Wasn't an intervention meant to help you move on after you broke up with someone? Or when you were dependent on something that wasn't good for you?

What did this have to do with Wes and me?

We hadn't broken up. We were still trying to make it work, but it wasn't easy. We'd gone out on two dates. Which were great, in case you were curious. And I still hung out with Everly and Wes, even though I'd moved out of his condo three weeks ago. Well, mostly I hung out with Everly, for her benefit. She had already lost her parents. Now wasn't the time for me to permanently disappear from her life, too.

All right, I'll admit it. I'd had a hard time walking away from her. Less than twenty-four hours after I'd moved out, I had already been missing her.

Wait! Was that what the invention was about? They were helping Everly move on by keeping me out of her life?

Right—that sounded crazy. They wouldn't do that.

Sensing my confusion—which was probably stamped on my face—Holly went on to explain their reason for being there. "Why aren't you and Wes together?"

"Sorry, pregnancy brain happening here." I gestured to my head. "What are you talking about specifically?"

"You two are perfect together and he loves you, so why are you living here and not with him?" Kelsey asked.

I dug my teeth into my lip, unsure how much they knew about my past and how much I wanted to tell them. Emma knew, but she and I tended to avoid the topic of our childhoods.

"Because I don't know if what he and I have is real. Or if it just felt real because I was living with him."

"You've been living on your own for the past three weeks. Does what you feel for him now feel any less than it did then?"

"No, but—"

"I get that you're scared," Emma said, flashing me a look that was a cross between pity and you've-got-this determination. "You grew up feeling like no one wanted you permanently in their lives. The people who were supposed to love you turned their backs on you. They should never have done that to you, but not everyone is like that. I love you, and I've never abandoned you. We've been best friends for over twelve years and I'm still here for you."

"I know, but—"

"And we love you, too," Holly piped in.

Kelsey agreed with them. "You're family to us. Both you and Little Bean are family to us. And it's not just us who feel that way. Our husbands would do anything for you."

"And Wes would do anything for you," Emma said. "He loves you. We know that. *You* know that."

She was right, I did know that. But it still wasn't enough to completely kick my fear in the butt. "I'm trying," I told them. "And it's not like I don't see him anymore. I still spend time with Everly and Wes. Maybe not as much as before, but I'm still there."

Emma slowly shook her head. "You forget that Wes is best friends with my husband. And I have ways of making Travis talk." The last part was said in a fake German accent that was supposed to sound evil. All it did was make me laugh. "You tend to show up at Wes's condo after he's gone to work. You go there to see Everly, but you've been avoiding Wes."

"That's not true." *Much.* "We talk on the phone every night, and we text several times a day." And I ate breakfast with them every Sunday morning.

It had become our tradition.

One I lived for.

"That's because it's easier for you to keep up your wall that way than it is when you're with him in person."

I had no idea if I was supposed to respond to that, so I sipped my apple juice instead. I wasn't *that* bad.

Was I?

Holly set her glass on the table. "We want you to give Wes a chance. Start a new chapter in your life with him. A chapter free of the past hurts you've endured."

The other three eagerly agreed.

"If Ava were here, she would also agree with us," Kelsey said.

It would seem Little Bean also had an opinion on the topic. She poked me in the side with her foot, although that could have just been her stretching.

I smiled softly at them and then at my belly. "Thank you. Your opinions on the subject have been duly noted, and I'll take them into consideration when I make my decision."

38

WES

The next three weeks after Hannah moved into her apartment went by in a blur. Between working hard to finish the software project for Liam's company and taking care of Everly, I didn't have much time to think, let alone do anything else.

I did keep my promise to her and took her out on dates whenever our schedules allowed.

Which had been a grand total of two dinner dates—excluding Valentine's Day.

"Do you have any questions?" I asked Liam's team. We were in their conference room, and I had just finished demonstrating the completed program I had been working on.

I was answering Jayden's question when Isabelle entered the room. "Sorry to interrupt, but Mrs. Jenkins is on the line, Wes. She said it's important. She called your cell several times, but it kept going to voice mail."

"Is Everly okay?" I asked.

"She didn't say what it was about." Isabelle pointed to the phone in the middle of the conference table. "She's on line three."

Liam leaned forward in his chair, folding his arms on the table, eyebrows drawn. "Go ahead." Like the rest of my friends, he cared a lot about my niece, too.

I picked up the landline and pressed the button with the blinking light. "Hi, Mrs. Jenkins. Is Everly all right?"

"She's fine, Wes. But it's Hannah. And well, Mrs. Hitchcock. Marylou offered to be Hannah's birthing partner."

"That's right. Hannah mentioned it to me."

"She was looking forward to it. However, she had an accident this morning and hurt her hip. So she's out of commission, and...well. Hannah is in labor."

"Labor? She can't be. She's still got two weeks until her due date." I could feel everyone at the table watching me, but I was too busy staring at the phone, shocked by Mrs. Jenkins's news, to look up.

"I don't think babies pay attention to the calendar. They come when they're good and ready. And it looks like her baby has decided today would be a good day to be born."

I was already out of my seat and would have been out the door the moment Mrs. Jenkins had mentioned Hannah was in labor if I had been on my cellular phone.

"Do you know where she is?" I asked.

"She's here. She was visiting Everly when the contractions became stronger. But she wants you to swing by her apartment first to pick up her suitcase and the infant car seat."

"That's not exactly on the way."

The sounds of a muffled conversation came through the phone line.

"Wes?" Hannah said a moment later. "I really need you to pick up my suitcase. It's by the door and has everything I'll need during labor, including my birth plan. I can't have this baby without it."

"We can pick it up on the way to the hospital. I'm not risking that I'm across town when you start wanting to push." If

Kelsey's and Emma's labors were anything to go by, I probably had plenty of time to get Hannah's things, but I still didn't want to risk it.

"You've got plenty of time. But if you come here first and get me, it will take us even longer to get to the hospital." She was right about that. Of course. The hospital where she was supposed to give birth was closer to my place than hers.

"*Please*, Wes." The note of desperation in her tone was something I wasn't used to hearing from Hannah. How could I say no to that…?

"I don't have the keys to your apartment."

"That's not a problem. I called my landlord. He's expecting you." The desperation had flipped to smug triumph.

"All right, I'm on my way."

"After you pick up my suitcase and the infant car seat…"

I mentally rolled my eyes. "Yes, after I pick up those things."

I hung up the phone and turned to Liam. "I'm going to need to reschedule—"

"Go. And keep us updated. I'll let Ava know."

That was all I heard before I was out the door. Fortunately, I'd done some reading on how to support your wife during labor. Travis had given me a book on the topic, but I couldn't be sure if he had given it as a joke, knowing how I felt about Hannah.

I guess the joke was on him—because I had actually studied it. Except that was over two months ago, before learning that Mrs. Hitchcock would be Hannah's birthing partner. Hopefully, I remembered everything I had read.

Traffic wasn't too bad on the way to Hannah's apartment, and fortunately, the landlord was waiting at the entrance with the suitcase and infant car seat when I drove up to the front of the building.

My luck with traffic came to a crashing halt once I headed to my place. It had upgraded itself to the status of major pain in the ass. The vehicles in front of me were moving, but a senior citizen with a busted hip and a walker could have moved faster.

"C'mon, c'mon," I muttered to myself, doing my best to stay calm. "If Travis, Josh, and Trent can survive childbirth, so can I."

Right, I wasn't the one who would be doing all the hard work. No man had ever died while his wife or girlfriend was pushing out their baby.

I mean, I assumed no man ever died. There was always the chance the woman killed him during childbirth because he had knocked her up.

However, that wouldn't be the case with Hannah. They weren't my swimmers who had resulted in her current state. I was merely the man who wanted to be there for her, for the baby, for forever.

I had the easy part.

Or I assumed it was the easy part.

After what felt like several lifetimes, I eventually arrived at my condo, did a crappy job parking my vehicle, and sprinted to the front entrance of the building. I jerked the door open, entered the building code for the inside set of doors, and ran to the elevators.

Make that *one* elevator. The tape across the other one warned it was out of order.

Shit.

I pressed the button to summon the working elevator and contemplated running up the stairs. But even though I was still in good shape—despite not training as hard as I used to—I lived on the twenty-fourth floor. The elevator was still the faster way to get there.

I removed my phone from my pantsuit pocket. Mrs. Jenkins didn't have a phone, other than a landline, but maybe I could text Hannah and let her know I was on my way up.

A dozen or so texts, all from my friends, were waiting for me to read them. Apparently, news of Hannah being in labor had gotten out fast.

The elevator door pinged open.

I sent her the text and stepped inside the empty space.

Me: Getting on the elevator now.

But as the doors began to close, I spotted Mrs. Roberge, a woman who I swore was probably a couple of centuries old, shuffling toward the elevator door, hunched over her walker.

I pressed the Open button so she could get on the elevator. And waited.

And waited.

And waited.

I couldn't even pick her up and carry her onto the elevator. I was afraid she would fall apart on me like a dry fall leaf.

She paused to grin at me and went back to shuffling slowly toward the open elevator doors.

After what felt like several more lifetimes, she stepped into the elevator, and I pushed her floor—which was two floors beneath mine.

"Thank you, Mr. Sexy." Her voice was low and reminded me of Rice Krispies being stepped on. She winked at me and grinned again. "That's what they call you in this building. Mr. Sexy."

That was news to me.

"Who calls me that?"

"Everyone in my poker group."

Ah, yes, I had heard about that group. As in, don't join it if you want to keep your shirt and pants on. You didn't literally lose them, but everyone in the group was supposed to be sharp and cunning. If you were a beginner or intermediate level player, you wanted to avoid it at all costs.

I just didn't know sweet Mrs. Roberge was part of it.

"And everyone else who is single in the building calls you that behind your back, too," she added. "Well, it's mostly the women who call you that, along with Charles in 2203 and that nice Mr. Edwards in 1709."

The elevator finally pinged open on her floor.

She shuffled toward the hallway while I pressed the Open button. "Say hi to your adorable little girl from me."

"Will do." I waited another lifetime for her to step off the elevator.

She paused and waved good-bye, then kept moving forward.

I jabbed the Close button and willed the door to shut faster than its current slow speed. It was like the elevator knew I was in a rush to get to Hannah and it was doing everything in its power to be a pain in the ass.

And succeeding.

The door had barely opened on my floor before I was sprinting down the hallway to my condo, keys in hand.

I unlocked the door and entered. The rich and delicious smell of dinner cooking filled the air, which was odd because cooking dinner wasn't in Mrs. Jenkins' job description.

Everly rushed over to me with an excited grin on her face. "Auntie Hannah was making us dinner, and now she's having her baby. I'm going to be a big sister."

I didn't have time to correct her, and at this point, her thinking she was going to be a big sister was the least of my concerns.

I scooped up her in my arms and walked toward the living room. "That's nice, sweetheart. Do you know where Hannah is?" She wasn't in the kitchen, and the living room was also empty.

"In your bedroom. Mrs. Jenkins said she would be happier there. Oh, and Mrs. Jenkins said Auntie Hannah broke a glass of water."

"She broke a glass of water?"

Everly nodded and pointed toward my bedroom as Mrs. Jenkins stepped from the hallway where it was located.

As soon as she saw me, her gaze went skyward, and she pressed her hand to her heart. "Thank you, Lord."

I lowered Everly to the floor.

"All right, Everly," she said, "how about you and I play Candy Land in your bedroom? And Wes, if I were you, I'd call 9-1-1." Her tone was calm, the opposite of how I sensed she was currently feeling.

That was all she managed to say before I was sprinting into my bedroom.

Hannah wasn't there, but my bathroom light was on and a long groan came from that direction. I was already dialing 9-1-1 when I entered the room.

She was bent over the sink. "Hee-hee...whoo-whoo." Then another groan. Louder this time.

A man on the other end of the line asked me what my emergency was.

"Oh, God, I need to push. Badly," was Hannah's reply to the question she hadn't heard.

Christ, that can't be good.

Correction, I knew it wasn't good.

"My girlfriend is in labor now." Hannah could argue semantics with me later about the girlfriend part. "I just got here, but I think her water broke and she says she needs to push."

"The ambulance has been dispatched, but there might be a delay in them getting to you. In the meantime, we need to establish how far along your girlfriend is. I need you to look between her legs and tell me what you see." He introduced himself, and I told him my name.

"Hee-hee...whoo-whoo."

"Okay, give me a moment." I put the phone on speaker and

parked it on the tile floor. I grabbed a couple of towels, folded them, and set them next to my phone.

I wrapped my arm around Hannah's shoulder. "C'mon, sweetheart. I'm going to help you onto the floor so that I can tell Simon how far along you are."

Her dress was damp with sweat, the hem soaked. Her panties were in a wet pile on the floor.

"I've changed my mind," she said, voice weak. "I can't have a baby. I'm not ready." Despite that, she let me help her sit on the towels, her back against the wall, her knees bent.

"I don't think you have a choice at this point, Hannah. But I'm here for you. I'm not going anywhere." I meant it in so many different ways, though I suspected at that moment none of them were registering with her. She was pretending, again, that she was blowing out a candle.

Yes, I might have remembered reading that in the book Travis gave me. It was meant to keep you from pushing when you weren't supposed to yet.

Personally, I thought it sounded like a pile of BS. It wasn't helping Hannah. She made another loud noise that sounded like she was bearing down.

"I'm just going to check how you're doing here, Hannah." I said it more for Simon's benefit than hers. I separated her knees and looked. Hair—almost like dark-brown peach fuzz—greeted me. "I see the baby's head."

"All right, Wes, it looks like you'll be delivering your baby. The ambulance isn't there yet. I'll talk you through it, so stay with me."

"It's not his baby," Hannah weakly said before giving in to another long groan, curling over her belly.

Once she was finished, I took her face between my hands. "Yes, the baby *is* mine." My tone was both gentle and fierce. "It's *ours* if you will let me be part of your lives. I don't care if you got knocked up by a turkey baster. I love you, and I love this baby." I tenderly kissed her forehead.

I was positive this would go down in history as the strangest call Simon had ever received. "What do you think, Simon? Should Hannah finally admit to herself that I love her, and love me in return once she's ready?"

"Hannah, I know I don't know Wes very well, but in the short time that I have known him—which has been about three minutes—he seems like a very nice chap. And it sounds like he does love you...."

I couldn't tell if he was trying not to laugh, but his 9-1-1 operator experience was shining through in his professional tone.

Hannah chuckled, then turned serious, her voice a whisper. "I was making you dinner. I thought I had plenty of time before I had to go to the hospital. But when I called Mrs. Jenkins, she told me that Mrs. Hitchcock was out of commission."

"You were making me dinner?"

She nodded. "I thought since we never have a chance to go on those dates because we keep having to cancel, I would make you dinner tonight." She paused as another round of contractions hit.

"I'm scared," she said once they had subsided for the moment.

She wasn't the only one who was scared, but no way in hell was I letting her know that. "I know, but you're not on your own. I'm here. We can do this together. Okay?"

She nodded, and the strong, determined woman I loved peered up at me and smiled softly. "Okay. But that's not what I meant. Not entirely, anyway."

"What are you scared about?" I had a feeling I knew, but I wanted her to spell it out for me so we could deal with it now.

Or at least, after the baby was born.

This might not have been the best time for us to discuss our future together.

"Us," she said. "What will happen if I say yes to being your girlfriend?"

We didn't have a chance to talk about it any further. Hannah started bearing down again.

"All right, Simon," I said. "Looks like this baby plans to come now. What do I do?"

Luckily for me—and Hannah—he was an excellent instructor.

"One more push, Hannah," I said at one point, hoping it was true, "and then you get to meet Little Bean face-to-face."

She gave another guttural groan that echoed off the bathroom tiles.

The head came out, and I followed Simon's directions on guiding the rest of the baby out. Little Bean then let out his first I'm-pissed-off-at-the-world, piercing scream.

That's right. Everly had predicted correctly. Little Bean was a boy.

I gently rubbed him down like Simon explained and handed him to Hannah. I brushed a damp strand of hair from her face and kissed her forehead again. "You did it. You were amazing." I smiled at her—relief and love and a billion other emotions flooding me.

She smiled back, tears wetting her face. "Thank you, Wes. I don't know what I would have done without you."

The ambulance arrived soon after. The paramedics did what they needed to do, and as a precaution, took Hannah and the baby to the hospital. I went with them. Mrs. Jenkins and Everly stayed behind...after Everly had a peek at the baby.

She'd had a huge grin on her face at the news that the baby was a boy.

"You can give him the special gift you got him once he's

released from the hospital," I had quietly told her before Hannah, Little Bean, and I left in the ambulance.

39

HANNAH

I don't know how long I'd been sleeping when I stirred awake to the low murmur of Wes talking.

How did I know it was him—beyond the sound of his voice?

My pulse spiked, and my heart attempted to scramble out of my chest to get to him.

The memory of the afternoon seeped into my brain. Of going into labor, but believing I still had plenty of time because Little Bean was my first baby, and Emma's and Kelsey's labors had seemed impossibly long.

Of learning that Mrs. Hitchcock was out of commission due to a bad hip.

Of Wes delivering my baby.

I slowly opened my eyes to the sunlight glowing softly in my hospital room. Wes was standing near the window with Little Bean cradled in his arms, telling him all about the wonders and adventures awaiting him outside. My breath caught at the adoring look he directed at the baby—a baby who wasn't biologically his.

Wes loved me, and he would never willingly abandon me

like so many others had. He had proved that when he helped to deliver my son. Emma and the girls were right. What happened to me in the past had been precisely that...in the past. Wes was my present and hopefully my future.

Hopefully Little Bean's and my future.

What Wes and I felt for each other was real. There was no doubt about it.

"How's he doing?" I asked.

Wes turned to me, and his smile caused another spike in my pulse. "He's doing great. How are you doing?"

"Tired. Sore. Grateful. For you both." I might have been exhausted, but that didn't stop the smile spreading on my face at the last part. "Have you been here the entire time?"

He walked over to my bed. "I told you I'm not going anywhere."

My smile widened. "I'm beginning to believe that."

Little Bean stirred in Wes's arms. I adjusted the bed so that I was sitting, and Wes carefully handed my son to me so I could feed him.

I hiked up the hem of my oversized T-shirt that I had packed in my suitcase, and helped Little Bean latch onto my nipple.

"Hey, little dude," Wes said to him. "I hope you realize those are on loan. They will be mine again once you've outgrown them." Smiling, Wes stroked my cheek. "Assuming that's okay with you."

"It's more than okay."

He leaned down and brushed his lips against mine. "I'm also hoping you and this little guy are planning to move back in with me. I've already had to live for three weeks without you. I'm not interested in doing that again."

"That can definitely be arranged," I whispered. "I love you, Wes—"

That was all I managed to say before his mouth claimed

mine, the kiss reaching down to my soul. Little Bean kept on sucking, unaware of the monumental occasion.

The kiss continued until Wes eventually pulled away. I didn't want it to end, but it was slightly awkward with me on the hospital bed and Wes standing.

He gave me one more sweet kiss. But instead of straightening once he was finished, he put his hands on either side of my hips and looked me squarely in the eyes. "I'm also hoping that you will be my wife."

I grinned at him, my heart having passed out from all the excitement. "Aren't you supposed to get down on one knee and ask me?"

"Since when have we done things the traditional way?" His gaze dropped to Little Bean, then lifted back to mine. Undeniable hope and passion and love filled his eyes.

An overwhelming emotion inflated me like a helium balloon, making me feel lighter. Happier. "I would love to be your wife."

He kissed me once more...and Little Bean kept sucking.

Most girls didn't exactly dream of being proposed to in that way, but it worked for me. Like Wes had said, nothing we had done so far would be considered traditional.

And I wouldn't have changed a thing.

His gaze returned to Little Bean. "So have you come up with a name for him yet? Or will his name legally be Little Bean? Because I'll just say this right now, if that's your plan, the wedding is off." His mouth transformed into my favorite cocky smile.

"I was thinking Eric for the middle name, after your brother."

"I think that's perfect."

"And I like Cameron as a first name."

Wes stroked the dark fuzz on top of Little Bean's head and directed his smile at him. "He looks like a Cameron."

I finished feeding my precious baby and handed him to Wes so I could take a photo of them together. Because how could I not?

The two of them made an adorable pair.

AN HOUR LATER, SOMEONE TAPPED ON THE HOSPITAL DOOR BEFORE cautiously pushing it open a few inches.

"Is now a good time for a visit?" Mrs. Jenkins asked from the other side of the door.

Wes went to let her in.

She wasn't alone. Everly and Mrs. Hitchcock were with her.

Everly bounced over to see Cameron, who was asleep in her uncle's arms.

I gave Mrs. Hitchcock a blatant once-over. "Wow, I see miracles really do exist. Your hip is already recovered."

"Funny how that happened." Flashing me a smug grin, she walked to my bed and patted my hand. "But don't worry, dear. If Wes hadn't shown up when he did, I would have been in the bathroom helping you. However, he did make it in time, so all is good."

She glanced between Wes and me. "All is good, am I right?"

Wes grinned at me, the love in his eyes undeniable to everyone in the room. He sat down in the armchair so Everly could see Cameron better. "Yes, everything is great."

"Then congratulations are in order." Mrs. Hitchcock strode over to him and peered at the condo building's newest resident.

Mrs. Jenkins joined them. "I hope you don't mind us stopping by for a visit. Your niece has been bouncing off the walls since the baby came into the world. I didn't think she could last much longer before she got to see him again."

Everly had a package in her hand, wrapped in pastel gift

paper. The item wasn't in a box, and it looked like Everly had helped wrapped it. A ton of tape was stuck to the paper.

She set it on Cameron's stomach. "This is for you."

Cameron stirred but otherwise continued sleeping.

THE HOSPITAL KEPT CAMERON AND ME FOR TWENTY-FOUR HOURS before releasing us. I couldn't have been happier to escape. It's one thing to be a nurse working in a hospital. It's something else when you're the patient who is stuck there.

By the time they released me, I was doing my own bouncing off the wall, eager to go home.

"The guys have already moved your stuff back into my condo," Wes said as he drove us from the hospital. Cameron was asleep in his infant car seat.

"Already?" I asked, more than a little surprised. I had thought I'd be returning to my apartment until I had straightened everything out when it came to my lease.

But I knew how he felt. As soon as I'd let Wes completely into my heart, the idea of being separated from him hadn't been too appealing. I'd gotten used to sleeping with him at night and waking up the next morning wrapped in his arms. The three weeks I had lived without that were the hardest three weeks of my adult life.

Did Emma and Travis know that Wes and I were now engaged?

You'd better believe it.

Wes had blurted the news as soon as they walked into my hospital room this morning. And judging from how many texts he and I received from our other friends within minutes of them leaving, it hadn't taken Emma and Travis long to fill them in on our engagement.

Everyone was ecstatic for us.

We arrived at Wes's building. He got out of the SUV and grabbed his son's infant seat.

You heard me correctly. That was one of the things we had discussed last night after everyone left my room. Because he was adopting Everly, Wes was familiar with the process for becoming Cameron's legal father.

Our son couldn't ask for a better dad. Even before Cameron was born, Wes had loved him like he was his own flesh and blood.

We had barely entered the condo when Everly and Mrs. Jenkins appeared in the hallway. Cameron was still asleep, with the floppy bunny Everly had given him on his lap.

Everly proudly showed the sleeping baby a picture she had drawn in crayon. "I drew you a picture. There's your mommy and daddy." She pointed to two stick figures that vaguely resembled Wes and me. Judging from the long brown hair on one of them, I was holding Cameron. "And this is my mommy and daddy. They're in heaven now." The two other adults in the drawing, both with halos and wings, brought tears to my eyes. "So I live with you, and that makes you my little brother," she proudly declared.

And of course, my hormones decided it would be fun to turn on the waterworks.

Damn pesky hormones.

I crouched to her level and gave her a big hug. "That's right. You're Cameron's amazing big sister, whom I love very much." I kissed the top of her head.

She hugged me back, then took hold of my hand, smiling broadly. "You have to see Cameron's room now."

I let her lead me into my old room. I stepped inside and gasped.

Travis had painted a mural on one of the walls, depicting a tree and woodland critters to go with the bedding and accessories I had bought Cameron.

"How?" I asked, voice not much more than a whisper. There was no way Travis could have done this in less than eighteen hours.

Especially since he and the team had left on a road trip after he and Emma had visited Cameron and me this morning.

Wes put the infant seat down and wrapped his arms around my waist, drawing me to him. "I told you I wasn't giving up on you. Travis painted it three weeks ago. You just never came into this room when you visited Everly, and somehow she managed to keep it a secret from you."

I was vaguely aware of Mrs. Jenkins leading Everly from the room to give us privacy. I was too busy gazing into Wes's gorgeous gray eyes to notice more than that.

"Thank you. It's perfect. You're perfect." And then I showed him how much I meant the words from the bottom of my heart.

EPILOGUE

WES

Sixteen Months Later

"They're here," my beautiful, glowing wife excitedly announced from the living room, waving two brown envelopes at me.

That's right.

My wife.

Were you hoping to witness our big day? Sorry to disappoint.

Let me flash back for a minute to the moment that brought us here.

Soon after Cameron had been born and I proposed to Hannah, we'd agreed on a short engagement. We weren't looking to have a huge wedding, one that required lots of planning. We chose a date for after Cameron turned four months old. In the end, Everly's adoption was finalized a few weeks before our big day.

Giving us another reason to celebrate.

Think that we got married too soon? That we were no better

than those celebrities who met and a few weeks later were walking down the aisle?

We didn't think so.

Hannah and I had known each other for over two years. It wasn't insta-love. Our respect for each other and our friendship had grown during that time. Neither of us felt like we were rushing things.

We were ready to become husband and wife—to be a family.

Our wedding was small and intimate. Just Everly, Cameron, our closest friends and their kids at a small resort in Napa Valley. In September.

The view was gorgeous.

But my breathtaking bride put it to shame as she walked toward me beneath a canopy of vines.

We didn't officially go on a honeymoon until two months ago. Because Hannah couldn't bear to be too far away from Everly and Cameron—who were staying with Josh and Holly and their two kids while we were gone—we spent our week-long Honeymoon in Napa Valley.

With lots of FaceTime with our kids.

Six months after our wedding, we could finally apply to legally adopt our stepchildren.

And let's just say that had been interesting—because by law you're supposed to contact the other biological parent to gain their approval. Both Everly's parents were dead, so I had to provide the courts with their death certificates.

It was Cameron's case that was more interesting. Remember that part about "You're supposed to contact the biological parent"? That means if you get knocked up by a one-night stand, you have to attempt to track the guy down first and get him to waive his rights to a child he might not know exists.

Can't find him? Then you have to show the courts the steps you took to contact him.

Used sperm from a known donor?

Then things are more complicated, unless he legally waived his parental rights before the fertilization process took place.

But since Hannah had used an anonymous donor, we didn't have to go through the process of contacting him.

We just had to live together for six months after our wedding, and then we could start the adoption process.

A process which I was beginning to feel like an expert in.

Six months after that, Hannah and I had stood in front of the judge, and he approved both adoptions.

So there you go—you are now up to speed on the past sixteen months since the birth of my son.

Cameron was playing on the floor with his sister in the living room. It was their favorite game. Everly would stack the colorful, soft blocks...and Cameron would knock them over.

True to form, as soon as she placed the final block on top, he lunged at them and giggled when they tumbled down. He then spotted me and pushed himself to his feet.

He toddled over and raised his arms above his head. "Dada."

I happily obliged him and picked him up. "Hey, how's my big boy doing?"

Grinning, he clapped his hands.

"He's doing fine," Everly said. "Except he keeps knocking over my tower." She didn't sound too upset about it. She never did. She just kept building them and seeing how long it would take before her brother bulldozed them down. "And Mommy is still sick."

That's right. She had been calling Hannah and me "Mommy and Daddy" for the past eight months. It had been her decision. I think part of it was because we were teaching Cameron to say Mommy and Daddy. And since she considered herself very much his big sister, it only made sense that she called us that, too.

But there were also times when she was being particularly stubborn. Then she'd put her hands on her hips and call me Uncle Wes. But that was usually when Cameron wasn't around.

She still remembered her biological parents. I made sure she never forgot them. Their family photo from when she was two was in her bedroom, and I'd tell her all kinds of funny stories about them and about her father and me growing up.

She still had the off days when their absence was too much and she cried. But those days were getting further and further apart.

I carried Cameron over to Hannah and kissed her cheek. I wanted to do a lot more than that to her later, once the kids were in bed. But for now, the kiss would have to do.

"You're still sick? I thought you were feeling better last night." I took the opened envelopes from her and peeked inside.

The smile hadn't left Hannah's face. "It comes and goes, but I'm feeling better now."

I removed the document from the first envelope and read it. My mouth responded with a matching smile.

Cameron reached out, attempting to grab the page from me.

"It's official, little buddy," I said, holding his birth certificate far enough away so he couldn't reach it. "You're definitely my son." My name now filled the space that listed his father's name.

Hannah removed the birth certificate from the other envelope and showed it to me. Everly's updated birth certificate now listed both our names as her parents.

"Okay, Cameron," Everly said. "I've made you a new tower to knock over."

My son squirmed to be put down. I placed him on the floor and laughed as his little legs propelled him toward the new target.

He squatted in front of the tower and knocked the blocks down with his hands.

"Yay!" Everly lifted her hands as if he had just scored a goal. Cameron copied her, raising his arms, and squealed with joy.

I chuckled at them and pulled Hannah into my arms. "Are you sure you're okay?"

She leaned into me. Her warm breath brushed against my cheek. "I'm definitely okay. But um...how would you feel if we were to have another child?"

For a microsecond, all I could do was stare at her, stunned.

Had we discussed having more kids? Not really. We had been so focused on the adoption process when it came to Everly and Cameron, the topic of having more kids hadn't really come up.

The grin on my face from earlier was nothing compared to now. "You're pregnant?"

She smiled back and nodded. "It would seem so."

I moved my hand to her still-flat stomach and stroked my thumb over the spot where our baby was hanging out. "Our honeymoon? No turkey baster this time?"

That's right. There had been one or two times during that trip when we had been a little too preoccupied, removing each other's clothes, to think about protection.

And afterward? When we realized our oversight?

We had just shrugged it off—because whatever happened was meant to be.

Hannah chuckled. "Definitely no turkey baster this time."

"Then I'd say I'm a very happy man." I captured my wife's sweet mouth in a satisfying kiss...until Everly started groaning about how gross we were being.

Laughing, I pulled away from Hannah.

"You were right," she said, grinning again. "The old-fashioned way of making a baby is so much more fun."

Amen to that.

READ ON FOR AN EXCERPT FROM DECIDEDLY WITH LUCK

KIERA

For as long as I could remember, I'd always loved fairy tales. Even before becoming an elementary schoolteacher.

More specifically, I'd always loved Disney's versions of the classic fairy tales.

Have you ever read Hans Christian Andersen's original story of *The Little Mermaid*? There are no singing lobsters, no happy endings. The little mermaid doesn't sail away into the sunset with her handsome prince.

Nope, not at all.

Spoiler alert!

She sacrifices herself so the prince can live, and the sea witch transforms the little mermaid into sea foam.

Unlike the original fairy tales, Disney leaves you with hope for a happily ever after, hope for a new beginning.

This was all fine and wonderful, but as I stood at the entrance to the hotel ballroom—my glittering silver stilettos feeling as though they were glued to the floor—I questioned if that would be the case for me.

Of course, it will.

Embracing that flicker of hope, I resumed reciting in my

head my goal for the evening: *Project Kissing Under the Mistletoe.* A kiss under the mistletoe from a handsome stranger. A happy-for-now ending to the night—and a baby step toward moving on after my husband's death a year ago.

I scanned the sea of ball gowns and tuxes and elaborate masks, searching for a particular blonde in a dress of black tulle. *That's right.* In addition to the Jingle Balls ball being a fundraiser for testicular cancer, it was a masquerade ball.

My sister waved at me from across the ballroom, next to the grand Christmas tree decorated with a flurry of gold and red ornaments.

Brittany and her husband were the reason I was here tonight instead of back home in San Francisco, knitting mittens for foster kids in Boston. They were the reason I was wearing the mask covering the upper portion of my face and the stunning burgundy gown.

Don't worry. This wasn't the anniversary of my husband's death. That had passed a week ago with me spending the day reading the love notes he used to leave all over our house.

Love notes I'd saved in a big floral box every time I found one.

On the day of the one-year anniversary, I'd sipped a glass of Enchanted Springs Chardonnay, the same wine we'd served at our wedding, and read the notes aloud.

Roses are red, violets are blue, I want to have hot sex with you.

A poet, he was not.

And then there was the note I had saved for last:

If I die before you, I want to be the star in the sky that grants all your wishes.

I inhaled a long, fortifying breath, channeling my inner Disney princess, and wove my way through the throng of merry partiers.

The conversation I'd had with Stephen after I'd found that note sashayed into my head. The conversation where he told me that if he did die before me—way, way, *way* down the line—he wanted me to fall in love again.

After this, he proceeded to list all the men he thought were viable options, in case they were available at the time.

"But definitely not Stinky Pete," he'd said.

"I don't think you have to worry about me ending up with the villain from *Toy Story Two*."

Stephen barked a laugh—the laugh he always made when he thought I was being cute and adorable. "I was talking about my teammate. Pete Mundy. His hockey skates smell like he melted Limburger cheese in them."

I grinned at him and kissed him sweetly on the cheek. "Okay, no, Pete Mundy. Anyone else?"

"Logan Mathews."

"Is he a yah or a nah?"

"A definite yah."

"I'm sure his wife would have something to say about that." Logan had been Stephen's best friend and teammate in college, and his best man at our wedding. Now, he played in the NHL—with the Chicago Blackhawks, last I'd heard.

"All right, I'll add him to the list," I'd said with a grin, even though my heart had been splitting into a billion fragments at the thought of Stephen possibly dying before me.

My sister's red lips curved into a wide smile under her black-feathered half mask as I approached.

"Kiera." She beamed at me like I was a baby who'd taken her first wobbly steps. "Let me introduce you to the charity's biggest supporter and my dear friend." The way she said it, you would've thought she was talking about royalty. "Lucinda, this is my little sister, Kiera. Kiera, this is Lucinda Mathews." The woman's surname came out in a hushed whisper.

I bit back the urge to curtsy to the much older woman standing next to Brittany. Lucinda's gold-and-cream gown, diamond earrings and necklace, and spritz of floral perfume gave her a queenly air.

"Hello, my dear." Her voice was dry and brittle, like antique parchment paper, yet filled with warmth and a spark of something.

Amusement, perhaps?

Remember the part about me resisting the urge to curtsy?

It would seem my body failed to get that message. Luckily, I'd had spent years perfecting the skill as a kid, back when I believed in fairy godmothers and dreamed of one day marrying my own prince.

Lucinda chuckled, and I felt my face heat as I straightened.

"And this is my grandson, Grayson." She gestured with a wave of her hand to the tall, dark-haired man next to her. His half mask was simple and black. If the way his tuxedo embraced his body was any indication, the man made keeping in shape a top priority.

I held out my hand for him to shake—because heck if I was curtsying for him. But instead of shaking it, Grayson lifted my hand to his mouth and pressed a soft kiss to it.

At the feel of his mouth against my skin, my body shouldn't have reacted like hot lava swirled within its depths. My breath shouldn't have hitched with sudden longing. And my lips shouldn't have tingled, craving to taste his mouth on mine.

None of those things should have happened—with a stranger, no less. A stranger who might not even be single.

Desire wasn't alone under the hotel chandeliers, their light-bulbs twinkling like stars. Hanging out with it was regret. Regret in knowing that Stephen was looking down from heaven and shaking his head at me, disappointed that the stranger I wanted to kiss under the mistletoe wasn't on the list of approved men he'd jokingly created.

"Brittany mentioned you're an elementary schoolteacher," Lucinda said.

I nodded and smiled warmly at the thought of my students. "That's right. I teach second grade."

"Oh, such a delightful age. My great-granddaughter is in that grade. Such a precocious little thing, just like her father was at that age."

My gaze flicked to Grayson, but he gave no indication the child belonged to him. So maybe she was his niece.

He chuckled, drawing my attention to his mouth. *Don't look at his mouth. Look away from his...* "I'm sure her father will be thrilled you said that. I know for a fact that he took great pride in keeping you on your toes."

She flashed him her perfectly straight, angel-white teeth. "I daresay you're right."

"And what about you?" I asked Grayson. "What do you do for a living?"

"This and that" was his non-answer.

Truth? I sort of appreciated that he was evading the question like a spy at a royal tea party. I preferred the mystery surrounding him. It made him even sexier—not that he needed help in that department as far as I could tell.

"Brittany also mentioned you live in San Francisco," Lucinda said to me.

For a masked ball, where our identities were a secret, my sister was certainly spilling the jelly beans when it came to all there was to know about me.

Please tell me you never mentioned my deceased husband.

"That's right," I said.

"She mentioned you used to live in Boston—"

I sensed she was going to say more, but Grayson coughed as though clearing his throat, and her words came to an abrupt halt.

She threw him a subtle smirk. He gave a barely perceptible shake of his head.

"Do you live in San Francisco?" I asked him. My tone was

edged with a curiosity I shouldn't have felt. I really didn't want to know anything about him. If I found out too much, the magic of the moment would be reduced to glitter.

"No, Chicago." His deep, sexy voice left my insides quivering like leaves caught in a stiff breeze.

"That's quite the drive just to attend the ball."

"You might say I happened to be in the neighborhood, and my grandmother asked if I would attend as her date."

Aww, that's so sweet.

"My poor Alfred died ten years ago from testicular cancer," Lucinda explained, "which is why this charity event is important to me. And why awareness and early detection is vital."

"I'm so sorry for your loss," I said to them both, praying Brittany didn't decide this was a good time to inform them about *my* dead husband.

Luckily, she remained silent on the topic.

"Thank you, my dear," Lucinda said. "I was fortunate to have a supportive family and friends to help me get through it. And you know the best part?"

I shook my head, clueless at what it could be.

"Just because you lose someone you loved doesn't mean you'll never love again." She winked at me, confirming she did know the truth. What else had my dear sweet sister shared? My social security number? "I found a new prince, and I'm just as much in love with him as I was with my sweet Alfred."

"I'm glad to hear that." My words had more to do with her falling in love with someone new than the chance of that happening to me again.

I shifted on my feet and twisted toward the orchestra, now playing a new piece.

I could almost imagine Cinderella and Prince Charming waltzing to the music with the other couples dancing.

"Would you like to dance?" The question was a low

murmur against my ear, and my insides quivered once again, in a way that would make a bowl of Jell-O envious.

ACKNOWLEDGMENTS

First, I want to say thanks to everyone who has fallen in love with the By the Bay series. After writing *Decidedly With Love*, I wasn't sure if I would be writing another book in the series beyond *Decidedly With Mistletoe*. But after so many readers ask me if Wes was getting a story, I knew I needed to write him one. And then the idea for the book came to me, and I couldn't wait to share it with the world.

I also want to thank my editor Bev, as well as Hope and Jessica from Flat Earth Editing for the copyediting and proofreading. All three individuals helped make this book sparkle. Naturally, I can't forget Brenda St. John Brown, who always shares her brilliant suggestions and wisdom when it comes to my romantic comedies. She's the best.

Hugs and kisses to the bloggers and reviewers who have fallen in love with the By the Bay series, to the wonderful members of my Facebook reader group (Stina's Sweethearts), and to the romance writers who are so free with their support and expertise. None of my books would be possible without you.

Finally, I would like to thank you to my husband Ralph, our three teens, and our cat Callie for your love and support. And for understanding that Pinterest is more than just hot men and cute kitty photos, it's an essential part of what I do (Okay, it is mostly hot men and cute kitty photos).

ABOUT THE AUTHOR

Born in Brighton England, Stina Lindenblatt has lived in a number of countries, including England, the U.S., Finland, and Canada. This would explain her mixed up accent. She has a kinesiology degree and a MSc in sports biological sciences.

In addition to writing fiction, she loves photography, and currently lives in Calgary, Canada, with her husband and three kids.

For news about her books and to sign up for her newsletter, check out her website at stinalindenblattauthor.com.